Dessa Rose

Dessa Rose

Sherley Anne Williams

Quill
An Imprint of HarperCollins*Publishers*

HarperCollins books may be purchased for educational, business, or sales promotional
use. For information please write: Special Markets Department, HarperCollins
Publishers Inc., 10 East 53rd Street, New York, NY 10022.

First Quill edition published 1999.

Designed by Beth Tondreau

Library of Congress Cataloging-in-Publication Data is available.

ISBN 0-688-16643-1

06 QW 10 9

Author's Note

𝓰𝓫

Dessa Rose is based on two historical incidents. A pregnant black woman helped to lead an uprising on a coffle (a group of slaves chained together and herded, usually to market) in 1829 in Kentucky. Caught and convicted, she was sentenced to death; her hanging, however, was delayed until after the birth of her baby. In North Carolina in 1830, a white woman living on an isolated farm was reported to have given sanctuary to runaway slaves. I read of the first incident in Angela Davis' seminal essay, "Reflections on the Black Woman's Role in the Community of Slaves" (*The Black Scholar,* December 1971). In tracking Davis to her source in Herbert Aptheker's *American Negro Slave Revolts* (New York, 1947), I discovered the second incident. How sad, I thought then, that these two women never met.

I admit also to being outraged by a certain, critically acclaimed novel of the early seventies that travestied the as-told-to memoir of slave revolt leader Nat Turner. Afro-Americans, having survived by word of mouth—and made of that process a high art— remain at the mercy of literature and writing; often, these have betrayed us. I loved history as a child, until some clear-eyed young Negro pointed out, quite rightly, that there was no place in the

American past I could go and be free. I now know that slavery eliminated neither heroism nor love; it provided occasions for their expressions. The Davis article marked a turning point in my efforts to apprehend that other history.

This novel, then, is fiction; all the characters, even the country they travel through, while based on fact, are inventions. And what is here is as true as if I myself had lived it. Maybe it is only a metaphor, but I now own a summer in the 19th century. And this is for the children—Malcolm Stewart, Patricia Grundy, Steven Allen, Evangeline Birdson—who will share in the 21st.

SHERLEY ANNE WILLIAMS

San Diego, California
September 14, 1985

Contents

Dessa Rose

Prologue

Someone . . .

        "Hey, hey . . ."

coming down the Quarters.

        ". . . sweet mamma."

Kaine, his voice high and clear as running water over a settled stream bed, swooping to her, through her . . . He walked the lane between the indifferently rowed cabins like he owned them, striding from shade into half-light as if he could halt the setting sun.

        "Say hey now, hey now—"

Even without the banjo banging against his back—she would have known him

        "Dessa da'ling . . ."

arms outstretched, fingers soundlessly snapping, their rhythm the same one that powered her heart . . . Mouth stretched wide in a grin, shadow running to meet him

"Don't you hear me calling you?
Hey, hey, sweet mamma, this Kaine's holla . . ."

Hoe thrown aside, running, running . . .

"Kaine calling, calling his woman's name—"

caught, lifted from the ground, pressed hard against his chest, hands locked behind his neck, the banjo banging against them. "What you doing down here so early?" *On the ground now and scared. Lawd, if Boss Smith saw him— And that no-good Tarver was still behind them—*

"They think I'm still up there at that old piece-a greenhouse trying to make strawberries grow all year round." *His warm breath tickling the side of her neck—almost, she lost herself in the sensation; dread held her quiet. Laughing, ignoring her silence, he stooped and picked up her hoe . . .*

The Quarters stirred. Smoke curled lazily from several stovepipes; children ran here and there. Already a few people waited a turn at the grinding stone near the center of the row, others at the well next to it.

"You just asking for trouble, coming down here like this," *she told him (she had told him . . . told him time and time again*

"Baby, I'm already in trouble."

He grinned but still the breath caught in her throat. "What you mean?"

"Mean a nigga ain't born to nothing but trouble," *David seemed to materialize out of the twilight as he spoke,* "and if a nigga don't court pleasure, he ain't likely to get none!"

"Naw," *Carrie Mae, fat brown baby slung on her hip, chimed in,* "Masa done sent his butt down here to get it out of trouble: taking care that breeding business" *baby . . . baby—*"he been let slide."

"Now yo'all know I be trying." *Kaine was laughing, too.* "But I got something here guaranteed to ease a troubling mind." *He patted Dessa's shoulder.*

Laughing, David and Carrie Mae passed on.

"*Kaine*—"

"*Lefonia gived me*—"

"*After how much talk?*"

"*Didn't take much*"

The laugh was choked out of her; she had looked into his eyes. They were alive, gleaming with dancing lights (no matter what mammy-nem said; his eyes did so sparkle) that turned their brown to gold. Love suffused her; she had to touch him or smile. She smiled and he grinned. "Don't take much, Dess—if you got the right word. And you know when it come to eating beef, I steal the right word if it ain't hiding somewhere round my own self's tongue." He tugged her up the steps to their cabin. She laughed despite herself; he could talk and wheedle just about anything he wanted. "And I pulled some new greens from out the patch and seasoned em with just a touch of fatback."

"*A touch was all we had. Kaine, what*—"

"*Hmmmm mmmmmm. But that ain't all I wants a touch of,*" *he said holding her closer, pulling the dirty, sweaty rag from her head. "Touch ain't never just satisfied me."*

She laughed and relaxed against him. They were inside, the rickety door shut against the gathering night. "Our greens going get cold."

"*But we ain't.*" *He stood with one leg pressed lightly between her thighs, his lips nibbling the curve of her neck.*

"*I got to clean up a little.*" *Teasing now, yet conscious, too, of the moist grittiness of her skin against the coarse cleanness of his shirt. Never end! Suddenly, fiercely, the wish was upon her. To be always in this moment, her body pressed to his, his warm in the bend of her arm.*

"*You ain't dirty,*" *he growled, hands grasping her shoulders, shaking her from the shadow of that wish. She leaned against him feeling the steady beat of his heart against her own; he ran the tip of his tongue down the side of her neck. "Ain't no wine they got up to the House good as this*—" *fingers caught in her kinky hair, palms resting gently on her cheeks. "Ain't no way I'm ever going let you get away from me, girl. Where else I going to find eyes like this?" He kissed her closed lids. "Or a nose?" He pecked playfully at the bridge, the tip. "Mouth."*

 His lips were firm and velvety as the tip of a cat-tail willow; her skin yearned under their touch. She trembled. "Mmmmmmmmmmm. I sho like this be-hime." Hands cupping her buttocks, he dared her, "Tell me all this goodness ain't mine. And when it get to moving— Lawd! I knowed it was going be sweet but not this doggone good!"

 Talk as beautiful as his touch. Shivering, she pulled at his shirt. This was love, her hand at his back, his mouth. "Sho you want," she asked him, "sho you want this old—?" His lips were on hers, nibbling, nipping, "Dessa," a groan in his throat. Her sentence ended in a moan. Thighs spreading for him, hips moving for him. Lawd, this man sho know how to love . . .

Desire flowered briefly, fled in dry spasm, gone as suddenly as the dream had come, so lifelike she had felt herself with him, knew herself among Carrie and them, been swept up in the warmth of their presence. And woke. She closed her eyes. Chains rasped, rubbed hatefully at her ankles and wrists. Coarse ticking scratched at her skin; corn husks whispered dryly beneath her at each move. Kaine's eyes had been the color of lemon tea and honey. Even now against closed eyelids, she could see them—Kaine's eyes, Carrie's smile . . .

I sent my Dessa a message

Dessa mouthed the words

   Chilly Winds took it,
    Blowed it everywhere.

and heard his voice in her ear

   Hey, hey Dessa da'lin,
   This Kaine calling, calling . . .

The Darky

"You have seen how a man was made a slave. . . ."
—FREDERICK DOUGLASS,
*Narrative of the
Life of Frederick Douglass,*
1845

One

❧

The Hughes Farm
Near Linden
Marengo County, Alabama
June 19, 1847

". . . Was I white, I might woulda fainted when Emmalina told me Masa done gone upside Kaine head, nelly bout
kilt him iff'n he wa'n't dead already. Fainted and not come
to myself till it was ova; least ways all of it that could git
ova. I guess when you faints, you be out the world. That how
Kaine say it be. Say that how Mist's act up at the House when
Masa or jes any lil thang don't be goin to suit her. Faint, else
cry and have em all, Aunt Lefonia, Childer, and the rest
comin, runnin and fannin and car'in on, askin, what wrong?
who done it? Kaine hear em from the garden and he say he
be laughin fit to split his side and diggin, diggin and laughin
to hear how one lil sickly white woman turn a House that
big upside down."

The darky had sat on the floor of the root cellar, barely visible
in its shadow. Occasionally her head moved toward the block of

light from the open door or her chains rattled in the darkness. There had been nothing in the darky's halting speech and hesitant manner to suggest the slave revolt leader she was convicted of being. Held spellbound by that very discrepancy, Adam Nehemiah had leaned forward from his perch on the cellar steps the better to hear the quiet rasp of her voice. He hadn't caught every word; often he had puzzled overlong at some unfamiliar idiom or phrase, now and then losing the tale in the welter of names the darky called. Or he had sat, fascinated, forgetting to write. Yet the scene was vivid in his mind as he deciphered the darky's account from his hastily scratched notes and he reconstructed it in his journal as though he remembered it word for word.

". . . I work the field and neva goes round the House, neitha House niggas, cept only Aunt Lefonia. Kaine, when me and him git close and see us want be closer, he try to git me up to the House, ask Aunt Lefonia if she see what she can do, talk to Mist's maybe. But Aunt Lefonia say I too light for Mist's and not light enough for Masa. Mist's ascared Masa gon be likin the high-colored gals same as he did fo they was married so she don't 'low nothin but dark uns up to the House, else ones too old for Masa to be beddin. So I stays in the field like I been.

"Kaine don't like it when Aunt Lefonia tell him that and he even ask Mist's please could I change, but Mist's see me and say no. Kaine mad but he finally jes laugh, say what can a nigga do? He been round the House, most a House nigga hisself—though a House nigga never say a nigga what tend flowas any betta'n one what tend corn. But Kaine laugh when Childer try to come the big nigga over him, tell him, say, 'Childer, jes cause you open do's for the white folks don't make you white.' And Childer puff all up cause he not like it, you don't be treatin him some big—and he was raised up with Ol Masa, too? 'Humph.' So he say to Kaine, say stedda Kaine talkin back at ones betta'n him, Kaine betta be seein at findin him a mo likely gal'n me. . . ."

"He chosed me. Masa ain't had nothin to do wid it. It Kaine what pick me out and ask me for his woman. Masa say you lay wid this'n or that'n and that be the one you lay wid. He tell Carrie Mae she lay wid that studdin nigga and that who she got to be wid. And we all be knowin that it ain't for nothin but to breed and time the chi'ren be up in age, they be sold off to anotha 'tation, maybe deep south. And she jes a lil bitty thang then and how she gon be holdin a big nigga like that, carrying that big nigga chile? And all what mammy say, what Aunt Lefonia and Mamma Hattie say, don't make Masa no ne' mind. 'Tarver known fo makin big babies on lil gals,' Masa say and laugh. Laugh so hard, he don't be hearin Mamma Hattie say how Tarver studdin days be ova fo he eva touch Carrie. Masa, he don't neva know it; but Tarver, he know it. But he don't tell cause the roots stop his mouth from talkin to Masa same as they stop his seed from touchin Carrie Mae."

Nehemiah paused, the pen poised above his journal. He couldn't bring himself to believe that negroes actually had some means of preventing conception, yet he could not keep himself from speculating. The recipe for such a potion would be worth a small fortune—provided, of course, that one could hit upon some discreet means of selling it. A contraception root would be very like slave trading, he thought with a low chuckle, something from which every gentleman would profit but which no gentleman would admit knowledge of. Probably he gave the negroes too much credit, but it would do no harm to question the darky further about this, he thought; he continued writing.

"Masa do wonder, but it's more'n one stud and Tarver is good fo drivin otha niggas inna field; good for to beat the ones what try for to be bad. Carrie Mae bedded wid David then and gots a baby comin . . .

"Kaine chosed me. He chosed me and when Emmalina meet me that day, tell me Kaine done took a hoe at Masa and Masa done laid into him wid a shovel, bout bus in his head, I jes run and when the hoe gits in my way, I let it fall; the dress git in my way and I holds that up. Kaine jes layin there on us's pallet, head seeping blood, one eye closed, one bout gone. Mamma Hattie sittin side him wipin at the blood. 'He be dead o' sold. Dead o' sold.' I guess that what she say then. She say it so many times afta that I guess she say it then, too, 'Dead o' sold.' Kaine jes groan when I call his name. I say all the names I know bout, thought bout, Lawd, Legba, Jesus, Conqueroo—anybody. Jes so's Kaine could speak. 'Nigga,' Kaine say, nigga and my name. He say em ova and ova and I hold his hand cause I know that can't be all he wanna say. Nigga and my name; my name and nigga."

"And what has that to do with you and the other slaves rising up against the trader and trying to kill white men?"

His tone had been a bit sharp, Nehemiah thought reading the question now, but he had been startled by that casual revelation of violence against a master. Perhaps he had made some overt sign of his excitement—after all, he was actually tracing the darky's career back, perhaps to her first mutinous act—for she had opened her eyes and looked at him. Nehemiah still marveled at how wide and black her eyes had appeared in the half-light of the cellar, the whites unmarred by that rheumy color characteristic of so many darkies. He had understood then something of what the slave dealer, Wilson, might have meant when he talked of the darky's "devil eyes" her "devil's stare."

"I kill white mens," her voice overrode mine, as though she had not heard me speak. "I kill white mens cause the same reason Masa kill Kaine. Cause I can."

It had been an entrancing recital, better in its way than a paid theatrical, the attack on the master, the darky's attachment to the young buck, that contraception root—all narrated with about as much expression as one gave to a "Howdy" with any passing stranger. And then that bald statement that seemed to echo in the silence. *This* was the "fiend," the "devil woman" who had attacked white men and roused other niggers to rebellion.

Nehemiah replaced the pen in the standish, seeing again the ghostly gleam of the darky's eyes in the dimness, the bulky outline of her body. Who would think a female that far along in breeding capable of such savagery? He shook his head, chiding himself; he shouldn't be surprised. Though the darky had no scars or marks of punishment except on her rump and the inside of her flanks—places only the most careful buyer was likely to inspect—these bespoke a history of misconduct. But the darky, according to the trial record, had been offered for sale at a bargain price (which Wilson jumped at) *because* she'd attacked her master. And neither the attack nor scars were mentioned in her description in the coffle manifest. How many others on Wilson's ill-fated slave coffle had carried a similar history writ about their privates? Nehemiah wondered; how widespread was such collusion?

Nehemiah leaned back carefully in the rickety chair, a sense of well-being spreading through him. This case was likely to yield more toward his book on slave uprisings than he had hoped. The obvious complicity between slave trader and slave owner in the resale of a dangerous slave was a theme worth investigating. It was the nature of the negro trader to buy cheap and sell dear— and warrant any one that could move as "likely" or sound. That was business and the wise buyer was ware. But to omit mention of a darky's mean streak went beyond sharp dealing and bordered on outright fraud.

Wilson, at least, had paid for his cupidity. That darky out in the root cellar and several bucks had somehow freed themselves, overpowered the guards, and freed the rest of the slaves on Wilson's coffle. The uprising had occurred on the trail, a couple of days east of Linden. Though the renegades had fled through the countryside, there had been none of the marauding and pillage rumor still attributed to them; the posse under Sheriff Hughes had caught up with them too quickly. Still, the toll in life and property had been horrifying. Five white men had been killed. Wilson himself had lost an arm. Thirty-one slaves had been killed or executed; nineteen branded or flogged: some thirty-eight thousand dollars in property destroyed or damaged.

The slave dealer was in comfortable enough circumstances, boarded at the home of a widow until permanent provision could be made for his care. But Wilson, while not violent—at least physically—was quite literally mad, by turns lucid and delusional. He could give a complete catalog of the names, dates, and places of purchase, the price paid for most of the hundred or so slaves in his coffle. A crackle of laughter or perhaps only the blinking of an eye and he would be plunged into tears and raving. Then he would call out to one or another of his companions on that ill-starred journey, or to Nate, the lone negro driver on the coffle who had died protecting him. Or "Step lively, there," he would cry; then, confidentially, "Lively niggers sing. Help em raise a song, Nate." Most often Wilson cursed the darky, "treacherous nigger bitch," and her cohorts, "fiends," "devils"—"Oh stop the bloody bastards, Nate!" his empty right sleeve waving as the nub within it jerked. It was an affecting spectacle. To see a white man so broken by nigras went quite against the grain. And Wilson, raving or lucid, blamed his condition on that darky out in the cellar, was obsessed with seeing, and selling, the kid she carried. A pickaninny that young would be more trouble than it was worth, but the court, fearing for Wilson's sanity, had delayed the darky's execution until after she whelped.

The unnatural, almost superstitious awe in which Wilson seemed to hold the darky had whetted Nehemiah's curiosity; slave dealers were not usually so womanish in their fears. The darky had been removed from the jail and placed in Sheriff Hughes' custody at his farm a few miles outside Linden—as much to remove her from the public eye as to have her near Hughes' cook who would act as midwife to the wench. Nehemiah had had no trouble persuading Hughes to let him see her, but he had been disappointed in that initial visit. The "virago," the "she-devil" who still haunted Wilson's nightmares had seemed more like a wild and timorous animal finally brought to bay, moving quickly and clumsily to the farthest reaches of the cellar allowed by her chains. Hughes had attempted, in a really remarkable approximation of the nigra's own dialect, to persuade her into the light provided by the open cellar door. He had not cared to compel her forcibly; she had been in a dangerously excitable state when first apprehended—biting, scratching, spitting, a wildcat—apparently unconcerned about the harm her actions might cause her unborn child. Her belly was almost as big as she and Nehemiah thought privately that birthing the kid she carried—a strong lusty one judging by the size of that belly—would probably kill her long before the hangman came for her neck. The stench of the root cellar that day, "composed," he had written, "almost equally of stale negro and whatever else had been stored there through the years," had almost suffocated him. They had withdrawn without coaxing her into speech.

He sniffed gingerly at his sleeve now, but could detect no telltale odor. Really, he must speak to Hughes about making provision for another meeting place. Being closeted with the darky within the small confines of the cellar was an unsettling experience. He took up his pen and wrote:

This is a long way from how those darkies escaped from Wilson's coffle but what there is of it is all here—even to that silly folderol about "roots" stopping some buck's mouth— as much in her own words as I could make out. It is obvious that I must speak with her again, perhaps several more times; she answers questions in a random manner, a loquacious, roundabout fashion—if, indeed, she can be brought to answer them at all. This, to one of my habits, is exasperating to the point of fury. I must constantly remind myself that she is but a darky and a female at that. Copious notes seem to be the order of the day and I will cull what information I can from them. I have at present no clear outline for the book—nor yet what I shall do with this darky's story, but I have settled upon *The Roots of Rebellion in the Slave Population and Some Means of Eradicating Them* as a compelling short title. It smacks a bit of the sensational, perhaps, but it is no more sensational than this story is likely to be.**

He double-starred the last word, denoting the end of the entry, replaced the pen in the standish, and stretched, slowly flexing shoulder muscles cramped too long over the makeshift table. The candles made a shifting pattern of light around him, leaving the rest of the small room in shadow. Leaning back in the chair, Nehemiah locked his hands behind his head. The idea for this book about the origins of uprisings among slaves had come from Nehemiah's publisher, Browning Norton. Anything to do with slavery, as the success of his last book, *The Masters' Complete Guide to Dealing with Slaves and Other Dependents*, seemed to prove, was assured some audience in the south and notice in the north. But Nehemiah had been reluctant to undertake a similar project so close upon the heels of it. He was gratified by the widespread recognition the *Guide* had brought him, but he had no plans to set himself up as an expert on recalcitrant negroes. However much the plantation south might rely on slave labor, the "negro tamer," like the negro trader, had no place in planter society. And Adam Nehemiah wanted just that.

Nehemiah was not a snob and rejected any suggestion of such an attitude; he did not undervalue the yeomanry, the small farmers, merchants, and craftsmen who made up the bulk of the white population in the south. He freely acknowledged that his own father had been a mechanic, owner of a small wheelworks in Louisville. Nehemiah, even now, would be in Louisville earning his livelihood in the family business had not the chance encounter with tales of the Old South—Cavalier Virginia, the landed gentry of Maryland and South Carolina—in a tattered, much circulated literary gazette provided a name for that singular quality that had set him forever apart among the people of his birth: He had taste, an instinct for fine food, fine clothing, fine conversation—fineness in its several manifestations. And there was something in his restless spirit that could not be satisfied by reading alone. He was drawn to the wealthy planters because they possessed many of the objects of his taste, the clothing and jewelry that delighted the eye, the foods that enchanted the tongue, the houses and furnishings that charmed and gratified some inner sense of continuity and style. He had thought education—schooling—the key to that world and had persisted in his efforts to continue his education despite his father's opposition. Though largely self-taught beyond grammar school, Nehemiah was well read in English literature, particularly the modern period, less so in the natural and physical sciences, and had some knack for mathematics. But land, not learning, was the entrée to planter society.

Nehemiah had turned his hand to first one thing then another, haberdasher, journalist (printing at his own expense a collection of his sketches that he sold, with indifferent success, through subscription), tutor, without penetrating beyond the fringes of society. Only teaching—he had specialized in preparing young men for university entrance—had admitted him to more than passing acquaintance with the better class of planters. The success of the *Guide* had changed that. It was little more than a handbook, the commonplaces of sound management (privately, he spoke of himself as a compiler or editor of its time-tested maxims); its novelty lay in the fact that no one had thought to compile such a volume before and in Nehemiah's constant reference to the practices of the wealthy planters among whom he'd lived as tutor and researcher. Instinct told him that too much emphasis on a knowledge of slave management could compromise the place in society that publication of the *Guide* had won for him. Still, Norton had pressed. A book on slave uprisings, touching as it must upon the secret fears of non–slave holder and slave holder alike, should be an immediate success, easily surpassing the heart- (and pocket-) warming sales of the *Guide*. The book would establish Nehemiah as an important southern author. And researching the *Guide* had opened the doors of countless Great Houses to him; Nehemiah had allowed himself to be persuaded.

Seated now at the makeshift writing table, in a chair rescued from the kitchen so that in his own mind he had dubbed it the "negro chair," just as one spoke of the rough homespun cus-

tomarily worn by darkies as "negro cloth," his only light two
malodorous tallow candles that smoked and flickered, in a stuffy
"attic-half" that was little better than a loft, Nehemiah had the
grace to laugh at his sanguine optimism. He ought, he knew, to
be grateful to Hughes. True, the fellow spoke English little better
than a negro (the darky, Sheriff Hughes told Nehemiah, was being
held "ex-communion"; the extenuating circumstances that had
delayed her hanging he called "excrutiating"; Nehemiah himself
was "Mr. Nemi," in what seemed a genuine expression of hale-
fellow regard), but Hughes had been the soul of cooperation, se-
curing permission for Nehemiah to read the court records—sealed
after the trials as too inflammatory for general perusal—even
turning over this "spare" room to Nehemiah's use while he ques-
tioned the darky. And the property, for all the lack of amenities
in the farmhouse itself, was a snug one, a little above three hundred
acres, such as Nehemiah himself was looking to purchase in Kentucky or middle Tennessee. But research for the *Guide* had taken
Nehemiah into Houses whose beauty was legendary, opening those
doors to him and on far more equitable terms than teaching had
ever done. He would be less than human, he told himself now,
did he not compare that with his subsequent circumstances. Research on this project had taken him into virtually every swamp
and overgrown road in southern Louisiana—where, according to
Norton, newspaper reports earlier in the year suggested some sort
of unrest among the slave population.

The hospitality of that region had been all that one could ask,
Nehemiah admitted now, but the reports of plots discovered and
insurrections foiled seemed always to originate in out-of-the-way
districts. He had seen a slave at Westwego, outside of New Orleans, said to have been cropped as a cohort of the outlaw slave
Squire, whose career had ended on the gallows some ten years before. The slave was a big, evil-visaged buck, black as sin, with great
flaring nostrils, wide enough—or so it had seemed to Nehemiah—
to drive a team through, and dainty holes at the sides of his head
where his outer ears had been cropped away. Whatever intelli-
gence the nigra might once have possessed had long since fled, and

Nehemiah had been unable to penetrate the smiling vacuity with which the darky now faced the world.

He had journeyed east to Lafayette on the short-turfed prairies of southwestern Louisiana to investigate a report that house slaves had discovered and betrayed a plot to rebel before it could begin. He had been told of the incident by a chance-met acquaintance at the home of Harrison Evans (second son of the Virginia Evanses) who had served in some measure as his sponsor in New Orleans. White men had actually been arrested in one or two cases, his informant had reported indignantly. There had been several newspaper accounts of reported unrest in the surrounding parishes of Iberia, St. Martin, and St. Landry, so, armed with a letter of introduction from Evans to Mr. James Carpenter, a major landowner in the area, Nehemiah had set out.

Carpenter had proved to be both a gracious host and the owner of the courageous darky Thomas, whose information had foiled the insurrection; he was thus much interested in Nehemiah's project. The plot had been a serious one: Four free negroes and nine of the slaves—over ten thousand dollars in property!—had been hanged; two white men from outside the district had been implicated, but as no negro could give evidence or bear witness in a court of law, they had not been brought to trial. Justice had been content with running the whites out of the area. Carpenter had been forced to give Thomas his freedom and safe passage out of the neighborhood as the only means of preserving his life from the vengeance of the other darkies; his name continued as a curse among slaves in the district.

These events, however, had occurred some seven years before, and though Carpenter spoke of "Uncle Tom's" departure with genuine regret (for the slave had been in the family since Carpenter's boyhood), even the remembered heroism of the loyal retainer had dimmed in his absence. And the planter had shrugged off the most recent rumors. The Creoles were an imaginative and emotional race—not that much better than the nigras as far as that was concerned; and most were nervous in the presence of three or more blacks. "Unless," he had added, winking at Nehemiah, "the blacks are women and the Creoles men." Nehemiah knew, of course, of such relations; more than one master used them as a means of increasing his capital and many used the *droit du Seigneur* to keep discipline in his Quarters. But no man of standing or sensibility made a parade of such practices as the Creoles were wont to do and he disliked hearing Carpenter make a joke of it.

And so it had gone, outdated reports, principals who were dead or moved from the neighborhood. Frustrated, Nehemiah set out on the coastal steamer at the end of May for South Carolina where he would make one of the J. T. Mims party at a newly popular and wickedly expensive resort on Lake Moultrie. He had hoped to be invited to an up-country manor or an island estate where he could while away the fever months safe from the agues that so often swept the low-lying costal areas during the summer. But the invitation from Miss Janet to be part of the select party of family and friends who gathered around the young Georgia couple during the summer months had been too flattering to turn down.

Mims and Miss Janet were among the best representatives of their class, people of means and taste who nurtured their inheritance and so savored its fruits to the fullest. Nehemiah knew there was some element of idealization in his view of the planter "aristocracy." There were few among them capable of the witty, erudite conversation that he craved; his more outrageous ripostes and marching figures were likely to be greeted with stares holding little more comprehension than that cropped buck's had. Yet, in the best of them, there was little of the ostentatious or affected. The mounds of victuals that so delighted shabby genteel "society" editors had no place on Miss Janet's table. Oh, there was a sumptuous amplitude about all Miss Janet touched. But what delighted, even inspired Nehemiah was not the quantity, but the quality, the subtle piquancy of the red-eye gravy or the feather lightness of a biscuit, sunlight falling across a Brussels carpet, the scrollwork on a ladder-back chair. The planters had wrought immense beauty in the wilderness that still dwarfed the nation and Nehemiah felt privileged to rub shoulders with its creators.

During the stopover in Mobile, Nehemiah had heard the tale of the uprising on the Wilson slave coffle, barely a month old and still causing shudders throughout the region. He had the tale from several sources; the name of the trader often varied; the coffle was said to have originated in Tennessee, Georgia, and Montgomery, to have been bound for Linden, Jackson, Huntsville. But always one thing remained the same. The slaves had killed white men in the battle in which they were finally subdued, and in the initial hand-to-hand action that had freed the entire coffle. That fact gnawed at Nehemiah. The slaves had killed white men. He had not heard of nigras doing that since Nat Turner's gang almost thirty years before.

Nehemiah rose, yawning. The darky's pregnancy was a stroke of luck; the rest of the ringleaders had been hanged by the time he heard of the uprising. Still, subsequent attempts to get the darky to talk had not been particularly fruitful. Nor, he admitted as he sat on the narrow bunk, was he particularly proud of the way he had handled them. He remembered one occasion in particular. He and Hughes had heard upon approaching the cellar a humming or moaning. It was impossible to define it as one or the other. Nehemiah had been alarmed, but Hughes merely laughed it off as some sort of "nigger business." The noise had sounded like some kind of dirge to Nehemiah, but Hughes chuckled when he suggested this.

"How else kin a nigger in her condition keep happy, cept through singin and loud noise?" he'd asked with a smug consequential air. "A loud nigger is a happy nigger."

"You make no distinction between moaning and singing?" Nehemiah asked tartly.

"Why should I?" Hughes replied with a hearty laugh. "The niggers don't."

Nehemiah had been obliged to rely on Hughes' judgment in the matter; as slave owner and sheriff, Hughes had had far greater contact with various types of darkies than Nehemiah would ever wish for himself. And he had heard much the same thought—a loud darky is a happy one—expressed again and again while doing research for the *Guide*. But the thought reminded him unpleasantly of Wilson's "Raise a song there, Nate," and Wilson's empty sleeve.

The sheriff had opened the door and the darky, caught in the stream of light, fell silent. Nehemiah, cautioning the sheriff to prop the door open as he left, descended into the cellar. The darky started to scuttle away and Nehemiah, fearful of being drawn into the shadows, called to her sharply. The darky stopped, crouching just inside the patch of light, and appeared unmoved when he reminded her that though the pickaninny she carried had saved her from a quick hanging, it would not save her from a whipping. Probably, she had seen that for the ruse it was. Except in the most extreme cases, even the meanest owner would not exact such harsh punishment of a darky so close to childbed. And one never threatened a slave. He had heard this axiom over and over again in his research for the *Guide*. One promised; and such promises had always to be kept.

The darky had greeted his statement with a flick of her eyes— almost as though he had been a bothersome fly and her eyes a horse's tail flicking him away. The memory of that gesture still had the power to outrage him; it had infuriated him then, and he had struck her in the face, soiling his hand and bloodying her nose, and stormed up the steps almost before he thought. He was immediately sorry; he had compounded the first error with another. It was seldom necessary to strike a darky with one's hand and to do so, except in the most unusual circumstances, lowered one almost to the same level of random violence that characterized the actions of the blacks among themselves. He was not, he told himself later, the first to have forgotten the sense of his own teachings; and the violence of his reaction had perhaps made any such response unnecessary in the future. Nonetheless, he had prevailed upon Hughes to institute the saltwater treatment: no food and nothing but heavily salted water to drink. That had gotten results; he glanced at where his journal, still open to the day's entry, lay on the makeshift table. Even so light a punishment would probably not be necessary again.

It was ironic, Nehemiah knew, that he who had never owned a

slave—nor wished to—should be counted an expert on their management. He had shrugged off much of the Calvinistic teachings of his father with the same ease with which he had put off the rough homespun his father's parsimonious nature forced the family to wear. But the elder Nehemiah's abhorrence of slaves still clung to him. He no longer saw the institution as quite the threat to white workingmen that his father had. Still, about the only thing a darky could do for him was to wash his linen—and that task he hired out. Such, he reflected, were the vagaries—and rewards—of life. Nehemiah pulled off first one boot, then the other and stood to take off his trousers. He would always take a special pride in the fact that he had been the first to hit upon the idea of compiling the *Guide,* but he felt in his bones that the new book would be an intellectual as well as practical achievement, a magnum opus, far eclipsing the impact of the *Guide.*

The *Guide* had not sold well in Alabama— It had done, Nehemiah amended, a brisk business in Mobile, and he smiled somewhat grimly: The rumors—and actual evidence!—of bands of runaway slaves in the area were too persistent for there not to be a high interest in the management of slaves among even the smallest slave holders. But, in general, Alabama slave owners prided themselves on taking care of their own. And it was true that there were not in the newspapers of the state the regular rash of alarums about rebellion plots discovered in the nick of time or advertisements for runaways that were a leitmotif in the papers and journals of most southern states. News of this uprising, despite the efforts of some civic boosters to keep it quiet, was rippling through the state, spreading consternation and fear in its wake. Hundreds of coffles a year went through Alabama, en route to Montgomery, Natchez, New Orleans—or the next town. Most of them averaged no more than twenty or thirty slaves except in the fall, when all roads in the state seemed to lead to the slave market in Montgomery. Even one desperate slave loose among the populace was fearful to contemplate and Wilson's had been a relatively large coffle of more than a hundred slaves. And white men had been killed. This was not news that would keep. If it sold no place else, Nehemiah thought with a chuckle, *Roots* would do "tolerable" well in Alabama! He adjusted his nightcap, blew out the candle, and climbed into bed. Ah, the work, *the* Work had begun.

June 20, 1847

    The darky demanded a bath this morning, which Hughes foolishly allowed her, and in the creek. She bathed in her clothes and dried in them also—as though there were not another darky on the place to spare her some sort of covering. A chill was the natural outcome, whose severity we have yet to determine. And were that not bad enough, she cut her foot, a deep slash across the instep and ball while climbing up the bank. Hughes thinks it a reasonably clean cut but she bathed near the place where the livestock come to water so there is no way of knowing. He claims that he was so nonplussed, "flustered," as he phrases it, at such a novel request coming from a nigger and a wench ready to be brought to light, too, that he had granted the request before he had time to think properly of the possible outcome. Since she was shackled during the whole business, he thought no harm could come of it—as though darkies were not subject to the same chills and sweats that overtake the veriest pack animal. It seems that I am never to be spared the consequences of dealing with ignorant people. Pray God this darky don't die before I get my book!**

"Sho was hot out there today."

"Yeah, look like it fixin to be a hot, hot summer."

The desultory conversation eddied around Dessa. The day's heat hung in the air; dust clung to her sweaty skin. The westering sun sent their shadows before them in wick-thin stripes dark across the sand-brown soil.

"*Hope it don't get too hot.*" Even the ones talking, Charlie and Sara and them, didn't seem too interested in what they were saying.

"*I see old crazy Monroe been over Masa Jefferson place again.*"

Dessa had seen Monroe that morning, chained out at one of the barns, looking miserable. He had been trying for the longest time to be with some girl over at the Jefferson plantation. But Young Mistress said all the girl was good for was housework and they didn't need another wench up to the House. That should have been that, but Monroe kept sneaking over to see her every chance he got. Which was to say, he made chances. As much as Boss Smith worked people in the fields, there was no way any of them were just going to "find" a chance to even sneak a "visit." And Master didn't like the men planting his seeds in the neighbors' gardens. Monroe want to chance that lash, Dessa thought, feeling suddenly evil; that was him.

"*Masa say he going sell him,*" Charlie said over his shoulder.

Sell him. For taking off a day to see a sweetheart. Sold away   Her temples throbbed with heat—

"*Lawd, won't these children learn?*" Sara asked of the air.

"*Can't learn a nigga nothing,*" Petey said quickly and they laughed.

"*Well,*" Santee said, "*I sho wished I knowed what that little girl got to make a nigga ask for a beating and walk fifteen miles a night to get em.*"

"*Don't know,*" Brady said loudly, "*but it sho gots to be goood.*"

"*This one nigga won't never find out.*" Charlie laughed and shook his head for emphasis. "*I don't want to love . . .*" and again that shake, "*where I can't* live."

"*Hey, hey sweet . . .*"

"*Listen to Charlie talk!*"

She didn't join their laughter . . . Someone . . . down the Quarters

"*. . . calling his da'ling's name.
Hey, hey sweet mamma . . .*"

Kaine's voice in the sunset, always, always the same.

"Someone sho is walking fast all a sudden."

They were laughing behind her. Dessa swung her short-handle hoe with elaborate casualness and paid them no mind. Kaine could always give you something to laugh about, changing words with the men, teasing the women. He made jokes on the banjo, came out with a song made up of old sayings and words that had popped into his head a second before he opened his mouth.

". . . *Kaine Poppa, calling his woman's name . . .*"

Fear touched her. There must have been something for Kaine to do back at the House. Childer could have found him a closet to turn out, some piece of furniture to move so the girls could clean behind it; Aunt Lefonia might have had some spoons or some such to polish in the kitchen. He could help serve supper if there was nothing else to do.

"Say now, hey now, Dessa da'lin . . ."

Heart pounding, she quickened her steps. Aunt Lefonia said Master was always complaining about how they couldn't afford to have a nigga sitting around eating his head off while he waited for some flowers to grow. Kaine could laugh, put it off on Master trying to get a rise out of his wife and her mother, but it must be something to it if it could put Young Mistress in tears. "What else she got to cry about?" Kaine, grinning wryly, eyes lit— Dessa wanted to run, to quiet his careless mouth with kisses . . . she hurried, hearing a quavering, high-pitched twang: "Place going to wrack and ruin cause he [meaning Master] don't know the difference between a gardener and a common field hand." Lefonia's ruddy brown face, twisted in comic mockery, shimmered before her eyes . . . hurrying . . . Mammy swore Aunt Lefonia could do Old Mistress to the life, the pinched mouth, the stuffed-nose quality to her voice. Lefonia knew, even if Kaine wouldn't tell her: "Long as it Vaugham money keep this House a showplace, that *nigger [meaning Kaine] better turn his hand to whatever need doing."* Not Aunt Lefonia's imitation now, but a voice so harsh and heavy it must have been Master's—when had she heard him speak? (that question wild within her, making her cold all the way through. Someday Master wouldn't care about Young Mistress's tears or Old Mistress throwing his family up in his face. He'd sell Kaine to Charleston or the next slave coffle that passed their way.

"Hey, hey . . ."

Dessa moved as if through molasses: Kaine was coming down the Quarters; temples pounding, she ran

≥∾

Nehemiah persuaded Hughes to allow the meetings with the darky to take place in the yard. He hoped that the novelty of fresh air would help him regain the rapport established during the last session with the darky and broken, he feared, by the brief respite while she recuperated from her chills. She was now fully recovered, suffering, so Jemina said, from no more than an occasional sniffle; the gash, while painful, perhaps, caused her no more than a slight limp. He sat now on a crude chair in the shade of the big elm in the side yard, pad and pen on his knee. The darky sat near him on the ground, knees drawn up to her chest, manacled hands clasped about them; her dress covered the leg-irons that hobbled her feet. A chain attached to her ankle-bead was wound around the trunk of the elm. From time to time she hummed, an absurd monotonous little tune in a minor key, the melody of which she repeated over and over as she stared vacantly into space. Each morning Nehemiah was awakened by the singing of the darkies and they often startled him by breaking into song at odd times during the day. Hughes, of course, found this comforting; thus far, Nehemiah reflected sourly, he had heard nothing but moaning from this darky.

"Who had the file you used to break the chains?" This was a shot in the dark; there was no proof that a file had been used, no indication, really, of just how this darky had first gotten free of her chains. And Nehemiah did not really expect an answer; except for that offensive flicking of the eyes, the darky had responded to none of his overtures. "Where did the file come from?" he asked sharply. "Was it another darky?"

The darky sat with her eyes closed and he nudged her with the tip of his boot to assure himself that she had not fallen into a doze. He had been told they fell asleep much as a cow would in the midst of a satisfying chew. He had not observed this himself and thought it an exaggeration for the darky did move, flicking her eyes up at him as she did so. He caught himself on an expletive, tapping his watch case impatiently. This was a damnable business.

The darky closed her eyes. Nehemiah contained his irritation and went on with his questioning. "Where were the renegades going?" They had been heading south when the posse caught up with them and Nehemiah was not the only one to speculate that they had been making for an encampment of runaway slaves long rumored to be in the vicinity of Mobile. The darky opened her eyes and stared off into space, humming again, that absurd tune. "Who were the darkies that got away?" He raised his voice so as to be heard over her humming. This, too, was a shot in the dark; there was no proof that any of the renegades had escaped the posse. But there was a discrepancy between the number of slaves listed on the coffle manifest and the accounting made by the court of those killed, executed, branded, and/or released. It might be, as Wilson's partner, Duncan, maintained, that those slaves—by Nehemiah's count there were at least two—had been sold en route and not immediately noted in the manifest. But the discrepancy remained a loose end in Nehemiah's opinion and he knew the darky could tie it up.

> "Lawd, give me wings like Noah's dove
> Lawd, give me wings like Noah's dove
> I'd fly cross these fields to the one I love
> Say, hello, darling; say how you be."

The darky's song burst in upon these reflections and before Nehemiah could react, she spoke.

"Kaine just laugh when Mamma Hattie say that playing with God, putting yourself on the same level's His peoples is on. He say Mamma Hattie ain't knowed no more about God and the Bible than what the white folk tell her and that can't be too much cause Masa say he don't be liking religion in his slaves." She had caught him by surprise, but he wrote quickly, abbreviating with a reckless abandon, scribbling almost as he sought to keep up with the flow of her words. ". . . Kaine just go on singing his songs to me in the evening after I gets out the fields. I be laying up on our pallet and he be leaning against the wall. He play sweet-soft cause he say that what I needs, soft-sweeting put me to sleep after I done work so all day. He really feel bad about that, me in the field and him in the garden. He even ask Boss Smith could I come work at the House or he come work the field. I scared when he do that. Nobody ask Boss Smith for nothing cause that make him note you and the onliest way Boss Smith know to note you is with that whip. But he just laugh; tell Kaine he a crazy nigga."

She laughed softly, shaking her head. "Kaine not crazy. He the sweetest nigga as ever walk this earth. He play that banjo, he play it so sweet till Mist's even have him up to the House to play and she talk about having a gang of niggas to play music for when they be parties and such like at the House."

Nehemiah stopped writing. More of that business with the young buck. He scowled, looking at the darky in exasperation. Sunlight filtering through the leaves dappled her face with shadow. In the cellar, her skin had seemed an ashen black, almost scaly in its leathery pallor. Now it seemed the color of pekoe tea, a deep lustrous brown that even in the shade glowed with a hint of red. Her voice had lost some of its roughness yet still held a faint echo of that desperate bravado that had fascinated him during their last meeting.

" 'Niggas,' Kaine tell me, 'niggas just only belongs to white folks and that be's all. They don't be belonging to they mammas and daddies; not they sister, not they brother.' Kaine mamma be sold when he little bit and he never know her face. And some time he think maybe his first masa or the driver or maybe just some white man passing through be his daddy."

Perhaps that was it, Nehemiah speculated, that strain of white blood that had made the young buck so rebellious. He should interrupt her, he knew; this was hardly germane. Yet he was reluctant to disturb the darky's trancelike state. He watched as her mouth quirked drolly, an eyebrow lifted skeptically. He wouldn't have thought the darky's face so expressive. Well, he thought, tapping his watch case again yet oddly arrested by the darky's display, he would let the darky talk this out.

". . . Kaine say first time he hear anybody play a banjo, he have to stop, have to listen cause it seem like it talking right at him. And the man what play it, he a Af'ca man, he say the music he play be from his home, and his home be his; it don't be belongs to no white folks. Nobody there belongs to white folks, just onliest theyselfs and each others. That in Charleston and I know that close to where I'm is and I wonder how it be if Masa had buyed Kaine then, when he little bit, stead of when Kaine be grown. But— It happen how it happen and that time in Charleston, Kaine not know all what the Af'ca man say, cept about the home and about the banjo, how to make it, how to play it. And he know that cause he know if he have it, home be his and the banjo be his. Cept he ain't got no home, so he just onliest have the banjo.

"He made that banjo hisself. Make it out good parchment and seasoned wood he get hisself and when Masa break it, it seem like he break Kaine. Might well as had; cause it not right with him after that. And I can't make it right with him. I tell him he can make another one. I pick up wood for him from Jim-boy at the carpenter shed, get horsehair from Emmalina's Joe Big down to the stables. But Kaine just look at it. 'Masa can make another one,' he say. 'Nigga can't do shit. Masa can step on a nigga hand, nigga heart, nigga life, and what can a nigga do? Nigga can't do shit.

'What can a nigga do when Masa house on fire?
What can a nigga do when Masa house on fire?
Bet *not* do [*mo'n yell, fire, fire.*]
[*Cause a nigga can't do shit!*]'

He sing that and laugh. And one day Emmalina meet me when I come in out the field and tell me Masa done shove in the side of Kaine's head." She looked up at the sun and blinked her eyes rapidly several times.

The woolly hair fitted her head like a nubby cap and for a moment Nehemiah fancied he could smell her, not the rank, feral stink of the cellar, but a pungent, musky odor that reminded him of sun-warmed currants and freshly turned earth. His skin prickled and he shook himself, cursing. The darky had led him back to the same point as the previous session and he had taken notes on nothing save the names she called in her first burst of speech.

❧

June 26, 1847

These are the facts of the darky's history as I have thus far uncovered them:

The master smashed the young buck's banjo.
The young buck attacked the master.
The master killed the young buck.
The darky attacked the master—and was sold to the Wilson slave coffle.

Nehemiah hesitated; the "facts" sounded like some kind of fantastical fiction. Had he but the pen of a novelist— And were darkies the subject of romance, he thought sardonically, smiling at his own whimsy. He didn't for a minute believe that was all there was to the young buck's attack on his master—a busted banjo! Yet, even if he never got to the bottom of that, the darky's case had already provided some interesting leads—collusion between slave owners and slave dealers and, the more he thought of it, the more it seemed that an argument ought to be made for a stricter separation between house servants and field hands. Clearly the buck had gotten ideas above himself, placing such exaggerated value on a primitive "banjar," even going so far as to try to order the work force to suit his own convenience. So, this incident with the buck was not wholly tangential to the events on the coffle. Nehemiah double-starred the last word. Obviously, mention of the buck was the key to getting the darky to talk.

ॐ

"Did this darky— What did you say his name was?" Nehemiah nudged the darky impatiently with his foot; she flicked her eyes at him. They sat under the elm, the darky chained as usual, Nehemiah stripped to his shirt sleeves against the heat. "Kay-ene— is that it?" People would give darkies these outlandish names, he muttered to himself, and throw the rules of spelling to the winds.

"You don't 'smell' it; you say it."

Startled, Nehemiah looked at the darky narrowly. Her eyes regarded him solemnly above the crook of her elbow and even as he stared, she quickly lowered them. She'd misheard him of course, but she had made, he realized, a slight jest. "That's quite a good joke—in what you said and," he added genially, "in my own rather slow reaction."

The darky ducked her head but not before Nehemiah saw the flash of even white teeth between the thick, long lips; seeing this, he relaxed himself. "Kaine did speak then, a great deal about freedom?"

She looked at him, alert. "Don't no niggas be talking too much bout freedom," she said flatly.

Nehemiah did not believe her, but decided, for the time being at least, to allow her to think he did. She was actually responding to his questions and he did not want to distract her. "Then what was your idea in trying to escape from the coffle?"

She picked up a twig and began to mark in the dirt and to hum— not the same tune as the previous day, but one equally monotonous. She looked up at him, finally, with widened eyes. "Was you slave, you want be sold deep south? I never been deep south, but Boss Smith, he always threats lazy niggas with that and they don't be too lazy no mo."

"And the others," he asked, "was this what was in their mind?"

She shrugged her shoulders. "Onliest mind I be knowing is mines. Why for you don't ask them first?"

This seemed more simple curiosity than insolence and Nehemiah allowed it to pass. "I didn't hear of this . . . incident until it was too late to speak with the others who were charged as leaders," he explained.

"Thank"—she spoke so quietly he almost missed her words— "thank it be a place without no whites?"

"What?" he asked sharply.

But she continued to herself, in a deeper dialect than she had heretofore used, really almost a mumble, something about Emmalina's Joe Big telling Kaine something and going, but where he could not make out. "They caught—"

"What?" he asked again.

The blank sullen look returned to her face; the humming started again. She moved as though uncomfortable and touched, almost as if frightened, the big mound rising beneath her dress. "This all I got of Kaine. Right here, in my belly. Mist's slap my face when I tell her that, say, don't lie; say, it must be Terrell, that how she call Masa, Terrell, say it must be his'n. Why else Masa want kill Kaine, best gardener they ever has, what cost a pretty penny? She say, well, Terrell live, he live knowing his slut and his bastid south in worser slavery than they ever thought of and Aunt Lefonia stop me before I kills her, too."

He was startled by the confession. There had been no hint of anything like this in the court records. And she did look fierce, poised on her haunches, staring into the sunlight. It was almost like listening to the first day's recital and he knew when she turned her head from him that, for the moment at least, he had gotten all that he could from her. This, together with the gathering heat, had made him close his notebook for the day.

June 27, 1847

I asked about the name of the young buck with whom this
darky lived, little suspecting what revelations this might lead
to. . . .

Nehemiah quickly wrote a summary of the exchange with the
darky, more satisfied than not with his progress. Miss Janet he
knew, would be interested in the gal's tale. She was eloquent on
the subject of slave concubinage, charging that the practice was
an affront to white womanhood. Nehemiah was not quite so ve-
hement—a man must, after all, have some outlet for the baser
passions—but he was sincere in his belief that a race could not
long prosper that sowed its seed so profligately. He found it
strangely stirring to think how even the appearance of immorality
had led to a barely averted tragedy. He continued in his journal:

It's obvious the buck shared the mistress's suspicion about
the master and this wench. Why else would the darky attack
a white man, his master? And she, that gal, now—

Nehemiah paused again. Lurking behind the darky's all too often
blank gaze was something more than the cunning stubbornness
which, alone, he had first perceived. That was a bad business with
the mistress, of course, though remembering the darky's playful-
ness that afternoon, he found himself rather unwilling to credit
her confession. He had not supposed that the thick-lipped mouth,
so sullen in its silent repose, could smile so . . . so freely, even
utter small jests. His own lips curved upward. She must be exag-
gerating, he thought, egged on, perhaps, by the young buck's ex-
ample and her own nerve in attacking the master. He continued
the entry:

This lapse does not unduly disturb me. I think the darky
begins to have less distrust of me. She was not overly free in
her speech but it is obvious that she inclines towards me more

than in the past. I fancy that I am not overly optimistic in predicting that one, perhaps two more sessions and I will have learned all I need from her. I shall have to think of a provocative title for the section in which I deal with the general principles apparent in her participation in this bloody business. Truly, the female of this species is as deadly as the male.**

Two

🦢

"June 28, 1847." Nehemiah wrote the date at the top of the new page. It was hot and clear, even as Hughes brought her up from the cellar, that the darky felt the heat, too. Her movements, always slow, were even slower, her walk not stumbling but heavy as though her feet were weighted. She eased her bulk onto the ground beneath the tree and leaned back against its trunk. Her dark hair seemed to merge into the deeper shadows cast by the low-hanging branches of the tree. Nehemiah sat in his habitual place facing her, stripped to his shirt sleeves, and felt stifled by even this light covering. The sharp bright sunlight was too painful to gaze at from the depth of the tree's shadow and his eyes wandered between the pages of his notebook, blank save for the day's date, and the darkness of her face. They were silent for some moments after she was seated.

"That writing what you put on that paper, huh?" He was startled by the question and did not immediately answer. "You be writing down what I say?" She was on her knees, turned to him now to see what was in the notebook.

Instinctively he held it away from her eyes. "Well." He cleared his throat. "Although I have written nothing today—we have said nothing so far . . ." He laughed a little, but this small pleasantry escaped her. "I do indeed write down much of what you say." On a happy impulse, he flipped back through the pages and showed her the notes he had made on some of their previous sessions.

"What that there . . . and there . . . and that, too?" He told her and even read a little to her, an innocuous line or two. She was entranced. "I really say that?" When he nodded, she sat back on her haunches. "What you going do with it?"

"I will use what you have said in a book I am writing." He was totally unsure of whether she would comprehend the meaning of that.

"Cause why?" She was thoroughly aroused by this time and seemed, despite the chain that bound her, ready to flee.

"Girl," he said, for at that moment he could not for the life of him remember her name, "girl, what I put in this book cannot hurt you now. You've already been tried and judged." She seemed somewhat calmed by the utterance, perhaps as much by the tone of his voice, which he purposely made gentle, as by the statement itself.

"Then for what you want do it?"

"I write—" He cleared his throat again, casting around in his mind for some appropriate words. "I write what I do in the hope of helping others to be happy in the life that has been sent them to live." He was rather pleased with that response. Certainly, it seemed to succeed in setting her mind at ease about the possible repercussions in talking freely with him; she appeared much struck by the statement, looking intently into his face for a long moment before she again settled into her customary pose. He allowed her to reflect upon this for a moment. She was silent for so long that he began to suspect her of dozing and leaned forward the better to see her. Her eyes were open (she seemed not to have the same problem as he with the harsh light), her hands cupped beneath the roundness of her stomach. "Your baby seems to have dropped; according to the old wives' tale, you'll be brought to bed soon." It was merely an attempt at conversation; he, of course, knew no more about that sort of business than he knew about animal husbandry or the cultivation of cotton. She jumped as though stung and he cursed his stupidity, knowing that his unthinking comment must have brought her own sentence to mind. After the initial start, she straightened her back and scooted nearer the tree, but said nothing. He waited, somewhat anxiously, for the blank sullen look to return. It did not, however, and emboldened, he ventured quietly, "Girl, where did the others get the file?" even as she spoke.

"Kaine not want this baby. He want and don't want it. Babies ain't easy for niggas, but still, I knows this Kaine and I wants it cause that. And . . . and, when he ask me to go to Aunt Lefonia . . . I— I near about died. I know what Aunt Lefonia be doing, though she don't be doing it too much cause Masa know it got to be some nigga children coming in this world."

Nehemiah started at that: baby murder! He had heard of African women fresh off the boat, as it were, engaging in such practices but this was the first time he had come across any hint of it among native-born blacks. Fancy that, blocking conception and child killing, too. And the owners not even aware! Oh, *Roots* would explode like an artillery shell among them. He was so startled by the disclosure and its implications that he almost missed her next sentence.

". . . anybody but Kaine, I do it, too. First time anyway. But—" She paused and licked her lips, touching her stomach again. "This Kaine and it be like killing part of him, part of me. So I talk with him; beg him. I say, 'This our baby; ours, us's. We make it. How you can say, kill it? It mine and it yours.' He just look at me. 'Same way Lefonia sons be hers when Masa decide that bay gelding he want worth more to him than they is to her. Dessa,' and I know he don't want hurt me when he call my name, but it so sweet till it do hurt." His voice seemed to ring inside her head. " 'Dessa,' just soft like that. 'Dessa, where your brother, Jeeter, at now?' I'm crying already, can't cry no more, not for Jeeter. He be gone, sold south, somewhere; we never do know. And finally I say 'Run,' and he laugh." Her mouth filled with the remembered bitterness.

"He laugh and say, 'Run, Dessa.' " (Lawd. No one had never said her name so sweet. Even when he was angry, Dessa. Dessa. She would always know the way he called her name.) " 'Dessa, run where?'

" 'North,' " she whispered. She'd never heard anyone talk about *going* north. North had been no more to her than a dim, shadowed land across a river, as mythic and mysterious as heaven: rest, when the body could bear no more. But, and she had understood this even as she breathed the word, if there was rest for the body, there must be peace for the heart. And it was her heart, *his heart*, that Kaine asked her to kill. "North."

"North? And how we going get there?"

"You know, Kaine." He knew. She knew he knew. He knew if he wanted to know.

"And what we going do when we gets there?"

She looked at him. He had to know.

" 'Dessa.' " Say my name again. " 'You know what is north? Huh? What is north? More whites. Just like here. You don't see Aunt Lefonia, I see her for you.' "

Oh, he had talked to her, the irreverent, half-uppity banter that could convulse her with laughter. "You think white folks piss champagne, huh? They bowels move the same way ours do; they shit stank just as bad." She remembered her own startled laugh, even though she didn't know what champagne was, even though she was shocked and a little frightened to hear him talk under white folks' clothes like that. He wanted, she knew, to shock her, to make her see that white people, except for their skin color, were no different from her, from him—from any of the people. Foolish, futile— But soon she was asking herself, what good was that white skin, anyway? They had been setting out rice in the one field Master now kept for it and that question had come to her as she watched Boss Smith talking with Tarver, one of the negro drivers. Even though the overseer's face was shaded by a wide-brimmed hat, she could see the winter paleness of his skin. As the spring progressed his nose would blister and peel and blister again until it achieved a semblance of the brown she was born with. But, white

people had houses and farms and horses— "And you think Masa'd have one pig or one chicken wasn't for us working for him,
wasn't for you and the rest of the people out there working from
'can see to can't'?"

"Boss Smith don't work us—" she had begun.

"Naw," Kaine had cut her off, "Masa don't let him work
yo'all from can to can't—no more; he just work you twice as hard
from sunup to sundown." That was true. Tarver was always there,
whether they were working rice, cotton, or corn, with his "Step it
up there; speed it up now."

They had seldom loved at night; the realization was like a fist
in her stomach. Nighttime was for holding, for simple caresses that
eased tired limbs, for sleep. Winter Saturdays they had loved in
the evenings after dark had shortened the gray afternoons into chilly
blackness, lighted by the flame on the fire-half, warmed by the heat
their bodies made. They had had only the one winter of love; and
the mornings. Memory of that fierce loving, muffled by the dense
blackness before dawn, flooded her, bringing quick heat to her face.
Sometimes, she had awakened him, suckling at his lightly haired
chest, hand searching the wiry thicket that began just below his
waist. Or she awakened, nipples tiny and hard, squeezed in his
fingers, and he already between her thighs. Molten now, she would
rear beneath him, open, drawing him deep; he would plunge.
Mostly hurried, always soon done. Sated, they would lie nested
together in the silence between cockcrows, dreading the mournful
bellow of the conch calling the day, summoning her to ceaseless
toil. And at night— The nights of which she dreamed were only
that, dreams and ghosts of dreams. I sat between mammy's knees,
she thought wildly, laughed with Carrie, argued with Jeeter, ran
with Martha. Loved Kaine—

She opened her eyes wide against a rush of tears, conscious now
of the white man, willing them not to fall, yet unable to halt the
memory of Kaine's voice bitter, beloved, and right: "And Masa'd
sell off any youngun on the place as soon as look at em cause he
know we can always make another one."

Fear had eaten at her insides; even if she saved their baby from

Lefonia, she would never be able to save it if Master wanted it. She cut her eyes at the white man. He was bent over the pad on his knee, his hand propelling the pen across its surface in intricate movements. What would this make him know about her, she wondered, about her life with Kaine? The white man looked up at her even as the pen continued across the pad and she recoiled, thinking in that first instance of seeing that his eyes were covered by some film, milky and blank. His eyes were "blue," she saw in the next moment, like Emmalina said Mistress's were, like sho enough white folks' were, like the sky. Hastily, she dropped her own. That's why we not supposed to look in white folks' eyes, she thought, with a shiver. There was only emptiness in them; the unwary would fall into the well of their eyes and drown.

"He, Kaine," she said, stumbling, taking up her tale again, "he tell me then how he been sold way from some masas, runned away from others. He run, he say, trying to find north and he little then and not even know north a direction and more places than he ever be able to count. He just think he be free of whippings, free to belong to somebody what belongs to him just so long as he be north. Last time he runned way, he most get there and he think now he know what way free land is, what is free town, next time he get there. But never is no next time cause the same time patterrollers takes him back, they takes back a man what been north, lived there and what know what free north is. 'Now,' Kaine say, 'now this man free, born free, but still, any white man what say he a slave be believed cause a nigga can't talk before the laws, not against no white man, not even for his own self. So this man gots to get another white man for to say he free and he couldn't find one quick enough so then the Georgia mens—that be what the north man call patterrollers—they takes him for to be slave. That's right. But even before the patterrollers catched him, white man hit him, he not allowed to hit back. He carpenter, but if white mens on the job say they don't want work with him, he don't work, and such things as that. He say it hard being a free man of color, he don't say nigga, say free man of color, but it better'n being a slave and if he get the chance, he going runned way.' "

Dessa had been almost overwhelmed by the story; wasn't there no place where a nigga could just be? And, "He—Kaine—say, he ask hisself, 'That free? How that going be free? It still be two lists, one say, "White Man Can," other say, "Nigga Can't," and white man still be the onliest one can write on em.' So he don't run no more. 'Run for what?' he say. 'Get caught just be that much worser off. Maybe is a place without no whites, nigga can be free.' But he don't know where that is. He find it, he say we have us babies then."

Dessa looked out at the sunshine and her lower lip trembled a little. "I know Kaine be knowing more'n me. I know that. He— he telled me lot a things I ain't even think about before I'm with him." Yet, everything that Kaine said that was supposed to make her see the foolishness of having a baby only convinced her that they must run. "No matter though," she said with her eyes closed. "Masa kill Kaine before it get time for us to go."

They were both quiet for some time.

"You think," she asked looking up at the white man, "you think what I say now going help peoples be happy in the life they sent? If that be true," she said as he opened his mouth to speak, "why I not be happy when I live it?"

June 29, 1847

As today is Sunday I held no formal sessions with Odessa. But, in order to further cultivate the rapport thus far achieved, I read and interpreted for her selected Bible verses. We were in our habitual place under the elm tree and I must admit that the laziness of the hot Sunday afternoon threatened, at times, to overcome me (as Hughes had warned it would. As a consequence he was loath to give me the key to the cellar. He felt my vigilance would be impaired by the heat. I replied that, in as much as the darky would remain chained as usual, there was no danger involved in such a venture—unless, of course, there was some question about the actions of his own darkies. He was stung by the retort as I meant him to be, but he did surrender the keys. It has really become quite tedious to plow the same ground with Hughes each time I want to do something with Odessa that he considers out of the ordinary. I shall make it my business to obtain another key to the cellar and to the chain with which she is bound to the tree—at my suggestion, this is the only one that in her quieted state she now wears. It is not to my liking to be required to request *permission* each time I wish to talk with the gal).

My drowsiness was compounded, I finally realized, by the monotonous melody she hummed. I have grown, it appears, so accustomed to these tunes that they seem like a natural part of the setting, like the clucking of the hens or the lowing of the cattle. Thinking to trap her into an admission of inattention, I asked her to repeat the lessons I had just imparted. She did so and I was pleased to find her so responsive. However, the humming became so annoying that I was forced to ask her to cease. She looked up at me briefly and though I had not threatened her, I believe she was mindful of previous punishments and of the fact that it is only through my influence that she is able to escape from her dark hole for these brief periods. She assured me it wasn't "no good-timing song"; it was about "the righteousness and heaven."

I asked her to sing it and I set it down here as I remember and understand it:

> Gonna march away in the gold band
>   In the army by 'n by,
> Gonna march away in the gold band
>   In the army by 'n by.
>
> Sinner, what you going do that day?
> Sinner, what you going do that day?
> When the fire arolling behind you
>   In the army by 'n by?

It is, of course, only a quaint piece of doggerel which the darkies cunningly adapt from the scraps of Scripture they are taught. Nevertheless, the tune was quite charming when sung; the words seemed to put new life into an otherwise annoying melody and I was quite pleased that she had shared it with me. We were both quiet for several moments after she had done. The heat was, by this time, an enervating influence upon me. She, too, seemed to be spent by that brief animation. After a few moments, I closed the Bible, prayed briefly for the deliverance of her soul, and would have returned her to the cellar. But, she spoke.

"They caught ev—" she said suddenly, turning to me.

Instantly I recognized in those few syllables the beginning of the question she had started to ask me the other day. "Some nigras did get away," I charged. "And *you* know where they are!" This was a bit impetuous of me, but to have confirmed what I have suspected all along made me incautious. The blank sullen look immediately returned to her face, but I count that as nothing. She will be brought to give up this information!**

Later:

Hughes says there is talk of a "maroon" settlement, an encampment of runaway slaves, somewhere in the vicinity. There have been signs of marauding about some of the farms and plantations farther out from town. In the latest incident, several blacks (the wife of the farmer could not give an accurate count) stole into a small farm about fifteen miles southeast of here, took provisions and the farm animals, and seriously wounded the farmer when he tried to protect his property. Fortunately, the wife was hidden during the raid and thus escaped injury. Hughes was inclined to treat this as an isolated incident—claiming that the other cases had happened so long ago that they had become greatly exaggerated in the telling—and thus dismiss the maroon theory as merely a fearful figment in the imagination of the larger slave holders. He put down the missing provisions and the occasional loss of livestock to the thieving of the planters' own darkies. I am aware, as I told him, that an unsupervised darky will steal anything which is not nailed down, yet, in light of Odessa's talk of a place without whites and her concern about "catching"—talk which I repeated—I cannot dismiss the theory of an encampment of some sort so easily. It is, of course, pure conjecture, but not, I believe, groundless to say, as I did to Hughes, that perhaps the unaccounted-for darkies had joined the maroons—which would certainly be one place without whites. And it's obvious the darkies from the coffle were making for *some*where when they were apprehended. Hughes was much impressed with my reasoning and invited me to join the posse which leaves at dawn tomorrow in search of the renegades. I readily accepted, for, even knowing the imaginative flights to which the darky's mind is prone, I put much faith in this information precisely because it was given inadvertently. What information Hughes and the prosecutor were able to obtain from the others—and from the darky herself regarding the uprising—is as nothing compared to this plum.**

🦢

Dessa had come to look forward to the talks with the white man; they made a break in the monotony of her days. She had slept a great deal when she first came to the farm, surrendering in the deep quiet of the cellar to the exhaustion she had held so long at bay. But, once she was rested, misery had come upon her in shuddering waves she hoped would kill her; and the dreams. She had paced restlessly, the chain that held her to the stake in the middle of the dirt floor clanking behind her. Sometimes she lay listlessly on the pallet or sat against the wall behind the dull sunlight that entered through the tiny window. Always, whether her eyes were open or closed, Kaine walked with her, or mammy. Jeeter tugged at her head-rag or Carrie Mae frowned her down about some little foolishness. Aunt Lefonia, Martha— They sat with her in the cellar. She grieved in this presence as she had not done since their loss.

Often she saw Leo, his bald head shining in the moonlight, his face a bloody mess, and felt his body heavy and supine where it had rolled against her knee. Her hands moved ineffectually above the gapping hole in his chest. Big Nathan whispered eerily, urgently, above her, "Help me get his jacket off. Help me!" Leo's skin was still warm, the flesh flaccid— She cringed away from that memory, that ghostly vision. They hadn't killed Leo; one of the white men had done that. And Leo— The white men would think Leo was Nathan, if they couldn't see his face. Nathan had been ferocious in battle but he could not look into Leo's dead face. He had raised the rock above his head and closed his eyes as it descended. She couldn't forget this. They had paid so much, so much for it all to end in this hole. Talking with the white man kept her, for those brief periods, from counting and recounting the cost.

Jemina said he was making some writing, a book, about the fight on the coffle. The big, light-skinned woman came to see her almost every night, often bringing some special fixings from the white folks' supper table that she passed to Dessa through the bars of the cellar window. At first, in her misery, Dessa hadn't understood why the house servant would take such risks for her, or even wondered why. She had merely accepted dumbly whatever the woman offered. Jemina's kindness had eventually penetrated her despair and, finally, Dessa had asked why.

"Why?" Jemina chuckled softly. "Why, honey, you's the 'debil woman.'" Hurriedly, she told how the people in the neighborhood had coined the name from the slave trader Wilson's description of the uprising. It expressed their derision of slave dealers, whose only god was money, and their delight that a "devil" had been the agency of one's undoing. Dessa had not liked the idea of such notoriety, but she was pleased to know that others knew of that daring, that brief moment of exultation in the clearing, when all had stood free, by their own doing, of beads and chains.

She was grateful for the brief companionship of the other woman for no one else came near her. Now and then she did hear a scrap of song or caught a word from a raised voice that might have been meant for her to hear. Often when she sat with the white man she saw one of the men or women going about some errand in the yard. Once, two wide-eyed, bare-bellied children had appeared suddenly behind the white man's shoulder. One had smiled quickly, tentatively, at her, then they had scampered away as silently as they had come. The white man never knew they were there. Twice a day, Jemina brought her meals. If her master had unlocked the door, Jemina set down the tray without a word. More and more often now, Beaumont, Jemina's husband, unlocked the door.

"Masa say he got better things to do than wait on some darky," Jemina had chuckled the first time Beaumont guarded the door. "Go on, look." She gestured toward the stairway. Dessa, her chain clanking, walked to the bottom step and looked up through the doorway. Beaumont, his foreshortened figure framed by the light, his face shadowed by a hat, cradled a rifle in his arms. He wiggled the fingers of one hand at her; his teeth flashed whitely and were gone. Jemina took up Dessa's slop jar and turned with a nod and brief smile and she, too, was gone. Dessa understood; even with Beaumont above, it would not do to tarry.

At night, Jemina hunkered down beside the window for a few moments' whispered conversation, meaningless words of encouragement that Dessa appreciated nonetheless. Sometimes Jemina brought news that she had overheard in the conversation of her white folks. That was how Dessa knew the white man had studied what the court said about the fight. She had no idea what a "court" was; she had never been more than five miles from where she was born before being sold, nor seen more than three or four white people together, except at a distance. She had no words to describe much of what she had experienced, or what those experiences had forced her to see. She understood "court" as white folks for trying to figure out if everyone on the coffle had been caught. She wanted to know this herself, so she watched and listened.

The white man was little, hardly taller than herself, she thought, but he kept a careful distance between them, even outside under the tree, sitting above and behind her, his chair tilted back on its hind legs, its back against the tree. He would lean forward long enough to wave her to a spot several feet from him, using the vinegar-soaked handkerchief she knew was meant to protect him from her scent. She no longer smelled—Jemina now brought her water to wash in—and it shamed and angered her that he still thought she did. Always above her, behind her if she turned her head, she heard tapping, in the silence between his questions, his finger flicking proudly against the gold chain he wore at his waistcoat.

She couldn't always follow the white man's questions; often he seemed to put a lot of unnecessary words between his "why" and what he wanted to know. And just as she had puzzled out what that was, he would go on to the next question. "Who had the file?" he would ask, and how could she answer that? There had been no file. Nathan had knocked out the trader where he slept and taken the keys to the chains from the saddlebags the trader used as a pillow. So, having no answers, she gave none, though she had listened carefully at first: Maybe this white man would tell her something she didn't know. But it was soon apparent to her that the white man did not expect her to answer. She had kept a careful expression on her face, now and then cutting her eyes at him to see if he required some response; but, despite her best efforts, her attention wandered. Once she had looked up and seen his face contorted with the violence of some unexpressed feeling. She had shrunk from him, her chains clanking about her, and he had hit her in the face. She had not taken the full force of the blow; she had been warned by that one startling glance. Her nose had bled some and she now kept her face vacant (better to appear stupid than sassy); but her mind continued to roam.

Had Master looked at Kaine like this white man looked at her? Why? White folks didn't need a why; they was: *his* voice, quiet and mocking, pulsing like a light through the darkness inside her. "Kaine—" She didn't know she had spoken aloud until she became aware of a voice in the stillness and knew it in the next instance as her own. How hoarse and raspy it sounded. She had not spoken above a whisper, except in muttered response to some white man's questions, in weeks. Caught in her own flow, she listened and continued, seeing as she spoke the power of Master as absolute and evil.

Terrell Vaugham, by virtue of his marriage to Mary Lenore Reeves, owned three farms, the large Home Farm and two smaller outlying properties, and a house in Charleston. Dessa didn't know how many people he owned. Somebody was always being born. Two or three times, a relative or family friend had died and left someone to one of the Reeveses, as Martha had been inherited by Young Mistress when an elderly cousin died. Master Vaugham had brought no slaves to the marriage (not even a manservant, Childer, scandalized, had reported), as Old Mistress had brought mammy, the dairy maid, and Lefonia, the personal one. All the children were separated early from their mothers and raised on the Home Farm under the care of Mamma Hattie and a couple of older or younger women—depending on who was just up from childbed or otherwise ailing. When the children were old enough to work, usually around six or seven, they were parceled out among the farms and the town house to fetch and carry, as Dessa had been put with her mother in the dairy. Often they were hired out to local farms or businesses or apprenticed to a craftsman on the Home Farm— as mammy had feared that Dessa would be apprenticed in the dairy. Carrie Mae, Dessa's older sister, already worked there; the only reason they would need three women in the dairy was that one was going to be sold. But Dessa, like many others, found a permanent place on one of the farms.

If they lived, they lived long. But the toll of those who did not, who died or were permanently debilitated by the annual fevers, by one or another of the ailments that walked through the Quarters with agonizing regularity, from punishments or their aftereffects, left a gaping need for more and more hands to plant, to reap, to make, to clean, to feed. Or, you were sold away. Increasingly, they were sold away. Even in dreams that threat had haunted her.

Master Vaugham had improved their working conditions. They

were never in the fields before sunup and seldom there much after sundown. They were given an hour-and-a-half break at noon, nursing mothers two. Roofs were repaired, weevily meal replaced. But they all knew, without, it seemed to her, ever having discussed it among themselves, that as soon as they learned some craft or task, they were liable to be sold. They were bred for market, like the cows mammy milked, the chickens that she fed. Dessa had not admitted this to herself, even under Kaine's prodding. She saw the past as she talked, not as she had lived it but as she had come to understand it. White men existed because they did; Master had smashed the banjo because that was the way he was, able to do what he felt like doing. And a nigger could, too. This was what Kaine's act said to her. He had done; he was. She had done also, had as good as killed Master, for wasn't her own punishment worse than death? She had lost Kaine, become a self she scarcely knew, lost to family, to friends. So she talked. She was reconciled to nothing, but the dreams or haunts that had crowded about her in the cellar now walked the sunlit air and allowed her peace at night.

Memory stopped the day Emmalina met her as she had come out of the fields. Dessa came back to that moment again and again, recognizing it as dead, knowing there was no way to change it, arriving at it from various directions, refusing to move beyond it. Out there was nightmare, Kaine's body, cold and clammy beneath her hands, Master laughing in her face, the horror that scarred her inner thighs, snaking around her lower abdomen and hips in ropy keloids that gleamed with patent-leather smoothness. Once the white man's questioning had driven her into that desert and Young Mistress had risen from the waste, clothes torn, hair screaming, red-faced, red-mouthed. The four red welts in the suddenly pallid face, the white spot where her thumb had pressed at the base of the red neck filled Dessa with a terror and glee so intense they were almost physical. Frightened at her own response, she was almost ashamed—not of the deed. No. Never that, but surely it was wrong to delight so deeply in anyone else's pain. She had seen the blood and bits of pink flesh beneath her own fingernails, felt again the loose skin of Young Mistress's neck. And clamped her mouth shut, clanked her arms across her chest. She should have killed the white woman; they would have killed her then. It would all have been over; none of this would have begun.

She didn't know where "this" had begun. There was no set moment when she knew that the negro driver the white men called Nate was paying attention to her or that the young mulatto boy who often walked the chain in front of her was being kind. Gradually she had realized that she never stumbled when the mulatto walked in front of her, that there was always something extra on her plate—a bit of home-fry when everyone else had only grits, a little molasses for her bread. She expected that one or both of them would come fumbling at her in the dark. The men and women were bound together at night; and, while it was more common for the white guards to take one of the women, the chains were no real barrier to a determined couple. They were encouraged to it. Pregnancy was proof of a woman's breeding capacity; and the boy was often chained with her at night. But neither man touched her.

Cully, the mulatto, talked to her about the stars when they happened to lie next to each other at night. She knew the drinking gourd, the North Star in its handle. He showed her a cluster he called Jack the Rabbit, put there, so he said, because of a low trick Rabbit had played on Brother Bear. Often he touched her stomach and marveled that the baby moved. This was all that she remembered of those nights. For at first she had paid him no attention. He talked just like a white man; except for his nappy yellow hair, he looked just like a white man. Later, he reminded her of Jeeter, her only living brother, who had been sold away. The big, bald-head driver, Nathan, had been with the trader the day she was bought. It shamed her somehow to know he had seen her so low and she was glad they could none of them hold a real conversation. The coffle walked twenty miles a day, and even around the campfire, talk among them was discouraged. But Dessa knew herself to be enveloped in caring. The pain and tiredness of her body numbed her mind; she was content to leave it that way. Even when the others spoke around the campfire, during the days

of their freedom, about their trials under slavery, Dessa was silent. Their telling awoke no echoes in her mind. That part of the
past lay sealed in the scars between her thighs.

Dessa couldn't understand why this white man would want to
take her out under the tree and talk about Kaine, and behind her
inquiring expression she resented his careless references. Wasn't
no darky to it, she would think indignantly. Kaine was the color
of the cane syrup taffy they pulled and stretched to a glistening
golden brown in winter. Or, Childer had said the words over them,
looking at each of them in turn, disapproving, Dessa knew, of
Kaine's choice (but he had chosen, Lawd! he had chosen her, brown
as she was, with no behind to speak of, and he had wanted her—
not for no broom-jumping mess, but the marriage-words and
Childer just had to accept that). Talking with the white man was
a game; it marked time and she dared a little with him, playing
on words, lightly capping, as though he were no more than some
darky bent on bandying words with a likely-looking gal.

Maybe she had been careless with the white man, she worried
now. She had lain awake in the early morning hours watching the
window as it slowly grayed with dawn light. The baby kicked vig-
orously in her side; she put her hand to her stomach, feeling it
ripple with the baby's movement, and crooned wordlessly to it.
She had slipped in asking anything of the white man that did not
turn his own questions back upon themselves; maybe she had
caught herself in time. He hadn't pressed her and she couldn't bring
herself to regret that betraying impulse. To know that someone,
Nathan, anyone had gotten away . . . She had forced Nathan and
Cully to abandon her, clambering noisily back toward the sound
of sporadic pistol fire, where she knew she would find the patterrollers. Her flight had been an act of total despair. Someone had
to escape. After what they had done, someone had to be free. She
was barefoot, pregnant— She had already held Nathan and Cully
back insisting that any who wanted to be free must be given a
chance. Nathan had grudgingly agreed. In the melee of a general
escape, the three of them would be harder to track. He had planned
at first to free only Dessa and Cully on some moonless night when

the two were chained together. He had a key, as did all the guards, to the shorter chains by which groups of five or six were chained together at night. Only Wilson had a key to the manacles and Cully argued against taking it. Best to let sleeping dogs lie; the three of them could be away while the camp slept and once free could worry about the manacles. But with more than half the coffle expected to run, they had to have the slave trader's keys.

Their numbers grew, David, Matilda, Elijah, Leo, two or three others Nathan felt could be trusted. They talked only of stunning the white men, tying them, taking their guns, of stranding them. The actual deed there in the clearing was more frightening and more exhilarating than any of them had imagined. Nothing went as planned. They had wanted a dark night, but there had been moonlight; Cully and Dessa weren't chained in the same group. The white men had delivered a big lot of people to an outlying plantation and were in a relaxed mood. They had sat long and drunk deep by the campfire, two of them falling asleep there; the rest managed to make their way to their bedrolls. Not long after the camp settled into sleep, one of the white men sought out Linda, a mulatto girl purchased in Montgomery, and led her into the bushes.

The other white men didn't even rouse up as the guard thrashed off into the underbrush with Linda, but everyone on the coffle was awake. Every night since Montgomery, one of the white men had taken Linda into the bushes and they had been made wretched by her pleas and pitiful whimperings. The noise from the underbrush stopped abruptly. Then came the rattle of chains and above it a dull thud, startlingly loud in the stillness, and the rattling of the chains again. In his lust and alcoholic daze, the guard had failed to secure the chain after he removed Linda from it. Someone in Linda's chain group moved and all their chains fell away. Seeing this as a sign, Elijah whispered urgently for Nathan, who was already moving stealthily toward Dessa's group. Linda appeared in the clearing, her dress torn and gaping, the bloody rock still clutched in her manacled hands. All hell broke loose.

The white men asked her later about attacking the trader, but whatever answer she had given (and she thought she had given several different ones), she could not remember the trader as distinct from the other white men. She'd tried to kill as many of them as she could. The one thing that stuck in her memory from that night was Nathan in the moonlight, crushing the face of his friend.

They had argued about which direction to take, some wanting to go north, following the drinking gourd to freedom. There was a mighty river to cross, David admitted, but once across it, they would all be free. Most wanted to go with Nathan, who planned to take Dessa and Cully south to the coast. They could find a ship there to take them to islands he had heard of where slavery had been abolished and black men were all free. Again, Nathan consented, not so grudgingly that time, she thought now, for he had fallen in with their plans. Matilda wrote a pass for them, stating that all of them were in the charge of Toby, a big mulatto, and Graves, a lean brown man approaching middle age, taking them to their master on a plantation farther south. The moon had set by the time this was decided.

They took wagons, weapons, and horses. The wagons proved too cumbersome for the quick cross-country trip Nathan said was imperative. They plundered, then abandoned them, piling the horses high with supplies, traveling, after the first day, by night and sleeping by day. The patterrollers came up on them one morning just as they were retiring, having, as they thought, eluded the white man for yet another day. Nathan and Cully, never far from her, took her hands and ran.

Afterward, when she burst into the clearing where the captured people were held, she had fought fiercely hoping by the strength of her resistance to provoke them into killing her. They hadn't; a blow to her head quickly ended her struggles. She kept count, on the trail and in the warehouse where they were held, scanning the faces of those who were recaptured, culling through the whispered names and descriptions of those who had been killed. Nathan—Nate, as the white men called him—was reported dead and no one of Leo's description was ever mentioned in her hearing.

Only Toby of the several mulattoes on the coffle had been taken alive and she mourned Cully, giving him up as lost.

Those who had not fought the posse too hard were early taken from the warehouse where Dessa and the rest were held. Those who remained learned their fates when some were taken out and didn't return, or returned whipscarred and branded. Yet, as the population in the warehouse dwindled, a pinprick of hope was born in Dessa. Perhaps their ruse had worked and Nathan had survived. Had it not been for that hope, her own sentence would have driven her mad. To be spared until she birthed the baby . . . the baby . . . Could she but do it again, she sometimes thought, she would go to Aunt Lefonia if that would bring her even a minute, real and true, with Kaine. But to let their baby go now, now . . . She would swallow her tongue; that's what Mamma Hattie said the first women had done, strangling on their own flesh rather than be wrenched from their homes. . . . She would ask Jemina for a knife. . . . She would take the cord and loop it around the baby's neck. . . . She . . .

A rooster crowed; the conch sounded. Dimly, so softly at first it might have been the echo of her own crooning, she could hear the people assembling for work, a mumbled word here, the chink of a hoe, the clunk of one implement hitting against another. A warbled call soared briefly above the dawn noise; sometimes this signaled the beginning of a song, one voice calling, another answering it, some other voice restating the original idea, others taking up one or another line as refrain. She never heard more than fragments of these songs; whatever commentary they contained did not carry beyond the Quarters, but she recognized many of the tunes. Now and then she mouthed the words or soundlessly improvised a response of her own. She came to recognize some of the voices, a nasal soprano she learned was Jemina's, a full-throated voice that skipped from baritone to soprano in a single slurring note, the clear tenor that ascended to falsetto and yodeled across the dawn much as Kaine's had done. He could have made another one, she thought as the tenor rose briefly and was silent. Kaine

could have made another banjo; he had made the first one. Why,
when they had life, had made life with their bodies—? The question gnawed at her like lye. She shut her mind to it; it would eat
away her brain, did she let it, leave her with nothing but a head
full of maggots.

On impulse, she moved to the window, her chain rattling behind her, and standing on tiptoe looked out. She could see nothing except the dusty yard that sloped away from the cellar, but
she sang anyway, her raspy contralto gathering strength as her call
unfolded:

> Tell me, sister; tell me, brother,
> How long will it be?

She had never sung a call of her own aloud and she repeated it,
wondering if any of them would hear her:

> Tell me, brother; tell me, sister,
> How long will it be
> That a poor sinner got to suffer, suffer here?

There was a momentary silence, then the tenor answered, gliding
into a dark falsetto:

> Tell me, sister; tell me, brother,
> When my soul be free?

Other voices joined in, some taking up the refrain, "How long
will it be?," others continuing the call; her voice blended with theirs
in momentary communion:

> Tell me, oh, please tell me,
> When I be free?

They had begun the chorus a second time when another voice,
a rough baritone that Dessa did not recognize, joined in, singing
at a faster tempo against the original pace.

Oh, it won't be long.
Say it won't be long, sister,
Poor sinner got to suffer, suffer here.

The words vibrated along her nerves; was this really an answer? She sang again:

Tell me, brother, tell me,
How long will it be?

Again the voice soared above the chorused refrain:

Soul's going to heaven,
Soul's going ride that heavenly train
Cause the Lawd have called you home.

Startled, Dessa drew away from the window.
"Odessa."
The voice cut across the singing and she was still a moment, heart thudding. "Who that?" she called. No one called her Odessa but the white folk; only Jemina came to the window.
"Odessa."
It came again and she bundled the chain in her arms and moved soundlessly back to the window. "Who that?" She saw the pale blur of a face at the window even as she recognized the voice of the white man.
"I'm leaving in a few minutes."
"You don't be coming back?" Jemina had not told her about this. She moved closer to the window, letting her chain drop noisily to the ground.
"Oh, I shall indeed return in a few days and we will resume our conversations then." He paused a moment as though waiting for some response from her; when she made none, he continued. "We are going in search of a maroon settlement."
"Maroon?" She caught at the unfamiliar word for he seemed to put special emphasis on it.

"An encampment of runaway slaves that's rumored to be some-where in this vicinity."

She clutched the bars of the window and peered at him through them. She had not understood the half of what he said, catching only the meaning of "camp" and "runaway." He stooped awk-wardly at the window, his face almost touching his knees. It was a ridiculous posture and she turned her face to hide her grin. "You a *real* white man?" she asked, turning back, as the thought struck her. "For true? You don't talk like one. Sometime, I don't even be knowing what you be saying. You don't talk like Masa and he a real uppity-up white man, but not like no po buckra, neither. Kaine say it be's white men what don't talk white man talk. You one like that, huh?"

She could hear him suck in his breath before he answered sharply, "I *teach* your master and his kind how to speak."

"Oh, you a teacher man," she exclaimed childishly. He was an-gry and she continued hurriedly, "Was a teacher man on the cof-fle." She was grinning in his face now, feeling him hang on her every word. "He teached hisself to read from the Bible, then he preach. But course, that only be to niggas, and he be all right till he want teach other niggas to read the Good Word. That be what he call it, the Good Word; and when his masa find out what he be doing, he be sold south same's if he teaching a bad word or be a bad nigga or a prime field hand."

"Is he the one who obtained the file?" the white man asked quickly.

Dessa laughed tiredly, wanting now only to hurry the white man on his way. "Onliest freedom he be knowing is what he call the righteous freedom. That what the Lawd be giving him or what the masa be giving him and he was the first one the patterrollers killed." She moved back into the darkness of the cellar, still laughing softly.

"Odessa!" he called again.

"Whatcho want?" she asked moving toward him. "Whatcho want?" stopping just outside the pool of gray light.

There was a shout from the yard and the white man's face disappeared from the window. She could see his legs clearly now as his hands brushed at the legs of his trousers. "You will learn what I require when I return," he flung at her.

The sound of his departing footsteps was lost in the new song the people had begun during their conversation. Dessa joined in, suddenly jubilant, her voice floating out across the yard.

> Good news, Lawd, Lawd, good news.
> My sister got a seat and I so glad;
> I heard from heaven today.
>
> Good news, Lawdy, Lawd, Lawd, good news.
> I don't mind what Satan say
> Cause I heard, yes I heard, well I heard,
> I heard from heaven today.

On the Trail
South and West of Linden
June 30, 1847

We set out early this morning, picking up the trail of the renegades at the farm where they were last seen. It led us in a southerly direction for most of the day and then, just before we stopped for the night, it turned to the west. The trackers expect to raise some fresher sign of them tomorrow for, by their tracks, they appear laden with supplies and we are not (a fact to which my stomach can well attest. Dried beef and half-cooked, half-warmed beans are *not* my idea of appetizing fare). And, I am told, if the weather holds humid as it has been and does not rain, their scent will hold fresh for quite a while and the dogs will be able to follow wherever it leads.

I did see Odessa this morning before we departed. I heard singing and, at first, taking this to be the usual morning serenade of Hughes' darkies, I took no notice of it. My attention was caught, however, by the plaintive note of this song (a peculiar circumstance, for Hughes, despite his disclaimer to the contrary, does frown on the darkies' singing any but the liveliest airs). I listened and finally managed to catch the words—something about the suffering of a poor sinner. I had no sooner figured them out—and recognized Odessa's voice—when another voice, this one lower and harsher, took up the melody, singing at a somewhat faster tempo while Odessa maintained her original pace. It gave the effect of close harmonic part singing and was rather interesting and pleasing to the ear, especially when other voices joined in, as they presently did.

This is the liveliest tune I have heard Odessa sing and I went round to the cellar window. There proved to be no time, however, for the kind of session such as now has become our custom—quite vexing. Odessa was a bit fractious, probably no more than a sign of her returning spirits. And no more than a careful master would soon put to rights. A pity she came under the influence of that fool buck so young. Even now, with prudent schooling— That Vaughram was a fool; of course one puts aside such things when one marries—as Mims did when he wed Miss Janet. Had *I* but had Odessa's breaking, that intemperate nature should have been curbed. What a waste that she should have fallen into such hands as those.**

Somewhere South and West of Linden
July 3, 1847

A wild goose chase and a sorry time we have had of it. I much doubt that there is an encampment, such as I first conceived of, at least in this vicinity. We have searched a large area and come up with nothing conclusive. Several times, we sighted what might have been members of such a band, but the dogs could not tree them and it was more than we ourselves could do to catch more than what we *hoped* were fleeting glimpses of black bodies. Whether they took, indeed, to the trees, or vanished into the air, as some of the more

credulous in the posse maintain, I have no way of knowing.
If they exist, they are as elusive as Indians, nay, as elusive as
smoke, and I feel it beyond the ability of so large a group as
this posse to move warily enough to take them unawares. To
compound matters, the storm that has been threatening for
days finally broke this morning, putting an end to our search
and drenching us in the process. We have stopped to rest the
horses, for Hughes estimates that if we push hard, we should
reach Linden by nightfall. A bed will be most welcome—and,
perhaps, I shall see also about something to warm it when
we get back. Hughes has given the call to mount and so we
are off.**

July 4, 1847
Early Morning

I put the date in wearied surprise. We have been out most
of the night scouring the countryside for signs of Odessa, but
there were none that we found and the rain has by now
washed away what we must have missed. It as though the
niggers who crept in and stole away with her were not human blood, human flesh, but sorcerers who whisked her away
by magic to the accursed den they inhabit. Hughes maintained that the devil merely claimed his own, and gave up
the search around midnight. But reason tells me that the niggers were not supernatural, not spirits or "haints." They are
flesh and bone and so must leave some trace of their coming
and going. The smallest clue would have sufficed me for I
should have followed it to its ultimate end. Now the rain has
come up and even that small chance is gone, vanished like
Odessa.

And we did not even know that she was gone, had, in fact,
sat down to eat the supper left warmed on the fire-half against
our return, to talk of the futile venture of the last few days,
to conjecture on God knows what. Unsuspecting we were,
until the darky that sleeps with Jemina came asking for her.

Hughes went to inquire of his wife—who had not risen upon our return, merely called out to us that she was unwell and that food had been left for us. I was immediately alarmed, prescience I now know, upon learning that the woman had not seen Jemina since the wench had taken supper to Odessa earlier in the evening. And Hughes' assurance that Jemina was a good girl, having been with the wife since childhood, did nothing to calm my fears. Such a slight indisposition as his wife evidently had was no reason to entrust the keeping of so valuable a prisoner to another darky who is no doubt only slightly less sly than Odessa herself. I protested thus to Hughes, too strongly I now see, for he replied heatedly that if I did not keep my tongue from his wife, my slight stature would not keep me from a beating. I am firm in my belief that these impetuous words of mine were a strong factor in his early abandonment of the search and I regret them accordingly. There are stronger words in my mind now, but I forebore, at that time, carrying the discussion further. I knew even then, without really knowing why, that time was of the essence. But Hughes shall find on the morrow that even one of my *slight stature* has the means of prosecuting him for criminal neglect. To think of leaving Odessa in the care of another nigger!

Hughes' darky was, of course, incoherent—when was a nigger in excitement ever anything else?—but we finally pieced together, between the darky's throwing her apron over her head and howling, "Oh, Masa, it terrible; they was terrible fierce," and pointing to her muddied gown to prove it, what must have happened. There were three niggers (she said three the first time; the number has increased with each successive telling. Perhaps there were only one or two; I settle upon three as a likely number. These were obviously the niggers with whom Odessa was in league in the uprising on the coffle. I could scream to think that even as we were out chasing shadows, the cunning devils were even then lying in wait to spirit her away. And to think that she—*she* was so deep as to give never an indication that they were then lurking about. Both Jemina and that woman of Hughes' swear that except for a natural melancholy—which in itself was not unusual—*I* have been the only one to succeed in coaxing her into animated spirits—there was nothing out of the ordinary in Odessa's demeanor these last days. And knowing now the cupidity of which she is capable, I must believe them). The three bucks overpowered the darky just as she opened the door to the cellar to hand down the evening meal to Odessa. At this point, Hughes ejaculated something to the effect that it was a good thing "my Betty" was not present, at which the darky began what must have been, had I not intervened, a long digression on the "Mist's' " symptoms and how she might, at long last, be increasing. But I could *feel* those niggers getting farther away with Odessa, and so could not bear the interruption. The darky swears she heard no names called, that except for one exclamation from Odessa, of surprise or dismay, she could not tell which, they fled in silence; swears also that she could not see well enough to describe any of the niggers, save to state that they were big and black and terrible, as though that would help to distinguish them from any of hundreds, *thousands* of niggers in this world who are equally as big and as black and as terrible.

Hughes' jocular, and inappropriate, prediction that we should find Odessa and her newborn brat—for what female as far gone as she could stand the strain of a quick flight without giving birth to something—lying beside the trail within a mile or so proved incorrect. Both the nigger and the one bloodhound Hughes keeps were alike worthless in finding their trail. And then the rain came up, driven by a furious wind, lashing the needlelike drops into our faces; washing away all trace of Odessa. Hughes, in giving up the hunt, charged that I acted like one possessed. I know this was merely his excuse for failing in his own lawful duty. But the slut will not escape me. Sly bitch, smile at me, pretend—. She won't escape me.**

The Wench

". . . I have plowed and planted
and no man could head me. . . ."
—Sojourner Truth

Three

"... I chooses me Dessa."

There was a murmur from the crowd gathered in the torchlit area between the corn cribs and the Great Barn. Dessa looked at Charlie. Ellis, Sara, and Neely, Charlie's first three choices for his team, stood beside him looking as surprised as she felt. She was young to have been chosen so early. Though she was a steady worker ("steady sometimes be better than quick," mammy said, "and it all ways better than flashy"), she was not as good at husking corn as Harriet, say, or Petey, or any of a number of other people whom Charlie could have chosen. He was probably joking, Dessa thought, trying somehow to show up Alec, the general for the other team of corn huskers. And Alec—Alec was obviously courting. He had chosen Zenobia at his fourth turn, passing over the experienced hands whose quick methodical shucking would make short work of the huge mound of corn piled in the middle of the area. That kind of funning was usually left until after the best workers had been chosen.

"Charlie going try for 'Youth' now he done lost 'Booty,'" someone called out.

People laughed and she hid her own grin in her hands. Charlie could choose whomever he wanted. Dessa, though young, was no more foolhardy a choice than Zenobia, who was not known for her quickness at any chore, had been. Alec's side had groaned when he called out Zenobia's name; Brud, his second-in-command, had tugged frantically at his arm. Alec had shaken him off impatiently. "This strategy," he said loudly. "Strategy." And taking Zenobia's hand, he pulled her to his side with a sweeping bow. That gesture had really loosened tongues and it was this amazed and ribald tribute to audacity that Charlie had sought to capture for himself in choosing Dessa. He probably meant to say Martha, she thought, as the older girl hunched her in the side.

"Come on over here, baby." Charlie beckoned to her, then folded his arms across his chest and waited with an air of such evident satisfaction that she was tickled in spite of herself. Still, she hesitated; maybe Charlie would choose Martha next. And— She glanced around. Mammy was sure to think that Charlie had chosen her because she had put herself forward and not because Charlie was just trying to shock people. Dessa craned her neck, her eyes searching among the dark faces, but she couldn't tell if mammy were anyplace in the crowd.

"Well, if that don't—" Alec slapped his thigh in disgust that no one took seriously. The good-natured wrangling over selections was customary—though that, too, usually took place later. Alec's public courting had swept them all into early gaiety.

Dessa eyed Zenobia curiously. She was not above average looking, her brown skin rather muddy and, even in the torchlight, given to ashiness. But Zenobia had, as Alec told anyone who would listen, ass-for-days (and said like that as one word, it wasn't cussing, just repeating what someone else had said. Anyway, she would never say it in front of mammy or any other grown person; with them it would be Zenobia's "long booty." Even this she would not say too often). And now that Zenobia was no longer with Jake, Alec was determined to have her.

This was common knowledge. Even the children know about it, Dessa thought with a smile as she watched the older woman. Zenobia looked like she wasn't studying about anything as she stood with her arm casually brushing against Alec's sleeve. She did jiggle when she walked; the way her firm buttocks jostled the coarse cloth of her dress was generally admired among the men and envied, at least a little, among the women (and not just a certain kind, as mammy and Aunt Lefonia maintained). Dessa herself preferred Martha's figure, she thought, and glanced at her friend, whose full bosom and high narrow behind seemed to be driving two or three young men on the plantation wild. And there was nothing about Zenobia—if you discounted her booty (and after tonight, no one in the neighborhood would)—that Dessa could see that would inspire a man to risk Master's accusation of playing around with the work. A corn husking was not, strictly speaking, work, true enough. Master provided music and food—Jeeter said his stomach itched everytime he thought of the night's feasting— and invited the masters of neighboring plantations to bring their people to the husking. The white folks, of course, danced and feasted at the Big House while the people shucked the corn. The food, the music, the competition over who would be the corn general, over which side would finish shucking its pile of corn first, all these made you want to come. And though some of the more religious people (for Master served up the persimmon beer in barrels) and some of the older people stayed away or only came later, like the white folks, to watch the dancing, everyone knew that all Master's corn, down to the last rounding, would be shucked before victual one was eaten or the fiddler bowed one note.

"In that case," Alec sputtered now, "I wants Martha."

Dessa felt a quick spurt of disappointment; they would not be on the same side after all.

" 'Booty' and 'Beauty.' " This from the crowd amid rising laughter.

"Martha?" Charlie squawked. He was definitely into his act now, playing to the laughing crowd. "Man, how you going choose Martha when Santee ain't been chosed, and Monroe; neither Hank?"

"Now, look here, Charlie, you know these two pretty little ladies don't be doing too much of no kind of work"—*here she started*

*up: Why Alec want to say something like that, even in fun?—"let
alone shucking corn, when they's right long side of each other."*

"And they don't be doing too much of that even when they ain't
together," Sara said laughing.

Though she and Martha looked indignantly at Sara, Dessa was
relieved that the older woman had spoken up. The whole business
of choosing sides had come to a halt. She felt torn between pride
at being the subject of the men's fast-talking raillery and mortification at having her name bandied about before every darky on
the place. Mammy would pitch a hissy ("Another one want to be
noted, huh? Note ain't never got a nigga nothing but trouble").

"Now, you just hold on a minute here, Sara—" Alec began.

"Aw, man, get on with the choosing."

"Don't make me no ne' mind which'n choose me." Martha spoke
for the first time. "I ain't never been particular about scratching
up my hands on no corn husks no way."

Dessa smiled at her whispered commentary. Martha was used
to all this; somebody was always trying to trade words with her,
to get next to her. But Martha paid none of them any mind. "Now,
if it was Masa . . ." she'd said once, looking at Dessa sideways
out of innocently widened eyes. Dessa had felt a faint brush of
fear at the idea. To do that with . . . She had turned away from
the thought uneasily and Martha had continued. "Why not? Least
that'd be one man can't be sold way from you."

"Sold way" the words echoed eerily in Dessa's mind and the
brightly lit, laughing faces of the people wavered before her eyes.
She heard a clanking noise, her own labored breathing. She stumbled and would have been dragged down by the pull of the ankle
chain had it not been for a hand on her elbow.

"Oh, drat!" Martha held out a stubby muscular hand, the nails
broken, the skin ashy. She licked a forefinger and rubbed it deli-
cately at a roughened place between her little and ring fingers.
"Them cotton boles do tear a hand up so."

Dessa laughed; Martha could tear up herself. That Robert boy
who worked with Luke's gang in the timber lots came into her
mind. Lawd. He was fine and maybe they would end up on the

*same side tonight or at least sitting across from each other. She
imagined the pile of corn reduced between them, his face appear-
ing above it in the moonlight, the pointed chin and little shiny eyes
that got lost in the crinkles of his face when he laughed. He had
some eyes for looking; they seemed to follow her whenever she
was around him. She couldn't see him in the crowd but there was
no doubt in her mind that he would seek her out before the evening was over.*

"Come on, girl." Martha tugged at her arm. "We on Charlie's
side."

*She stood a moment, her eyes frantically searching the scene:
Someone was missing. They rested a moment on mammy's wide
dark face, her uncovered head, the thin hair gathered into three
plaits that stuck out from her head   Dessa's heart beat fast*

*Mammy didn't go out without something on her head— She
turned . . . Jeeter? Her insides opened up. Jeeter? Was this the
hole in the blackness? The brother sold south*

*It was dark; the square was lit almost as bright as day by flar-
ing torches and moonlight, but there were shadows on the faces.
The people milled about—men, women, children (When I wasn't
nothing but a chile . . .)—oh, someone was missing*

*Charlie and Alec scrambled up the corn pile and finally suc-
ceeded in laying the rail across the top of it to everyone's satisfaction. Last year, the mound had been so lopsided and there had
been so much argument back and forth about which side—if
either—were larger that Master had had to divide the pile*

*No. That hadn't happened since she was a real little girl. When
Old Master was alive. Master Vaugham didn't get any closer to a
shucking than that wagon seat. She could see his face gleaming
whitely across the heads of the people. Blood had crusted on his
temple and a cut above his eye oozed wetly. She backed away, her
head pounding, suddenly, painfully . . . Masa? Masa bleed—
Someone*

"Slip shuck corn a little while," Alec gave out. He stood at the
top of the pile, hands on his hips, his feet planted solidly in the
corn. "Slip shuck corn a little while.

"Little while, little while I say."

She was a steady worker, picking up an ear with her left hand, stripping it with her right, tossing the shuck onto a pile at her right side and the ear into a basket in front of her.

"Slip shuck corn a little while."

Charlie and Alec strode across the pile of corn, shouting encouragement to their teammates, now and then husking an ear of corn with a flourish or dropping down to work and trade words among the shuckers seated around the edge of the mound. And most of all lining out some tale or commenting on some topical situation, improvising on an old theme that the singing made new.

"Little while I say."

She saw mammy down the line and waved. That Robert boy caught her eye and winked. She dropped her own as Martha nudged her with a sly laugh.

(I wasn't nothing but a child

"Possum up the gum stump, racoon in the holler;"

Someone was missing

"Rabbit in the old field fat as he can waller."

Maybe it was the torchlight on the faces that made such shadows   The people talked and laughed but someone was missing

"Nigga in the woodpile can't count seven . . ."

The twang of the straws beaten against the fiddle strings rose above the sound of shuffling feet. Little Simpson could really handle the straws. Little Simpson wasn't nothing but a child

"I was grown when I met you." She'd said that once in response to some comment of Kaine's about her bull head and what
she would never learn. And he had laughed. *"You still ain't nothing but a child—"* Oh, Kaine's fingers like the notes off that banjo
on her skin—and here they'd thought that there wasn't anything
half so fine as Gustus on that fiddle with Little Simpson to beat
the straws.

"Whee-ee-yooo, whee-ee-yoo . . ."

"Gentlemens to the right." Brud strutted away from her on the
call; she whirled to the left, double-timing on the flight of half notes
Kaine played just for her while his heel and toe stomped the syn-
copated rhythm to which the rest of them danced
"Whee-eee-yoo, whee-ee-yoooooo," he sang above the music and
the dancing feet.
She rocked back on her hips, clapped her hands, and glided into
the turn. Brud's fingers were light as a feather at her waist and on
her fingertips as he guided her through the figure.
Whee-ee-yooo, whee-ee-yoo, her heart answered.
She snuggled

২৯

The raftered ceiling had been whitewashed and recently, the walls,
too, and where the sunlight struck them, they gave off a sharp
light that hurt her eyes. She closed them, but even behind her lowered lids, she could still see the light striking the white walls and
it filled her with terror. Where was this place? And the white face
white? eyes as gray as glass under arching red brows and lashes.
"Harker?" The name she screamed was dredged up from a place
she didn't know existed but she felt safety in the name and she
screamed it again and again, her eyes screwed tight against the
white walls, against the white face. "Harker. Harker! Har-
kerrrrr . . ."
The hands were thin and strong; she could feel the fingers bit-

ing into her shoulders as the hands shook her. Harker? whispered through her mind but . . . Harker's hands were . . . She didn't know. Harker? She peeked through partly opened eyes. The white wom— She could feel a scream, hear it rising and rising as she fought to untangle her arms and legs from covers. The white woman would kill her kill her and . . . the baby. Baby. Her ba— She freed an arm and smashed it into the white woman's face just as hands grabbed her from behind. She twisted. Black. "Harker?" But the face did not respond. She raised a leg to kick and the side of her face seemed to explode. She fell back on the bed. "Harker." It was only a whimper, the last sound she heard before her mind went blank.

ಕ⋙

Dessa watched the white woman. She knew she had lain like this before, body rigid, heart hammering against her ribs, watching the white woman through half-closed lids. The white woman stood at the door. This, too, had happened before . . . maybe. A white woman moving quietly around her bed—*bed?* (Feel like it feather, too! Dessa barely stifled a laugh. Lightheaded in a feather bed.) She was in a bed, a white woman *white* stared at her from the shadows of some room— She would be still. The white woman moved. Her heart thudded in her chest. The white woman passed beyond her line of vision. She heard a soft swish off to her right, someone moving about, a voice talking. She couldn't understand a word. This a dream. Her heart slowed, muscles relaxed; she snuggled . . .

Dessa watched the white woman, who stood now with her back to the door. She lowered her lids even more, looking at the white woman through the spikes of her own lashes; finally she could no longer see her. A white woman. The image filled her mind, the hair pinned carelessly on top of her head, orange tendrils hanging about the pale blur of the face. She opened her eyes slowly. The face seemed to float toward her. She clenched her hands convulsively and was still.

"I know you-all ain't doing a thing but playing possum." The face grinned.

Dessa's mind raced; she could not put two thoughts together. Oh, why this dream so hard? Mammy would have a time trying to explain this dream. A white woman— Is that your enemies? . . . could be . . . *could be*

" 'To dream of death is a sign of marriage.' "

The teeth of the comb bit into her scalp as Carrie Mae parted off another thin line of hair. Dessa flinched from the comb and frowned at mammy. Dessa and Carrie sat on the steps that led up to mammy's cabin door, Carrie Mae on the top step, she on the next step between Carrie's legs. Carrie's fingers tugged sharply on each strand of hair as she began the intricate corn row. Sometimes it was so hard to get mammy to talk some sense. That was grief had her bowed down, so Aunt Lefonia said—pappy, whom Dessa remembered a little (didn't she? somewhere; when she was little: a prickly cheek against her own small hand, a wide chest against her knees, hard arms supporting her bottom . . . ?); Jeeter, whom she knew she loved; that boy and girl mammy seldom spoke of, children sold away— Lawd, there was that word again. Mammy had to talk. Dessa turned her head under Carrie's hands and looked at her mother. She waited. The old woman sat on a three-legged stool in the doorway, her heavy hips and thighs overflowing its seat, arms folded tight against her chest, eyes closed. Maybe she should go see Aunt Lefonia. But Lefonia would only send her back to mammy; mammy was the one who read dreams. "This a white woman I'm dreaming of, mammy, not no burying shroud."

Mammy sat on a three-legged stool by the bottom step, head bowed, sucking on the little corncob pipe Jeeter had made for her. Dessa wanted very much to see mammy's face, the full lips that were the color of ripening blackberries, the broad, pockmarked cheeks and furrowed brow, the large flaring nostrils. The whites of mammy's eyes were yellowed, the red-brown pupils covered by a milky film. This she knew from memory. Mammy would not turn her head.

" 'A dream of marriage is a sign of death.' "

"I know that, mammy," she said patiently. "This a white woman I'm dreaming of, not no wedding gown."

"Maybe," Carrie said; the comb's teeth bit into Dessa's scalp again. "Maybe, it's like silver money; you think, mammy? (Hold your head this way, Dessa.)" She tapped Dessa on the shoulder with the comb. "You know, 'Silver money a sure sign of trouble.' "

What a nigga doing dreaming of money, anyway? Dessa thought impatiently. Course something like that bound to mean trouble. She had never seen a white woman so close—the fine red-gold fuzz on the top lip, the lines radiating from the corners of the eyes, the bluish shadow at the temples, the skin as pale as hoecake dough—so much detail she could almost think it real. "Mammy—!" Lawd, she wished she could give herself up to Carrie's strong fingers massaging her scalp, to her nonsense about the baby's talking at six months. "Mammy—"

" 'A bright Christmas mean some white folks going die.' That the only one I knows." Martha grinned. (This was too much, Dessa thought frantically; Martha would tell her something she didn't want to know. Something mammy would say she didn't need to know.) " 'A dark un mean some nigga going go.' " Martha was laughing now. "But I guess we don't need no dream to tell that. Girl"—Martha sobered—"don't be running round here trying to figure out no dream when you got life right here to get through." Her skin was the golden brown of an autumn sycamore leaf, with just that much red, stretched smooth and taut over the thin-bridged nose, the delicate nostrils. "Don't be studying about no dream." And Martha walked away.

"You scrape—oh, about the same amount you use if this was a regular cup of tea—scrape that much from the horn of a cow; this is if they real sick with the fever, now. I wouldn't use this for just every little common heat. But I take the scrapings from the horn, you see, and make that into tea, just pour some hot water on it, honey. Let it steep till it cool, then reheat it and this will cure any fever—long as it ain't determined to kill. Now if the fever determined . . ."

"Mammy, I came about my dream." Dessa was exasperated. She stood in front of mammy's cabin. Like all the others in the Quarters, it stood on stilts above the ground. Three rickety steps led up to its lone door. Mammy sat in the doorway on a three-legged stool. Dessa started up the steps. Mammy was going to tell her something about this dream today.

" 'Never tell a dream until you broke your fast.' "

"Fast? Mammy, you say yourself I'm fifteen, going on sixteen. Me and Kaine be just down the Quarters, there." They were inside mammy's cabin, the dark smoky room where she and Jeeter and Carrie Mae had been raised. A crude fireplace had been arranged in one corner, bricks and a stovepipe that vented the smoke from the fire through a hole in the wall. A rude table and four three-legged stools stood before it. Pappy had finished the last stool just before he'd hired out that last time. That was before Dessa was old enough to work the fields. She had slipped away from Mamma Hattie as she often did and run off to the spring house. Mammy gave her a piece of cheese and continued churning the butter: swish, creak, squeak, and beneath that a top-pa-ta, top-pa-ta, as the stick thumped against the bottom of the churn. The sound of the churn filled the room and mammy's voice rose above it: "This little light of mine . . ." Dessa rocked herself to the beat of the churn and chewed to the rhythm of mammy's singing. "This little light of mine . . ." Dessa chewed and rocked and hardly noticed the creaking of wheels as a wagon lumbered into the yard. Someone had come running, shouting. Mammy had jumped up screaming, knocked over the churn, and slipped and slid in the soft butter and yellowed cream, and screaming had run behind the wagon and the pine box that knocked against the wagon sides. Mammy sat now on one stool, Carrie Mae, a big chicory-brown baby (. . . baby? asleep on her shoulder, on another. Dessa sat down on a third. One place was empty.

"We be just like Carrie-nem." Someone was missing "Kaine through with all that foolishness he done when he first come here—acting out and talking back." Someone "Mammy, you going talk to Boss Smith for us?"

" 'Dreaming about dollars is a sure sign of a whipping.' "
Mammy nodded her head wisely and turned as though to talk to
Carrie. In that moment Dessa saw her face clearly though she could
not say by what light. Deep lines ran from nose to mouth and
something gleamed on one cheek. " 'Never spit in the fire; it will
draw your lungs up.' "

The banjo again. He could make it tinkle like the first drops of
spring rain spattering on the roof or sheet like creek water run-
ning over a rocky course. Someone was sweeping her house after
sundown, someone was sweeping her out of the family
house "Mammy. Mammy. I dreamed—"

" 'Put graveyard dirt in your shoes and can't no dog track you.' "
She snuggled

છ૰

The white light the raftered ceiling Dessa had seen this all before. She watched the white woman sitting in the light from the
long window. Her hair was the color of fire; it fell about her
shoulders in lank whisps. Her face was very white and seemed to
radiate a milky glow; her mouth was like a bloody gash across it.
Dessa closed her eyes. Only the Quarters had been a dream.
Mammy, Martha. Kaine's face danced before her eyes. She was
the one who was missing; she had been sold away. This was a bed
and these were sheets. She clutched them in her hands.

The white woman sat in a rocker across from the bed. Next to
her was a large cradle; next to it another piece of furniture Dessa
couldn't identify. A large cupboard stood in a corner on the other
side of the rocker; near that corner was a door. Dessa stared at it
but could not move.

They had come for her at night. Nathan, Cully, and Harker,
whom she hadn't known. Jemina, praising the Lawd in scared
whispers, had opened the cellar door and unlocked her chains. Free,
and scrambling up the steep steps, Dess had focused all of her attention on the stranger's whispered instructions, refusing to think

beyond the next step. She was free and she walked on, mindful of his hand on her arm, uncaring of anything else save his cautions and the putting of one foot in front of the other. Silently, she had thanked the Lawd, Legba, all the gods she knew, for Harker and Cully and Nathan, for Jemina herself. She would not be a slave anymore in this world.

They had walked for a long time, Harker going before her, holding back low branches and vines, his voice whispering the presence of obstacles on the path so she could avoid them. It had taken a while for her feet to remember the gliding shuffle that, slow as it appeared, ate up ground. The coffle had taught her that, just as it had Cully and everyone else who had ever spent more than a day on one. She had learned quickly after the first few hours of hobbling along with the manacle rubbing her ankle raw. She had known without being told that if she fell, one of the drivers would be along with the whip. Her feet were remembering: The muscles of her calves and thighs protested some and it took all of her concentration to keep their protests from drowning out the remembrance of her feet. She didn't speak. She didn't think either. She was free; maybe not as free as she would ever be but she knew, without needing to think about it, that she'd never be less free than she was now, striding, sometimes stumbling toward a place she'd never seen and didn't know word one about.

She remembered laughing weakly, leaning against the thin mulatto boy, an arm around her, an awkward pat on her shoulder. ". . . the midwife back at the farm say less your time real near . . ." (Farm? Had he— A *white* woman—) Her own foot in the stirrup, Cully pushing from behind, she mounted the horse before Harker. And leaning back against his chest, tears sliding silently down her cheek. She had not known how bad she felt, how scared, how— She had lost track of place, of time, dozing only to be jostled awake by the dull throbbing in her back, some pounding in her head, starting up out of some unremembered dreams to feel the sinewy arms around her, the beard-stubbled cheek against her face, "Got you" on a smoky breath. At some point they rested, probably more than once; she remembered the sky through a canopy of trees, the smell of roasting meat, "Rest," her face against some coarse material, the warmth of someone's flesh and the dull throbbing in her back. She was bumped up and down and something, in her womb, she guessed, somewhere deep inside her, the baby pinched its lining in its fist. It had rained, hard and soaking, and Harker laughed, "There go the trail and the scent," as he pulled out an oilcloth and draped her in it. But the wetness of the rain was mixed with that other, sudden, drenching liquid that made the horse rear, nearly killing them both, embarrassing her half to death. What would Harker think, her having no more bladder control than this? And little else: the anxious broad-nosed face, a fiercely muttered "Shush!" and "Bear down, bear down! You got to help." The core of her body uprooted, Lawd, the pain, the blood . . .

The white woman's mouth was like an open wound across the milky paleness of her face. She sat, one shoulder bare, a child held against her breast. "Got enough?" She tickled the baby under the chin and raised it to her shoulder, patting its back and murmuring. The baby was big, a year old, maybe, or more, with plump white arms and legs, wisps of light-colored hair on its smooth white head. The child burped loudly and grinned; the white woman laughed. "Well, I guess you did get your fill."

Dessa closed her eyes; her lashes clotted wetly against her cheeks. Her stomach was flat, the muscles flaccid; her breasts, swollen and tender, felt on fire. Lawd, where my baby at; where is my child? She could feel the sodden rag between her thighs, sticky with blood. "Where my child?" She didn't know she had spoken aloud until she heard the gasp,

"Right here."

And opened her eyes.

The white woman, the shoulder still bare, the curly black head and brown face of a new baby nestled at her breast, faced her now. "See?"

"Naaaaaawwwww!" The scream rushed out of her on an explosion of breath. She saw the glass-colored eyes buck before her own squeezed tight. The covers weighed her arms and legs; some voice screamed, "Annabelle. Annabelle, get Ada! She starting up again!" Hands, herself crying weakly, a cool cloth on her forehead and something at her breasts.

"See? See? He know his mama. See, he just want to eat."

Dessa looked down. The brown baby was in her arms, his dark eyes staring up at her unwinkingly. She touched a tiny fist; it opened to grasp her finger. She looked up. She had never seen the tall brown-skinned woman before.

"Let me fix them pillows so you can nurse more better." The woman bent over Dessa, her hands moving deftly. Dessa lay quietly but warily. "There, now; you turn just a little on your side and you both be more comfortable. Well, go on; put the nipple in his mouth."

Dessa looked down quickly, then up at the woman's smiling face. She did as she was told, gingerly touching her breast and awkwardly guiding it toward the baby's mouth. The nipple touched his cheek and he turned his head toward it, his mouth opening to grasp and clamping tightly around it, all in one sudden movement. A sharp pain shot through her breast at the first tug and she gasped.

"You got to get used to that," the woman said conversationally. "Pain going get worse before it get better—that is, if you ain't dried up. It's a mercy if you not, way you been carrying on." She laughed. "Attacking white folks and scaping all crost the country in the dead of night." Laughing again and shaking her head. "I told her don't be coming in here less one of us was with her. But you think Miz Ruint going listen at me?"

At least she could understand these words even if they still made no sense to her. Who was this woman? Where was "Harker?"

"She sent the boy at him. He be here directly. You go on see at that baby. He getting some, huh?" she asked, peeking over at the nursing baby. "It be all right, now."

Every pull of the baby's lips sent a thrill of pain through Dessa's breast. She looked up at the woman and smiled before she closed her eyes.

❧

Rufel watched the colored girl, not as she had at first from the rocker by the window, rocking gently as she nursed the babies or shelled peas. The colored girl was young. Don't look no more than twelve or thirteen, Rufel had thought. Couldn't be more than fourteen, she would say to herself, don't care what Ada said. She disliked disagreeing with Ada. The older darky had an abrupt way of speaking that Rufel found daunting. Rufel herself was not, of course, a child to be corrected by some middle-aged darky— Who knew no more about birthdays, she would continue sullenly to herself, than "planting time" and "picking time." Why, even Mammy hadn't known how old she was or even her own birth-date. That was why they—*she*, Rufel, "Miz 'Fel," had chosen Valentine's Day as Mammy's birthday. Mammy had refused to accept a date— "This way I don't have to *age*, see," she had joked, "I just gets a little older." Eyes full and shiny, a smile fluttering about her bee-stung lips— Rushing from the wound of that memory, Rufel would silently declare, All darkies know about is old age.

Rufel would sew or rock for a minute, until another point occurred to her. Thirteen, even fourteen was young to have a baby, even for a darky. Well. Rocking again, maybe sewing, fifteen. But no older and Ada talked about her as if she were a grown woman. Even if the girl were eighteen, as Ada said, she was too young to live as a runaway, hand to mouth, Rufel thought scornfully, like the rest of these darkies. And Ada was no better than the rest of them. Why, any white person that came along could lay claim to them, sell them, auction them off to the highest bidder. They should thank their lucky stars she was a kindhearted person. Bertie— But she resolutely closed her mind against the thought of her husband. She had done what she could do. He would see that when he came. Rufel would resume her task, all the while watching the colored girl. If she didn't want to go back to her people—

The wench was the color of chocolate and Rufel would stare at her face as she tossed or, more frequently now, slept quietly, at the thin body that barely made an impression in the big feather bed. The girl would be all right. Rocking again or returning to the rocker if she had stood as she sometimes did to fetch some article, to stretch, or just to look more closely at the colored girl.

Ada and Harker said she—they called her Dessa—had been sold south by a cruel master. She certainly acted mean enough to have been ruined by a cruel master—kicking and hitting at whoever got in the way the few times Rufel had seen her roused from stupor. But the girl's back was scarless and to hear Ada tell it, every runaway in the world was escaping from a "cruel master." Ada herself claimed to have escaped from a lecherous master who had lusted with her and then planned the seduction of Ada's daughter, Annabelle. Rufel didn't believe a word of that. She could see nothing attractive in the rawboned, brown-skinned woman or her lanky, half-witted daughter—and would have said as much but Mammy had cut her off before she could speak, thanking Ada for her help and God that Ada had escaped from her old master.

Vexed, Rufel had bit her lip, remembering then what the utter nonsense of the darky's statement had made her forget. They needed Ada. That was the plain fact of it.

Often, misery washed over her. She would struggle against the familiar tide, feeding her indignation at Ada's story. At least Uncle Joel and Dante, the darkies Bertie had brought back from that last trip, had stayed, she would remind herself then. And, forgetting her angry, and silent, exasperation at Bertie's conviction that he had somehow gotten the best of a deal that netted him an old darky and a crippled one, took some satisfaction in their loyalty to the place. Mammy said they had been some help at harvest, but the real work was done by the darkies Ada knew. Still, Rufel hadn't been able to resist pointing out Ada's lie to Mammy.

"No white man would do that," she'd insisted; unless he tied a sack over her head first, she had continued maliciously to herself. Mammy, folding linen—*black hands in the white folds, Mammy's hand against her face, and even then, maybe, that scaly, silvery*

sheen creeping over the rich, coffee-colored skin—had paused.
"Why, Mammy, that's —" Rufel wasn't sure what it was and
stuttered. "That's—"

"Miz Rufel!" Mammy had said sharply. "You keep a lady tongue
in your mouth. Men," Mammy had continued with a quailing
glance as Rufel opened her mouth, voice overriding Rufel's attempt to speak, "men can do things a *lady* can't even guess at."

Rufel knew that was true but could not bring herself to concede
this openly. "Well—" She had tossed her head, flicking back locks
of hair that tumbled in perpetual disarray from the artless knot
atop her head. "Everyone know men like em half white and
whiter," she had finished saucily.

"Miz Rufel," Mammy had snapped. "Lawd know it must be
some way for high yeller to git like that!" Shaking out a diaper
with a low pop and folding it with careful precision across her
lap. "Ada have a good heart and at least she know how to work
that danged old stove."

Mammy's retort about the stove had silenced Rufel. She shared
Mammy's antipathy for the beastly and expensive contraption Bertie
had so proudly installed in the kitchen lean-to during the first
months of their marriage. Its management had baffled every cook
they ever owned; meals were most often late or the food burned,
when the darky could manage to get the fire going at all. None of
them had ever understood how to regulate cooking temperatures
by sticking a hand into the oven and counting until it had to be
withdrawn, the method prescribed by the manufacturer. And it took
Mammy's constant supervision to see that the stove was kept clean
and blackening applied to prevent the rust of its many surfaces
and joints. To his credit, Bertie had seldom complained about the
tardy and overdone meals (often he was not there to share them),
and usually laughed when Rufel apologized for the quality of the
meals set before him. How, he would ask, could she be expected
to teach darkies to regulate the temperature of the stove when most
of them couldn't count beyond one or two? Still, Rufel felt she
had failed in a crucial duty and she was both relieved and piqued

that Ada seemed to have an instinct where the operation of the stove was concerned.

Despite Ada's considerable skill in the kitchen, Rufel still itched sometimes to throw the lie back in Ada's face (White man, indeed! Both of them probably run off by the mistress for making up to the master), but she was glad she hadn't provoked Mammy that day. Mammy had probably not believed Ada's story herself, Rufel thought now, but had not wanted to antagonize Ada. Mammy, perhaps even then foreseeing her own death, trying to secure the help Rufel would need until Bertie came back, knew Rufel would need that scheming Ada. No, Rufel had concluded, hurrying now lest she be trapped in grief and fear, the "cruel master" was just to play on her sympathy.

But—maybe—there were no people for this wench to return to. Timmy had said the other darkies called her the "debil woman." His blue eyes had rolled back into his head and he had bared his baby teeth in a grotesque grin as he said it. Repulsed by his mimicry, she had scolded him for the mockery. "But that's the way they do it, mamma; and laugh and slap their thighs." He had imitated that also and she had relaxed, a little surprised at how seriously she had taken the joke. And it was a joke, she told herself, a foolish nickname, "debil woman" (He talk plain when he with me, she thought defensively). What could there be to fear in this one little sickly, colored gal? Oh, she was wild enough to have some kind of devil in her, Rufel would think, smiling, remembering the way the girl's eyes had bucked the first time she awakened in the bedroom, just the way Mammy's used to when something frightened her. Mammy, Mammy's hands in her hair— Sudden longing pierced Rufel. Mammy's voice: "Aw, Miz 'Fel"; that was special, extra loving, extra.

Rufel squeezed her eyes tight. She—the colored girl—had probably been scared out of her wits at finding herself in a bed. Even in her fevered state, she would know that no darky could own a room like this. It was a spacious and light-filled chamber, handsomely proportioned and stylishly finished from the highly polished golden-oak flooring to the long, French-style windows that faced the morning sun. Even the open-beam ceiling, so long an ugly reminder of that good-for-nothing darky's unfinished work, seemed, since Mammy had hit upon the idea of painting the rough wood white, almost elegant. The highboy and matching cupboard, the cedar clothespress and thin-legged dressing table with its three-quarter mirror had come with her from Charleston; the crib and the half-sized chest had been made by the estate carpenter at Dry Fork as the Prestons' christening gift for Timmy. She had only to look at these to see Dry Fork again—not as she had come to know it during her lying-in with Timmy and the weeks she had spent there regaining her strength, as a bustling, virtually self-sufficient, miniature village, but as she had seen it on her first visit, the year she and Bertie went to Montgomery to buy a cook: the stately mansion built in the English style with an open court in front, the circular carriage drives and broad walks, the gardens opening before it: large flower beds and mounds, empty at that season but since pictured in her mind in a riot of blooming colors, rose, snowball, hyacinth, jonquil, violet. A mockingbird sang perpetually from bowers of honeysuckle and purple wisteria, perfumed and heavy with spring blossoms.

There was no comparison, of course, between the Glen and such magnificence; you couldn't build an establishment like Dry Fork in five or even ten years. Not without slaves, not without "capital." Unconsciously, Rufel quoted Bertie, and shrugged, impatient with herself. What could a darky have to compare the Glen with? Certainly it offered a better home than any runaway could hope to have. Even that scheming Ada didn't want to go back out in the wild.

And, if the darky wasn't from around here— No angry owners or slave catchers had descended on the house as Rufel had half expected would happen. She had been in the yard drawing water from the well, because that idiot girl of Ada's had forgotten to do it, the morning Harker rode in with the girl. She had been startled by the sight of darkies on horses and frightened when she recognized Harker. What would these darkies steal next? And: She would

have to say something; people might not come way out here looking for a chicken or a pig, but somebody would want to know
about these horses. The darkies had been as startled as Rufel, but,
after the briefest hesitation, had continued walking their horses
toward the kitchen lean-to. "Harker." She had stepped into their
path—and seen the girl strapped in the litter Harker pulled behind his horse. There was something in the ashen skin, like used
charcoal, the aimless turning of the head that had kept Rufel silent. The baby had started to cry, a thin wail muffled by layers of
covering. The girl's eyes had fluttered open and seemed to look
imploringly at Rufel before rolling senselessly back into her head.
"Go get Ada," Rufel had ordered without hesitation. "Take her
on into the house; bring the bucket," she said as she bent to look
for the baby.

She shouldn't have done it; Rufel had been over that countless
times, also. If anybody ever found out. If they had been followed.
But nothing of that had entered her head as she picked her way
carefully up the steep back steps, the baby hugged close to her
body. The girl's desolate face, the baby's thin crying—as though
it had given up all hope—had grated at her; she was a little crazy,
she supposed. But she could do something about this, about the
baby who continued to cry while she waited in the dim area back
of the stairs for the darkies to bring the girl in. Something about
the girl, her face— And: She—Rufel—could do something. That
was as close as she came to explaining anything to herself. The
baby was hungry and she fed him. Or she would imagine herself
saying to Mammy, "Well, I couldn't have them bringing a bleed-
ing colored gal in where Timmy and Clara were having breakfast," wheedling a little, making light. As long as the girl wasn't
from around here— Though it would serve the neighbors right,
she thought, resentful now, if the darky did belong to someone
around here. Many times as Bertie had gone looking for a darky
and been met with grins and lies. Truly, it would not surprise her
to learn that some jealous neighbor had been tampering with their
slaves, just as Bertie had always said, urging them to run away.

Harker and Ada swore the darky wasn't from around here. In

fact, Harker said the girl was from Charleston. Not that Rufel believed that for a minute; Ada had probably put him up to that, hoping to touch Rufel's heart. But, if the girl were from Charleston. Here Rufel would stop short, hearing once again Mammy's anxious voice, urging her to write the family, for surely they would send for Rufel to visit, seeing again the glittering ballrooms of her first Charleston season. Usually—for if it wasn't this longing or memory, it would be some other—she would put aside whatever task she worked on, gather up the babies if she had been nursing, and find something in the sitting room that needed doing.

No one asked and she rarely thought to question herself after the first day or so. She knew there was more to the girl's story than the darkies were telling, and now and then she did wonder briefly what could have forced the girl out into the woods with her time so near. Even in the comfort and splendor of Dry Fork, having Timmy had been an ordeal, and Rufel refused to dwell on the agony of Clara's birth. Well, darkies did have their own way of doing things and whatever the real story was, it couldn't, she thought, amount to much. Rufel sometimes suspected that the girl was the sweetheart of one of the new darkies, and was made uneasy by the idea. They couldn't start using the Glen like a regular hideaway, she would think fearfully, and push the speculation aside. The colored girl would wake and tell her story— Whether or not she believed it, Rufel, recalling the long hours she had spent with Mammy, talking idly or in companionable silence, thought it would be something to pass the time.

Rufel leaned now against the bedroom door and watched the colored girl, who lay curled on her side in the big feather bed, facing the door. The colored girl had not stirred at the sound of the closing door and after a moment Rufel continued across the room to the curtained doorway in the adjacent wall. This girl couldn't go on acting crazy forever, she thought impatiently, talking all out of her head, laying up like she was still half dead. Rufel pushed aside the curtain with a swish and entered the narrow antechamber where her seven-year-old son, Timmy, slept. It had been her dressing room in the original plan of the house. The boy had slept in the room since early spring and its plain neatness was a sign of his growing independence. He acted more like nine or ten than the eight he would be in November, spending long hours with Uncle Joel and Dante as they tended the stock and garden, with Ada in the cook-shed, or with Annabelle, when she could catch him and there was nothing better to do.

She should keep him closer, Rufel thought as she put away his clothing in neat piles on the open shelves above his makeshift bed, keep him away from the darkies. Send him to the field school at the crossroads— But Bertie would return and be mortified to find his son sharing a desk with common red-necks. And where would she get the two dollars a month to keep him there? I can't just keep him cooped up in here with me all day, she thought wearily. And the darkies talked before him as they would not with her; it was through him that Rufel kept some kind of track of the comings and goings in the Quarters. She was not entirely convinced that some of those darkies were not Bertie's nigras taking his continued absence as an opportunity to slip back and live free. Neither she nor Timmy would ever recognize them. Mammy had been the one who knew them all.

Finished, Rufel turned and stood in the doorway, peeking between the curtains; she could just see the top of the girl's head in the pillows. Rufel shrugged between the curtains and started toward the bedroom door but stopped as she neared the bed. The girl had turned over; her profile was a sooty blur against the whiteness of the pillow. Her eyes were closed, the lashes lost in the darkness of her face. When open, they looked like Mammy's, a soft brown-black set under sleepy, long-lashed lids. And big. Once, when Rufel had had to restrain her, the girl had seemed to look at her, to recognize her. Even as Rufel watched, the girl's expression had changed to fear and loathing. It was over in a moment. The girl had renewed her efforts to get out of the bed and Rufel had called to Ada for help. Sometimes, when the girl's eyes fluttered open, their gaze sweeping past her without recognition, Rufel thought she had imagined that momentary expression. And it was silly to suppose the girl had really recognized her, even if she were from

Charleston. And never, never had Rufel done anything to anyone to deserve such a look. But to see eyes so like Mammy's, staring such hatred at her. It had given Rufel quite a turn. She wanted the girl to wake up, wanted to see that look banished from her face.

The girl lay unmoving and Rufel continued to the door. It was time for this darky to wake up. Rufel turned as a thought hit her, and, back to the corridor door, eyed the colored girl. Perhaps she had changed her position slightly, but she lay still now under Rufel's gaze. "You not doing a thing but playing possum," Rufel said loudly. The girl did not respond and, turning with a flounce, Rufel stepped into the wide central hall, closing the door behind her.

The big front door stood open and the wide hall was cool. Rufel could see Annabelle, Ada's daughter, through the open parlor door opposite the bedroom. Annabelle sat on the backless lounge near the front window, head bent over the magazine she held in her lap. The girl couldn't read a lick, but she would, if Rufel let her, spend hours staring at the illustrations in old *Godey's Lady's Books*, turning again and again to favorite pictures and staring off into space.

"You supposed," Rufel said loudly as she entered the parlor, "to be folding nappies." Clean laundry lay piled about on the settee and chairs ready to be sorted, folded, or ironed, and put away.

Annabelle looked up at Rufel's words and, putting the journal aside, stood. "This'n just start crying," she said, pointing at the newborn baby, who began the first tentative notes of what Rufel knew to be his hungry cry. Then, pointing to Clara who crawled toward Rufel across the bare wooden floor, face screwed up to cry, "That'n—"

"And see at these children," Rufel shouted as she reached for Clara.

"—been fretting off and on. Spect she hungry," the girl continued as though Rufel had not spoken. "Nappies in the chair." She pointed.

"Well, put them away," Rufel snapped. The girl had to be told everything and she would do just what she was told and no more.

Rufel wiped at her daughter's motley face. She would have to speak to Ada, she thought with a tightening of her stomach; the girl was just too, too—slow. That was what Mammy had maintained. Slow and big for her age. Rufel certainly agreed with that last. Ada seemed to tower over both Rufel and Mammy who were themselves somewhat above average height. Annabelle, whom Ada claimed was no more than thirteen, was already eye level with Rufel. And Rufel could not rid herself of the idea that Annabelle's slowness was assumed, that the girl somehow used this means to mock her. There had been incidents. Once, Rufel had stood posing in front of the mirror, lifting her hair from her neck, tugging at the waist and bodice of her dress. It was the first time she had taken an interest in her appearance since Mammy's death and she prattled to the girl, as she used to with Mammy, about fashions and hair-styles, which had lifted both their spirits, and happened to look up in midsentence to see the girl's retreating image merging into the shadows of the great hall. Reflected in the mirror, the dusky doorway seemed to yawn at Rufel's back and she turned, suddenly furious. "Why— I'm telling you more joy and, and happiness, yes! and excitement, too, than you can ever imagine in that paltry black hide. Nigger," she started forward, "you come back here." The girl stopped in the hall so suddenly that Rufel almost ran into her. She retreated a step before the other's silence. "You." And then again, this time stronger. "You know you don't just walk away from a white person without a by-your-leave."

Hands on hips, Annabelle leaned toward Rufel, grinning in her face; the dark shoots of her tangled hair seemed to writhe in the yellow light from the fan-glass over the door. A thousand imps seemed to dance in her eyes as she said on a rising note of incredulity, "Mistress '*Fel? Miz Rufel?*"

Rufel flushed, hearing the name on the darky's lips over a sudden pounding in her head. "Miz Rufel" was a slave-given name, discarded by white people when they reached adulthood. Annabelle had put Rufel almost on the same level as herself by its use now, making Rufel appear a child, Young Missy in tantrum, rather than Mistress of the House. Shaking, Rufel screamed, "My name is 'Mistress' to you!" and fled before the silent laughter in the girl's eyes.

Shaken and angered by the incident, Rufel had complained to Ada. And Ada, while allowing that the girl was slow and oftentimes silly, had defended her, reminding Rufel in that abrupt way she had that neither of them belonged to her, that in fact they did her a favor by working for her at all! Outraged, Rufel had wrung from Ada a promise that Annabelle would do better. Annabelle was more civil now—almost foolishly so. At times, Rufel itched to strike the girl and hid her own anger behind an elaborate show of patience. And, despite her anger at the way the girl had turned the name against her, she could not break herself of the habit of thinking of herself as "Rufel," "Miz 'Fel," the pet name Mammy had given her so long ago.

Rufel curbed her temper now and turned to look at the baby. He lay on his back in the bedding-stuffed basket that served him as a daybed. She patted his chest and made soothing sounds at him before turning back to Annabelle, who had not moved during the pause. "After you put away the nappies," she said carefully, "change the baby and bring him into the bedroom. Don't forget to wrap him up." He would be all right until Annabelle came back for him.

Clara quieted under the expectation of eating and Rufel retraced her steps to the bedroom. She sat Clara in the crib while she unfastened the bodice of her dress, loosening her milk-plumpened breasts. Annabelle came in with the nappies but Rufel ignored her as she picked up Clara and sat in the rocker. She leaned back in the chair, allowing Clara to accept her nipple, and, feeling the muscles in her back and pelvis loosen, relaxed under the baby's deep pulls at her breast. Clara liked to explore, her fingers wondering at Rufel's dress, her underthings, tracing imaginary patterns across Rufel's skin. Often when she finished, Clara would lie with her head resting under Rufel's bosom as she explored herself, her fingers, her nose. The baby let the milk gurgle in her throat and smiled around the nipple when she saw Rufel watching her, in perfect charity with the world. Rufel smiled, too, holding her quietly, barely rocking, now and then smoothing wisps of hair from the baby's face as she continued to nurse.

Clara finished and Rufel burped her, talking gently to the child, who was now so sleepy she could barely keep her eyes open. Rufel laid her in the crib and settled herself once more in the rocker. Annabelle had come back so quietly that Rufel had scarcely noticed her. Now she handed the infant to Rufel and waited, shifting her weight from one foot to the other, for Rufel's dismissal. The girl would now stay—except for sneaking off to look at those danged magazines, which not even Ada seemed able to do anything about—until Rufel told her to move. "Bring his basket in here," she told the girl, turning away from her. "You can go sit in the parlor when you finish that." It would be a relief to have someone around with a little conversation and initiative. She glanced at the colored girl, still asleep, on her back now, and quiet, as she gave the baby her other breast.

The new baby suckled with insistent shallow pulls. "Your mammy will have a time when she start nursing you," she chided him, speaking aloud as she often did when she nursed the babies alone. Sometimes this one stared at her with eyes as bright as new brown shoe buttons and almost lost in the brown folds of his face. Rufel had taken the baby to her bosom almost without thought, to quiet his wailing while Ada and the other darkies settled the girl in the bedroom. More of that craziness, she knew; but then it had seemed to her as natural as tuneless crooning or baby talk. The sight of him so tiny and bloodied had pained her with an almost physical hurt and she had set about cleaning and clothing him with a single-minded intensity. And only when his cries were stilled and she looked down upon the sleek black head, the nut-brown face flattened against the pearly paleness of her breast, had she become conscious of what she was doing. A wave of embarrassment had swept over her and she had looked guiltily around the parlor. Annabelle was settled in a corner, oblivious to everything but the page of the journal in her lap; Timmy, she realized with relief, had slipped out soon after breakfast. No one would ever know, she had assured herself, and, feeling the feeble tug at her nipple, he's hungry and only a baby. Lulled as she always was by the gentle rhythm and spent by the drama of the morning's events, she had dozed—and awakened to the startled faces of Ada and Harker. Their consternation had been almost comic. Ada had stuttered and Harker had gaped. In the pause Rufel had recovered her own composure, feeling somehow vindicated in her actions by their very confusion. She had confounded them—rendered Ada speechless. Still, she had felt some mortification at becoming wet nurse for a darky. She was the only nursing woman on the place, however, and so continued of necessity to suckle the baby. Whatever care she might have had about the wisdom of her action was soon forgotten in the wonder she felt at the baby.

The baby had lost what Timmy called his bird look, the grayish sheen over his skin that Ada said was common to newborn darkies. His color had been blotchy, pale patches of nut-shell brown, darker patches of chocolate, red, even green. "That why they called them colored, mamma?" Timmy had laughed. He was as fascinated with the baby as Rufel, taking an interest in him that he had never shown in Clara, wanting to measure him, to watch when he was bathed or changed, to wake him if he were asleep, to hold him if he were awake. She herself liked to watch the baby as he nursed, the way he screwed up his face and clenched his fist with the effort, the contrast between his mulberry-colored mouth and the pink areola surrounding her nipple, between his caramel-colored fist and the rosy cream of her breast.

"Where my baby at?"

Startled, Rufel looked up. The colored girl had risen on one elbow in the bed and was watching Rufel.

"Why— Why—" Rufel said, rising from the chair thinking, Finally. About time this girl woke up. "He right here," she said smiling, bending her arm so that the girl could see him better. The movement dislodged the baby's mouth from her nipple and he started to cry. She started toward the girl, rocking the baby in her arm. "Here's your baby right here." She could see the girl's body stiffening, her hands fumbling at the covers as she tried to rise from the bed. "Annabelle," Rufel called shrilly, "Ada! This girl starting up again."

ॐ

Sutton's Glen was not the largest property in the district—no one really knew what that was. Much of the land along the Witombe River (thought to be some of the best in northern Alabama) was undeveloped, owned, it was rumored, by various eastern interests that expected to make a killing when the market was right and so refused all fair offers for the land. People pointed to the sparse settlement in the neighborhood as proof of this allegation, implying that their own residence in the area had been achieved through the hardest work.

There had been, over the years, a few attempts to cultivate cotton on a large scale along the river (generally forgotten when the "stranglehold of eastern interests" theory was expounded), but none had survived beyond a few seasons. Worms two years running were said to have proved the undoing of several; rust, a malnourishment of the stems and leaves that often plagued cotton, the undoing of others. Travelers on the Great Road between the river port at Iverton, on the south, and Double Springs, the county seat to the north, might see an occasional white frame house in the dells or on the hilltops that dotted the rugged landscape; more often the dwellings were log huts of one or two rooms. Even these were not numerous. Most of the holdings in the county were small, some no more than forty or fifty acres. Sutton's Glen, with almost two hundred of its five hundred acres cleared for cultivation, was thus a substantial property.

The Great House at the Glen sat some six miles from the Road in a small meadow above Ives Creek, and was known in the neighborhood for its fancy cook-stove (the first in the neighborhood with a removable ash-box and a built-in tank said to keep gallons of water hot) and the fanlight and double windows that graced its front— Not that many in the neighborhood had seen the House close up. There was bad blood between Sutton and several of his neighbors, though few now remembered the ins and outs of the original quarrels. Whatever the initial fault, Sutton's high-handed manner in these disputes—it was rumored that he had once tried to whip a white man off his place—had served to alienate most of the neighborhood. Sutton had never encouraged visits, anyway, and had always eschewed the harvest "bees" and the house and barn raisings that provided most of the opportunities for socializing in the area. The charitable, mostly women who thought Sutton a handsome, albeit mysterious, figure, called him reclusive, and wondered that his wife put up with such habits. Others, and these were in the majority, declared the Suttons would-be swellheads, victims of "planter fever": that flashy House, they muttered, and passel of niggers in a region where there were few slave holders and few of those who owned more than two or three slaves, all that land planted in cotton when any fool could see this was corn country. Sutton had stuck it out longer than most, so popular wisdom ran, but the hill country did not take kindly to cotton culture—nor its people to the "hoity-toity" ways of those who planted it.

The Suttons were seen so seldom that folk in the district could go from one season to the next without giving them so much as a thought. They bought provisions in Iverton, bypassing, so it was claimed, Barton's Emporium at the tiny crossroads hamlet some nine miles from the Glen, to make the longer trek into town for even the smallest purchase. Few now recalled the last time they had attended the occasional church services held by itinerant preachers at the crossroads store. Now and then, a hunter or traveler on the Elmira-Dexter track, which ran within five miles of the Glen, might notice woodsmoke curling above the trees in that general direction, and mention this at one or another of the neighborhood gatherings. Even such comments as this had ceased, over the years, to draw much response.

The long double windows at the Glen faced east toward the steep, wooded slope that formed the eastern bank of Ives Creek as it snaked through Sutton land. Hills rose behind it, heavily timbered, stretching without break to the far horizon. Often Rufel, as she sat in the rocker by the windows, fancied that sunlight danced briefly at a pane of glass. The tail of a curtain fluttering through an open window in the breeze might catch some traveler's eye. The Georgian facade of the House would gleam whitely through the trees, as fleeting as a dream, lost from sight as the Road dipped, the river curved, hidden again by the trees. That was Sutton Glen as Bertie had first described it to her in Charleston, his lilting voice holding her mesmerized so that she saw what he saw and loved it, she thought, as he loved. "If you was to take a ride on that river . . ."

The daughter of a prosperous cotton factor in the city, whose shyly engaging manner made her generally well liked, Rufel had been expected to do well for herself—not a brilliant match (that would be for her younger sister, Rowena, the beauty in the family, to make), but someone with prospects. She could not, as the saying went, look as high as she chose—her father, Benjamin Carson, was the *junior* partner in his uncle's cotton factorage; the firm itself was up and coming rather than established. Still, her father and Uncle Carson would come down handsomely with whomever she chose to marry. The son of some up-country planter come to town for the racing season perhaps, or one of the aspiring young lawyers in the city, a doctor from one of the outlying counties—someone would approach her father soon. If not this season, then the next.

Bertie had made that "someone" seem as dull as dishwater. They met at the come-out ball of Abigail Sorenson, in Rufel's only season in Charleston society. The ball had been one of the largest of the year and Rufel and Bertie had literally run into each other in the crush. He had caught his foot on the hem of her gown; she had narrowly missed spilling punch on him. They had both taken the mishap in good part, Rufel nervously good-natured, somewhat awed by the handsome stranger. He had worn no hat, of course, but his bow when he introduced himself gave the impression, even in the press of bodies, that he had just swept one off. When Rufel discovered a small rip at the waistline of her gown, he offered to convey her to her mother. Rufel, who had felt rather lost in the crowd where she knew few people and those only slightly, had been flattered by his solicitude and gratefully accepted. He had chatted amiably as he wove their way expertly through the crowd and, under the gentle flow of his conversation, she had relaxed. She never remembered afterward just what they had talked of as they strolled through the ballroom; he was by turns worldly-wise and boyish, seeming at times no older than she. But he was obviously someone; she could tell that by the way he dressed and his soft drawl.

He courted Rufel through the rest of the spring, not assiduously at first, he was too well bred for that. But they met often at subscription balls and now and then at one of the large private parties that highlighted the racing season in Charleston. He teased and flattered her, but always with a subtle deference that made her feel older than her seventeen years, and fragile as though she might break from rough handling. In his more serious moments, he told her of the Glen, the mansion he was building above the river, and the virgin land he was plowing. Blousett County boasted no city as fine as Charleston—few areas did, he added with a quick smile. But northern Alabama was not a wilderness or frontier. There were towns and roads. Not many people, he admitted with a wry grin that went straight to her heart: "We have every class *but* the aristocracy," laughing and as quickly sobering. That would come, of course—pushing back the shock of brown hair that was wont to curl on his brow. And the Suttons would be part of it; earnest, emphatic on this point. At first she couldn't believe that he had singled her out, could think of nothing about herself that would attract him. Later, this very circumstance became proof of his love. Under Bertie's gaze, her rather carroty hair became flame, the freckles across her nose and cheeks, a golden veil. Finally, he had declared himself: She could be the wife of some bumpkin or mistress of FitzAlbert Sutton's heart.

Charleston meant nothing to her then. To stay and be married off to some younger son seemed, under the spell of Bertie's high-flown speeches, a fate worse than death. Mrs. Carson, for whom there was no better reference than to be accepted within the no-

toriously closed circle of Charleston society, needed little persua-
sion. Some of the best families in South Carolina had taken up
lands in Alabama in recent years and Bertie seemed on easy terms
with many of them. More familiar with the vagaries of cotton cultivation, Mr. Carson and his uncle were less enthusiastic. They had
hoped to see Rufel married closer to home—to a man of property,
to be sure, but one also less dependent on the land than the run-
of-the-mill planter. Even had Alabama been the scene of fierce In-
dian fighting, Rufel would have gone with Bertie. Her father and
Uncle Carson had yielded to her mother's arguments and her own
tearful pleas; she and Bertie were married and sailed for Alabama
at the end of the spring.

This was the story Rufel told herself as she sat in the rocker by
the windows, looking at the trees, rocking as she nursed the babies or shelled peas, or simply sat, rocking gently.

Sometimes she relived her first trip to Montgomery, the ball the
Prestons had given at Dry Fork in their honor, their annual trips
to the cotton market at Mobile; even the summer after her second
miscarriage, when she had "taken the waters" at White Sulphur
Springs, became one of a gay succession of amusements that she
re-created in loving detail, lingering over isolated images: the great
hall at the Glen as she had first seen it from the threshold, held
aloft in Bertie's arms, so wide she'd thought it a room, high-ceil-
inged, oak-floored, an elegant stairway at its end; sunlight slant-
ing across the black and white tile in the bathhouse at Dry Fork;
a steamboat on the river, majestic as a dowager, chaste as a maiden
by day, a torrid beauty by night; droopy vermilion flowers planted
in the doorway of some rude cabin along the banks of the
Black River.

More often she recalled some scene from her season in society,
an oversubscribed luncheon at the Jockey Club during the racing
meet, an afternoon musicale in the garden of some stately home,
the ballroom at the Sorensons' (a real one, not the double parlor
that served for dancing in the houses of most of her friends),
opening out onto a veranda and a garden, barely perfumed so early
in the spring, the chill darkness a welcome retreat from the heat

and light, the music and laughter of the big overcrowded room. This was how she remembered her courtship, a lighted room, heat, noise, herself and Bertie strolling somewhere in the throng.

She had not always longed for Charleston, nor missed the company that seldom came. There had been the trips—their anticipation and recollection—and Timmy, born in the second year of their marriage, the ordering of the household; Rufel sketched a little, hooked rugs, sewed. In the days spent with Mammy, her treasured "weddin gif," she recalled the glittering scenes again and again, knitting them firmly into the commonplace fabric of their days.

There had been the inevitable disappointments and sorrows. They had never gotten far enough ahead to complete the second story, never had much luck with slaves, ill health and runaways plaguing them so they never had more than eight at a time—not counting Mammy and whoever was acting as Bertie's man. There was the continuing unpleasantness with the neighbors over runaways and grazing rights. They resented the fences Bertie put up to protect the cotton fields from the hogs and cattle that habitually roamed at will in the neighborhood. He accused them of harboring his slaves, even encouraging them to run away. Rufel had miscarried twice after Timmy was born, and somehow they had lost touch with the many friends met on excursions outside the county and with her family.

Rufel never, even in her most private thoughts, referred to the four-year-old estrangement from her family as more than having lost touch. Someday, she told herself, she would write her mother and set the record straight, refute those malicious slanders against Bertie and herself. Perhaps she and Bertie had been a bit free in asking money of her father and Uncle Carson in the first years of their marriage. Even big plantation owners were often short of hard cash and waited upon the harvest to purchase ready-made goods or pay for services. Her mother just never understood how much it took to establish a decent living in these backwoods. Anyway, the loans had not amounted to much; certainly not the exorbitant sums her mother had mentioned in that last hateful letter. Four or five thousand dollars, indeed! And the second story still no more than a Georgian front and an empty, slant-roofed shell, the kitchen barely a lean-to covering that monstrous cook-stove. They could not have borrowed so much in just four years of marriage. And whatever the correct sum, her father must have known that Bertie would repay it as soon as they were on their feet.

It was all, of course, a stupid misunderstanding, which though hurtful, Rufel would have been ready to forgive, had it not been for the libelous names her mother had called Bertie, scoundrel, wastrel, gambler. All of this caused by Rufel's request for some trifling sum whose purpose she couldn't now even remember. Rufel had brooded over that letter in secret. It seemed to reveal a mean and petty side of her mother's nature that she herself had sometimes suspected but always excused; she could not bring herself to show the letter to Bertie or even mention it to Mammy. To do so seemed somehow to give validity to those stupid charges. In truth, she cared more for the consequences of the letter than for the content of the letter itself. She could not now hope to visit Charleston with her family's help. But someday, she told herself, when they were on their feet, she would write her mother; she would see the record set straight.

These were the dreary parts of the story and Rufel tried never to tell herself those. She did not sneer at the neighbors as Bertie did, but she knew them to be rough and uncouth. The women, as Bertie maintained, were dowds, for the most part, and gossips. Now and then—always unbidden and fleeting—she had thought, as Mammy had more and more frequently muttered aloud, that there ought to be something more showing on the eastern horizon than a bird lifting above the trees. And always, close upon the heels of that feeling, silencing that vagrant thought as she had Mammy's whispers, came the knowledge that Bertie had wrested a good living for them out of these backwoods. Rufel had never had to turn her hand to more than an occasional piece of sewing or the soil in a flower bed. She knew Bertie had bought her leisure at some cost and she would not criticize him.

Worms, spreading from a new field into the established cotton acreage in the fifth year of their marriage, had devastated the harvest and come close to wiping them out. Bertie had proposed an extended business tirp, like the shorter ones he went on once or, more frequently now, two or three times a year. Most often he had returned with a little of the ready money they were always so short of. He traveled the rivers, the Mississippi, the Missouri, and Ohio, where, he said, northern capital met southern enterprise and made "deals," made cash money. Rufel had only a hazy idea of what Bertie was talking about, something, she thought, like what her father and Uncle Carson did, something to do with planters and cotton, with the buying and selling of goods. And this was only to tide them over, to make ends meet until more land could be cleared, more cotton planted.

Bertie had returned before the last cotton picking, with money, a bolt of watered silk for her, a saddle and the crippled darky for Timmy. Their own harvest had been smaller—not enough land planted to cotton, Bertie had explained; they would remedy that come spring. And he had gone again in the slack time between the last chopping and the first picking of the cotton, back to the river, to get capital to feed the land. Mammy hadn't liked it. Rufel was expecting; she had miscarried twice and had a hard time with Timmy before that. There wasn't a decent driver on the place and the responsibility for directing the half-wild negroes who then worked their fields would fall largely to her. But Rufel could not bring herself to say no; Bertie was always so sure and she was, she thought, in good health. Those expensive waters had done her some good, she had laughed, pleased to be pleasing Bertie, who thought it so important that he go. Had he not gone the last time, she told herself, they would scarcely have made it through the winter, even Mammy could see that.

It had laddered like a stocking; four of the six hands had taken off soon after they finished stripping the corn fields in August; the baby, Clara, had come early and hard. Bertie had not come at all. Perhaps, as Mammy said, he had gone too far north in search of business, been caught there when a river iced over. Rufel had no clear idea of geography and was calmed by Mammy's confidence.

She had, as Mammy often reminded her, a healthy baby girl; they had taken care of the harvest—though what Master Bert would say about how they had done it, using runaways. Mammy laughed, sure that Bertie would see the joke they had played on the neighbors, and Rufel herself thought it funny after a while. Payback, Bertie would call it, for all the Sutton slaves these shiftless farmers had helped escape.

Rufel worried less about Bertie's reaction than her neighbors', though Mammy assured her that none of the darkies were from the area. Her fears that she would be denounced or arrested for harboring runaways receded as autumn wore on, but she was never as sanguine as Mammy about the arrangement with the runaways. True, they seemed to work with a better will than darkies on the place had ever done; but she could not like Ada, the raw-boned darky whose aid Mammy had enlisted when Rufel's labor with Clara had proved so long and difficult. Ada had stayed on to cook; Annabelle was to help in the House. The darkies had lightened Mammy's load considerably but Rufel sensed something sly in the way they seemed to avoid her, and secretly fretted that Ada seemed to take up so much of Mammy's time. Rufel had nothing much to do with the four or five other runaways who had harvested the crops—Mammy and Ada made what arrangements were necessary—but she could not rid herself of the suspicion that, having run away from one place, these darkies would run away from the Glen, too.

Rufel got into the habit, as she nursed Clara, of sitting by the window, rocking gently, watching the trees. She thought then of Charleston, began to speak of it with hesitant longing as she sat and watched the trees. She did not think, as Mammy teased her at first, that Charleston would appear on the eastern horizon, but she hungered for the city of her come-out with a strength she tried guiltily to conceal. Mammy, concerned and fearful at Rufel's lingering lethargy, urged Rufel to try one of the foul-tasting teas Ada swore would help a new mother regain her strength. Ada, Mammy told Rufel, might, if asked, stay on when the master returned. As if Bertie were due back any minute! And she spoke casually of

Rufel's deepest fears: It was sure bad of Master Bert to get out of touch like this; Rufel shouldn't spare him her tongue when he returned. Her calm certainty that he would return bolstered Rufel's own faltering belief. Bertie, she told herself as she gazed out the windows, would be homebound as soon as the river up north thawed in the spring.

Rufel remembered hardly anything of that winter (and felt a faint surprise, if she thought of it, that she had no recollection of privation or even scrimping), except that she had been miserable. She had paid little attention to the preparations for spring planting until Mammy began to talk of it. They should marl the cotton fields and put manure on them; they should rotate the crops, putting corn where Bertie had always planted cotton; put in oats or hay or peas; expand the potato field. Plant less cotton altogether. Rufel had been uneasy as the suggestions diverged more and more from Bertie's practices, but Mammy, citing as justification the experience of the new darky, Harker, who had wandered into the Glen sometime during the winter, had easily quieted Rufel's hesitant questioning. She was baffled by the larger questions of crop management that were implicit in these changes and found it easier in this, as in so much else, to rely on Mammy's judgment.

A cold had settled into Mammy's chest at the tail end of spring. It had seemed nothing serious at first and Rufel, roused at last from lethargy and anticipating Bertie's return any day, had enjoyed pampering Mammy, playfully bullying her into drinking Ada's noxious brews. The cough had worsened and with frightening suddenness, Mammy died. Rufel could not get used to that fact. Nothing in the days and weeks since Mammy's death had filled the silence where her voice used to live. Bertie would not return. Rufel never voiced this fear aloud or even phrased it to herself. It had been unthinkable to say when Mammy lived; it was impossible now that Mammy was dead. Who would scold her or laugh away her fears? But they were there, darting into consciousness. Only Charleston kept foreboding at bay, the dreamlike images of her first season serving as a refuge from her dull days and the neverending trees.

Rufel herself had never seen Sutton Glen through the trees. Oh, she had imagined the elms that would someday line the lane from the Road to the House, their branches meeting overhead, the House standing squarely at lane's end. But Ives Creek was too narrow, its course too winding for convenient travel and the House wasn't visible from the Road. She had come to understand these things silently as she nursed Clara and stared out the windows or simply sat singing tunelessly. It was like being swallowed up by the forest, she thought, wanting Charleston again with all her heart. Like the forest had swallowed up everything east of Ives Creek: "If you was to take a ride . . ."

Yet, she would tell herself, even now, as far as she knew, there was a spot—on the opposite slope, say—where just so much of the House was visible, just so much and no more. It made no difference, of course, what she or anyone else might see from some distant perspective. She looked out upon the barely kept yard, the slopes rising beyond it, the changing light, changing colors, the empty sky. The trees grew fat, got lean; some water glinted silver, imagined among the trees. And now she watched the colored girl.

ॐ

The days drifted by. Dessa slept, waking to the colored woman's gruff urgings to "eat. Eat," the taste of some strongly flavored broth, the mealy texture of cereal, thinned she thought with milk, the changing of the bloody cloth. Acutely embarrassed and weak as a kitten, she bore the woman's gentle touch. Often she woke to find the baby asleep in the curve of her arm and, hand heavy, powerless to caress him, she pursed her lips and breathed him love . . . Or opened her eyes to some smiling face—dark, peach-colored, hair like night or the sun—whose name she ought to know. She would grin feebly; they would pat her arm. Nathan, she would think. Cully. But already they were gone.

The colored woman chatted in a companionable way as she tended Dessa. Not enough to require an answer or force Dessa to questions, but she did listen, her mind holding enough to know the baby was doing well; the white woman meant no harm; she could sleep. She did not dream but she became cautious in her waking. The white woman seemed often in the room and Dessa woke, now and then, to find her settled in the rocker, hands quiet in her lap, dreamy-eyed, looking toward Dessa but apparently talking to herself. ". . . bonnet . . ." Dessa heard several times. Half-listening, fascinated, she watched the red mouth move. She knew she could understand what the white woman said if she would let herself. But if she understood the white woman, she would have to . . . have to, have to do— Something And— ". . . picnic," the white woman said. Dessa wanted to laugh. Where did you go to pick nits? Or was that something else only white folks did? She peered at the white woman; her dress looked neat enough. So they had bugs, just like some trashy buckra or freshwater negro who didn't know enough to keep clean. "Mammy . . ." That made no sense. Mammy's name came up often. What could this white woman know of mammy; or mammy of "dropped waists" and "Dutch sleeves"—unless these were cows?

Once she woke in arms, her face tangled in a skein of fine webbing that seemed alive, it clung and itched her skin so bad. She almost suffocated in her terror for she knew the white woman held her and they were together in the big feather bed. And, really, it was the white woman's breathing that saved her, brought her to her senses; its calm regularity imposing order on her own wildly beating heart. That breathing, punctuated by a drawn-out sigh of utter satisfaction and the small fragile bundle that nestled at her spine. Turning cautiously, moving with infinite patience, she inched herself and the baby toward the edge of the bed. Squirming carefully into the soft mattress she managed to nudge out a slight rise between herself and the other woman who, still breathing regularly, had likewise turned away. What kind of place had she come to? she thought as her heart thudded against her ribs. Her fingers touched briefly the satiny hair, the thin velvet of her baby's skin. It was a long time before she slept again.

The colored woman's name was Ada, Dessa realized one morning. The long windows had begun to gray with dawn light. No conch or bell sounded here; people must get up with the rooster's crow. This was the Sutton place except Master Sutton wasn't here. Ada called the white woman "Miz Ruint." There was something funny about the way Ada said the name, as though— Was the white woman crazy? Dessa sweated; the thin stuff of her shift clung to her. *Shift.* Dessa clutched at the garment. She had never in her life owned cloth as fine as the material her hand rubbed against her side. She moved uneasily between the unbelievable smoothness of the sheets. The white woman's breathing was barely audible in the stillness. Maybe she was crazy, Dessa thought, but not a killer. No, not a killer. Nathan and Cully would not have brought her here. Not a killer; but touched, maybe; strange in the head. What else could explain her own presence in this bed?

Touched; and Ada said, Miz Ruint said the master was coming home this harvest for sure. The other woman had laughed quietly. Ada said the white woman had said the same thing about the master's return last year and he hadn't come. Dessa remembered that; Ada had rolled her eyes as if to say— Dessa couldn't quite put her finger on it. Crazy—maybe, she assured herself now, but not no killer. Ada spoke also of "Dorcas." In her mind's eye, Dessa saw a thin, loam-colored face, surmounted by a tangle of even darker hair. No. That was Annabelle, Ada's daughter, seldom seen and then only briefly, a slender figure who hummed quietly and showed no interest in Dessa. Dorcas was someone Ada quoted, someone Dessa didn't think she had yet seen. Never mind, she told herself. Her hand moved to soothe the baby. There had to be someplace else to sleep. She would ask Ada.

Neither Ada nor her daughter belonged to the white woman; none of them did. Ada's words plucked at Dessa's attention. Ada's face beneath her bandanna was placid and Dessa wondered if she had heard right. Free? Dessa wondered silently, as she watched Ada stir the bowl she held. Dessa tried to gesture but her hand fell limply to her side. She swallowed. "Yo'all—" she croaked.

Ada paused with the spoon halfway to Dessa's mouth. "Free?" she said smiling, brown eyes looking closely at Dessa as she replaced the spoon in the bowl untouched. "Cat let loose your tongue, huh? Come on, it just a bit more." She stirred the remaining grits and lifted another spoonful toward Dessa. "Come on; eat up."

Dessa opened her mouth obediently. The grits had been thinned with milk and seasoned with butter and Dessa held the spoonful in her mouth savoring the richness.

"I wouldn't zactly call it free," Ada said, doubtfully. "We runned away," she added brightly, as though this explained it all. "She let us stay here; she need the he'p. Man gone; slaves runned off." Ada shrugged and smiled. "White folks think we hers but didn't none of us never belong to this place." She spooned the last of the cereal into Dessa's mouth and rose.

"Ada." Dessa managed to grasp a fold of the woman's skirt. "Ada, sleep with you?" She struggled to one elbow, then fell back weakly, her eyes seeking to hold the other woman's. "Me and the baby?" She couldn't spend another night in the white woman's bed.

"Honey." Ada bent over her, eyes warm with concern. "Honey, me and Annabelle sleeps in that little lean-to they calls a kitchen; it just barely big enough for us and it ain't no wise fitting. You ain't even out of childbed—"

"Quarters, we could—"

"Worse than a chicken run." Ada sat on the bed, stroking Dessa's hand. "Tell you, honey, these some *poor* white peoples. Oh, this room and the parlor fine enough, but you know what's outside that door? A great big stairway lead straight up to nothing cause they never did finish the second floor." She laughed. "The 'Quarters' is a cabin, one side for the womens, one side for the mens. 'Sides," she added when Dessa would have protested further, "she the only nursing woman on the place. Even if you go, you ought to leave the baby here."

Dessa had suspected from the way the baby turned from her, fretting and in tears, that she had no milk to speak of. Her baby, nursing— Her breathing quickened and her heart seemed to pound in her ears. There was more, but Dessa turned away.

Ada talked as much to herself as she did to Dessa, almost in the same way that the white woman did, never really expecting an answer. Already she seemed to have forgotten that Dessa had spoken. Dessa surrendered to the familiar lassitude. Runaways. Ada, Harker, how many others? And the white woman let them stay, nursed— Dessa knew the white woman nursed her baby; she had seen her do it. It went against everything she had been taught to think about white women but to inspect that fact too closely was almost to deny her own existence. That the white woman had let them stay— Even that was almost too big to think about. Sometimes it seemed to Dessa that she was drowning in milky skin, ensnared by red hair. There was a small mole on the white woman's forehead just above one sandy eyebrow. She smelled faintly of some scent that Dessa couldn't place. Why had they all run here? Because she let them stay. Why had she let them stay?

". . . behind. She was that put out about it, too." The white woman was sewing this time, setting big, careless stitches in a white cloth draped over her knees. Against her will Dessa listened. ". . . night of the Saint Cecilia dinner and of course Mammy had to dress mother for that."

No white woman like this had ever figured in mammy's conversations, Dessa thought drowsily. And this would have been something to talk about: dinner and gowns—not just plain dresses.

". . . all by myself. And scared, too—the Winstons was related to royalty or maybe it was only just a knight." The white woman paused a moment. "Now, often as Daphne told it, you'd think I'd know it by heart." She shook her head and laughed softly. "Mammy would know it."

Maybe, Dessa thought, with a sudden pang, Mammy hadn't "known" about Kaine, about Master selling Jeeter . . .

". . . Mammy doubted that, when it all happened so long ago wasn't no one alive now who witnessed it."

I seen it, Dessa started to say. Master sold Jeeter to the trader same as Mistress sold me. But the white woman continued without pause.

". . . the pretty clothes. Well, I know Mammy didn't know a thing about history, but I knew she was right about the clothes.

She used to dress me so pretty. Even the Reynolds girls—and their daddy owned the bank; everyone said they wore drawers made out of French silk. They used to admire my clothes."

Dessa stared at the white woman. She was crazy, making up this whole thing, like, like—

". . . pretend their clothes came from a fashionable *modiste*, but I always said, 'Oh, this a little something Mammy ran up for me.' So when I walked into the great hall at Winston, I had on a dress that Mammy made and it was Mammy's—"

"Wasn't no 'mammy' to it." The words burst from Dessa. She knew even as she said it what the white woman meant. "Mammy" was a servant, a slave (Dorcas?) who had nursed the white woman as Carrie had nursed Young Mistress's baby before it died. But, goaded by the white woman's open-mouthed stare, she continued, "Mammy ain't made you nothing!"

"Why, she—" The white woman stopped, confused. Hurt seemed to spread like a red stain across her face.

Seeing it, Dessa lashed out again. "You don't even know mammy."

"I do so," the white woman said indignantly, "Pappa give her—"

"Mammy live on the Vaugham plantation near Simeon on the Beauford River, McAllen County." This was what they were taught to say if some white person asked them; their name and what place they belonged to. The white woman gaped, like a fish, Dessa thought contemptuously, just like a fish out of water. Anybody could make this white woman's wits go gathering.

"My, my— *My* Mammy—" the white woman sputtered.

The words exploded inside Dessa. "*Your* 'mammy'—" Never, never had that white baby taken Jessup's place with Carrie. "*Your* 'mammy'!" No *white* girl could ever have taken *her* place in mammy's bosom; no one. "You ain't got no 'mammy,' " she snapped.

"I do— I did so." The white woman was shouting now, the white cloth crushed in her trembling hands.

"All you know about is this kinda sleeve and that kinda bonnet; some party here— Didn't you have no peoples where you lived? 'Mammy' ain't nobody name, not they real one."

"Mam—"

The white woman's baby started to cry and the white woman made as if to rise and go to it. Dessa's voice overrode the tearful wail, seeming to pin the white woman in the chair. "See! See! You don't even not know 'mammy's' name. Mammy have a name, have children."

"She didn't." The white woman, finger stabbing toward her own heart, finally rose. "She just had me! I was like her child."

"What was her name then?" Dessa taunted. "Child don't even know its own mammy's name. What was mammy's name? What—"

"Mammy," the white woman yelled. "That was her name."

"Her name was Rose," Dessa shouted back, struggling to sit up. "That's a flower so red it look black. When mammy was a girl they named her that count of her skin—smooth black, and they teased her bout her breath cause she worked around the dairy; said it smelled like cow milk and her mouth was slick as butter, her kiss tangy as clabber."

"You are lying," the white woman said coldly; she was shaking with fury. "Liar!" she hissed.

Dessa heaved herself to her knees, flinging her words in the white woman's face. "Mammy gave birth to ten chi'ren that come in the world living." She counted them off on her fingers. "The first one Rose after herself; the second one died before the white folks named it. Mammy called her Minta after a cousin she met once. Seth was the first child lived to go into the fields. Little Rose died while mammy was carrying Amos—carried off by the diphtheria. Thank God, He spared Seth." Remembering the names now the way mammy used to tell them, lest they forget, she would say; lest her poor, lost children die to living memory as they had in her world.

"Amos lived for a week one Easter. Seem like he blighted the womb; not another one lived till she had Bess." Mammy telling the names until speech became too painful.

"Them was the two she left, Seth and Bess; Seth was sold away when she come with Old Mistress to the Reeves place. Sold away like Jeeter, whose real name was Samuel after our daddy—only Carrie kept saying Jeeter when she meant Junior and that was the name he kept. Bess, born two years before Old Mistress married Old Master Reeves; left cause she was sickly; died before Rose reached her new home."

Even buried under years of silence, Dessa could not forget. She had started on the names of the dead before she realized that the white woman had gone. Both children were crying now but Dessa's voice continued through their noise:

"Jeffrey died the first year she come to the Reeves plantation; Caesar, two years older than Carrie: head kicked in by a horse he was holding for some guest. Carrie was the first child born at the new place to live. Dessa, Dessa Rose, the baby girl."

Anger spent now, she wept. "Oh, I pray God mammy still got Carrie Mae left."

Four

How dare that darky! Seething, Rufel blundered blindly out of the back door, slamming it behind her. She went quickly down the steep steps, pushing roughly past Ada—who had just set foot on the bottom step—without a word. Wench probably don't know her own name and here she is trying to tell *me* something about Mammy. She strode across the yard, automatically turning down the path to the stream. Uppity, insolent slut! Ought to be whipped. And if she was mine, I'd do it, too, she thought venomously. She took the faint path to the left and entered the thin strand of trees that boarded the upper creek. It was cooler here in the dappled sunlight and Rufel slowed her pace. Of course she knew they were talking about two different people. Though how that crazy gal could think *she* could know anyone I would know—forgetting that she herself had half-hoped the same thing. Rufel knew the darky often shammed sleep but she had also sensed the girl's puzzled wonder at her words, and her wide-opened eyes had seemed to invite confidences. Rufel had not talked of Charleston with the raw yearning that Mammy had come to hate and fear, but as simple proof that that life had existed; the darky's credulous, if drowsy, attention had seemed somehow to confirm that existence. Rufel flushed angrily. She had acted no better than the wench; she had fallen into reminiscing with a strange darky.

Mammy would say she was too trusting, Rufel knew, too open-hearted. The wench had been sassy, but it was Rufel who had first forgotten her place, gossiping like common trash. She could hear Mammy's voice plain as day. I was just trying to cheer her up, she thought defensively. Must be dull as straw laying up in that bed all day. If she had chatted a bit long, well, Rufel admitted that she was lonely, that the silence since Mammy's death sometimes came near to crushing her. And to be invited to speak— Resentment flared in her. Anyway, she thought sullenly, there had been no call for the wench to turn so hateful. Making up all that stuff just to be mean.

Rufel came out on the narrow shoreline and was almost upon the dark figure by the tree before she noticed him, or he her. One of the darkies who came to see the girl, recognized in the instant before she could scream. Fishing: the pole propped between his knees, his back propped against the tree trunk, battered hat over his face. Sensing or only hearing her, he moved. Hat slipping, pole falling, body struggling to rise, he seemed at first all arms and legs, a shapeless darkness contained by ragged clothes, topped by the light-colored hat, and she covered her mouth to laugh. Balanced now, he rose, fluid, looming black against the sky, stopping the laugh in her throat. She would have screamed, but he spoke.

"Don't." Softly, arm out, hand up, open, looking straight into her eyes. "I'm just fishing." He gestured with the pole toward the creek. "No trespass intended." But he made no move to go.

Confused she stopped. "Why—" It was *her* place, she thought indignantly. "You—" Everywhere; they were everywhere, her house, her bed— And Mammy— Rufel burst into tears. Of course she knew Mammy's name, she told herself, and she would think of it as soon as she got over being so upset. She—

"Mis'ess." Close to her, body heat drawing her . . . "Miz—" She threw her arms around the shoulders, her head seeking that spot where the frayed collar lay open against the black neck.

"Mammy," she hiccuped against the soft, supple cloth, and, remembering with painful clarity: "Dorcas. It was Dorcas."

Dorcas. Pappa had not given her Mammy as a birthday present as Rufel sometimes claimed. Dorcas was a lady's maid extraordinaire who had traveled with her former mistress in France and, at eleven hundred dollars (you could get a good field hand for that!), far too expensive a present for a thirteen-year-old girl. Dorcas did for all three of the Carson ladies, sewing, laundry, hair, dressing them, choosing their clothes. They called her Mammy because Mrs. Carson thought the title made her seem as if she had been with the family for a long time. She cared for them all, restraining Mrs. Carson's taste for low-cut dresses and Rowena's penchant for gaudy furbelows. She kept five-year-old Benjamin junior in starched shirt fronts when company came and introduced the senior Carson men to the comforts of the soft tie, which had not then come into the general vogue. She made Rufel stand up straight, rinsed her baby-fine hair in malt water and lemon, and arranged it becomingly about her childlishly thin face. And loved her. It was Rufel Mammy had loved, Rufel whose heart she had stolen from the moment she smiled.

"Dorcas," spoken promptly in response to Rufel's startled question at finding a strange slave in her room. Her face was like coffee with nothing of cream in it, Rufel had thought in confusion, feeling gangly and graceless, conscious of her rumpled pinafore and the hair that straggled limply about her face. "Dorcas" was neat as a pin: Her long, narrow white apron was spotless, pinned under the bust rather than tied at the waist of her dark gown; a white kerchief was arranged in precise folds over her broad bosom; a cream-colored bandanna— No, Rufel corrected herself. The silky-looking cloth on the darky's head bore little resemblance to the gaudy-colored swatches most darkies tied about their heads. This was a scarf, knotted in a rosette behind one ear. Rufel, used to the rather haphazard dress of the other house slaves, was made uncomfortable by the darky's tidy appearance. Why, she thought, again in confusion, she's almost stylish. "I'm to be taking care of you and Miz Rowena and your mamma," the darky said pleasantly. She put away the last of Rufel's undergarments in the chest, closed the drawer, and turned, for Rufel had remained silent. "You are Miss Ruf—?"

"Ruth. Ruth Elizabeth," she said then, the spell broken. The darkies never could get her name straight, slurring and garbling the syllables until the name seemed almost unrecognizable. The careless pronunciation of the two household servants annoyed Mrs. Carson; often she dealt offenders a sharp slap across the mouth. Automatically, sure of herself now, firm and clear, "Ruth Elizabeth."

"That's quite a mouthful for a young beanpole like yourself."

And Ruth Elizabeth, drawing herself up in offended dignity— for she was agonizingly conscious of her height, her suddenly expanding breasts, and tried to minimize both by slouching—was arrested by the smile flashing like a firefly across the dark face. The eyes lit with laughter, yet for a moment, Rufel sensed some hesitation, felt the dark eyes question, May I? Is it all right to tease? Drawn by that firefly grin, yet disturbed by the darky's obvious assurance, Rufel was relieved by that hint of uncertainty; it made the darky seem more natural and herself a bit more comfortable.

Rufel had been lonely, had felt herself ugly and awkward. Mammy talked with her, admired her hair and rather full-lipped smile, showed her how to walk erectly. She praised where Mrs. Carson had criticized, hugged where Rufel's own mother had scolded. Whatever Rufel had not taken to that pillowy bosom seemed insignificant to her now; and she had been taken to that cushiony bosom, been named there 'Fel, Rufel. To hear the names on Mammy's lips was to hear, to know herself loved.

The hands in her hair now were hard, the chest, the arms. Rufel sat up sniffing. A dark hand obligingly offered her a ruffled cloth. She blew her nose with dainty precision, only then realizing that she had used her own petticoat. She turned to the darky aghast, and caught her breath. Never had she seen such blackness. She blinked, expecting to see the bulbous lips and bulging eyes of a burnt-cork minstrel. Instead she looked into a pair of rather shadowy eyes and strongly defined features that were—handsome! she thought shocked, almost outraged. She looked again, surreptitiously this time, conscious of herself, the darky, a *male*, herself, on the ground, together. He had dropped his arm from her shoulder at her first start of surprise; stiffly now, she drew further away from him.

"Dorcas." He cleared his throat. "Dorcas; that was the lady that died?"

Rufel sniffed again and nodded. "She treated me just like, just like—" She stuttered and could have wept again, seeing with an almost palpable lucidity how absurd it was to think of herself as Mammy's child, a darky's child. And shuddered. A pickaninny. Like the ragged, big-bellied urchins she had seen now and then about the streets of Mobile, running errands, cutting capers, begging coppers. Mammy was a slave, a nigger, and, and "She— She was my maid," she finished lamely, confused; "my personal servant." But Mammy was my friend, she thought. Embarrassed by her own recoil from the cherished memory, she said stoutly, "She loved me. And no darky can tell me different!" she added fiercely. She hiccuped and scooted closer to his comforting warmth. "That wench," she continued angrily, "the one you-all always making over—"

"Dessa?"

"—said Mammy didn't love me, couldn't possibly have loved me."

"I don't see that as much to take on about." The darky spoke quietly. "Something some darky said."

"She—"

"Dessa didn't even know Dorcas, and just met you. Why you so upset?"

Rufel opened her mouth to speak, closed it, and turned away. "I was just remembering Mam—" tongue stumbling over the familiar name, "remembering her." Unable then to recall the familiar face, she blinked away angry tears, seeing then the loved features, the coffee-black skin and cream-colored head-scarf, the full lips, but subtly altered so the face seemed that of a stranger.

"Guess you must have cared for Dorcas a lot."

She nodded and wiped her nose, warming to the quiet voice. "I talked to her every day of my life from the time I was thirteen. I don't think I ever thought a thought during all that time that I didn't tell Mam— Dor— That I didn't tell her. Well," seeing his skeptical look. Had he known Mammy? she thought wildly, and looked away. "Not everything. When I was— After I got married, there was certain thoughts a married lady can't share. But I told her everything else," she said hurriedly, grabbing among memories she and Mammy had shared. "I'd come home from a ball or even just a little walk with the Misses Greyson, Regina and Dolly— they were my particular friends."

There was no special day she remembered, just the feel of those strolls about the city with Pompey, one of the Greysons' darkies, walking along behind, or the taste of the buttery little biscuits the Greysons' cook made for afternoon tea. Mammy had not always been there when Rufel returned from an outing; often as not, Mammy had been dressing Mrs. Carson or trying to comb the tangles out of Rowena's thick, honey-blond curls. But always she found the time to review the happenings of Rufel's day, to exclaim over any small triumph, to console, advise, coax, chide— Rufel had started to describe the dress she had worn to Abigail Sorenson's ball when she became aware of movement at her side. The darky stood, hat in one hand, fish at his side in the other; Rufel stood also, her face burning. She had done it again, she saw; memory, mouth had run away with her— As if darkies could ever know the life she spoke of.

"Scuse; scuse me, Mistress, for intruding." The darky was bowing and backing away. "Scuse me." He was gone.

Rufel stamped her foot angrily. They were jealous of course, jealous of her memories, jealous that her life had been so much better than theirs, that it would be again. She was crying because she missed Mammy, she told herself as she sat under the tree and wept.

Ada had made the darky a pallet on the floor in the bedroom, she reported when Rufel returned to the House. Rufel, her breasts throbbing, said nothing to this as she bent to pick up Clara.

"I fed Little Missy a soft egg and some custard," Ada said quickly.

Rufel ignored this, too, as she fumbled to open her bodice. She could hear the baby crying through the closed bedroom door, but she shrank from the thought of nursing him, a *pickaninny*, seeing this for the first time as neighbors might—*would*—see it. His dark skin might as well be fur.

"When the baby sleep through the night, Dessa move back of stairs." Ada spoke loudly.

Just like the reason I don't answer is cause I can't hear, Rufel thought irritably. Clara had done as much playing as nursing and now settled sleepily in the curve of Rufel's arm. The tightness in one of her breasts had eased but the other continued to throb.

"Where Dorcas used to sleep," Ada continued. "—if that all right with you," she added quickly.

So you finally realized you have to ask the mistress round here, Rufel thought spitefully, enjoying Ada's obvious discomfiture. Aloud, she said angrily, "I don't care where that wench sleep." She would have to feed the baby, Rufel thought wearily. She took the sleeping Clara into the bedroom and laid her in the crib. The darky was awake but Rufel avoided her eyes as she picked up the squalling infant. Ada hovered in the background looking uneasily from one to the other.

Mammy would have had the story out of us in a minute, she thought as she returned to the parlor, forced an apology from the instigator—if not from both!—as she used to do when Rufel and Rowena quarreled. Rufel caught herself up short. There you go again, she told herself angrily, expecting all darkies to be like Mammy. Like family, a voice wailed silently within her.

Rufel sank gratefully into the rocker in the parlor and freed her breast to the baby's searching mouth. The baby planted a tiny fist on her breast, sucking hungrily, his shoe-button eyes glittery with tears. She turned her head from his stare, uncomfortable under his unwinking gaze. Almost of their own volition, her fingers stroked his silken curls, so different from the bald heads of her own newborns, the utter brownness of him a striking contrast with the pallor of their skins. Willfully, she closed her eyes and, sighing, gave herself over to the sensual rhythm of his feeding.

Later, lying awake in the big bed, she welcomed the soft regularity of the girl's breathing in the larger silence of the night. She hated the stillness, the quiet. Listening to the crickets, hearing Timmy turn in sleep, or Clara's occasional sighs, was like listening to some extension of the hush, as if she were the only waking, thinking being in the vast emptiness she had not even been aware of when Mammy was alive. Ada had said the name so easily, had always called Mammy "Dorcas," Rufel knew. Dorcas. She mouthed the name, seeing Mammy's face now, but finding no comfort in the familiar image. It was as if the wench had taken her beloved Mammy and put a stranger in her place. Had Mammy had children, Rufel wondered, suckled a child at her breast as she did the wench's, as she did with her own? And how had Mammy borne it when they were taken away— That's if she had any. Rufel interrupted that train of thought. She had only the wench's word for that. And they were not, she repeated, talking about the same woman. But Mammy might have had children and it bothered Rufel that she did not know.

Mammy had liked blackberries, Rufel knew. Every summer they had put up jam and Mammy had coaxed tarts from whatever darky was trying to cook. They had not had much luck with cooks, with the cook-stove, but Mammy could talk the roughest field hand through a creditable tart, Rufel thought with a smile. Mammy had liked to work with silk and had directed the work of the household from a chair under the oak tree in the kitchen yard as long as fair weather held. Had she a sweetheart? A child?

In all the years she'd known her, Rufel had never seen Mammy without the rosette-knotted cloth on her head and the snowy kerchief tied across her bosom, until Mammy got too ill to rise from her pallet back of the stairs. So changed, the dark face framed by darker hair with a strand or two glinting silver, softer than a skein of the silkiest wool. And yet the same, making light of her ailment, humoring Rufel, who had the darkies move the mattress from the cramped quarters under the stairwell into the parlor where Rufel nursed her. Both of them enjoyed the brief reversal—though Mammy only let Rufel do so much and no more—neither believing that Mammy could come to harm over such a little cold.

Mammy was kind and wise and strong; her short black hair curled about the fingers with a will of its own; she had narrow-fingered hands, the thumb and second finger calloused from sewing because she hated wearing a thimble; she liked blackberries and silk and the oak tree in the kitchen yard. That much and no more, Rufel thought, somehow shamed; eleven years and only then to know the feel of a loved one's hair under a loving hand. Truly, such ignorance was worse than grief. She thought feverishly. Mammy had not liked France. Oh, it was pretty enough, she said when Clara Carson asked, or so Mrs. Carson had reported often to their friends, when she still talked about her new slave before company, before she learned, Rufel thought with new bitterness, that it was better to have an old servant named Mammy than to have a "French" maid who couldn't talk French. Had Mammy minded when the family no longer called her name? Was that why she changed mine? Rufel thought fearfully. Was what she had always thought loving and cute only revenge, a small reprisal for all they'd taken from her? How old *had* Mammy been? Why had they gone to France? Rufel had never asked. Had she any children?

The wench's breathing seemed to fill the room. Slaves were free in France, Rufel thought; it was like going north where the Yankees tried to entice slaves away. Had Mammy loved that other mistress so much? Sudden, foolish jealousy spurted through her, about a woman you don't even know, she berated herself. Mammy made the same choice for you, staying when she could have run like the rest of those shiftless darkies. But Rufel knew, even as she told herself this, that escaping to the woods or even running away to the north was not the same as being free in France. And Mammy had passed that up to return. She would have returned if she had a child, Rufel knew, thinking of the wench's words that afternoon. *Mammy have children.* What had the colored girl called her Mammy? *Rose.* Dorcas. *Rose—smooth black.* She remembered the phrase, the fresh airish smell that seemed to follow Mammy—Dorcas. Rose? Would the wench call that coffee-dark skin "smooth black"? Rufel herself had seen Mammy's eyes in the wench's face. The wench was from Charleston. Mammy had returned to Charleston all those long years ago.

Rufel was awakened sometime before dawn by the baby's muffled cries. She lay still a moment, consciously struggling out of sleep, feeling puffy-eyed and heavy-lidded, breasts throbbing faintly. He had been crying, she realized as she stumbled out of bed, for some time, and wondered why the stupid wench hadn't brought him to her or at least called her. She bent to pick him up, her muttered complaints abruptly silenced by the memory of how reluctantly she had nursed him earlier in the evening. Wench still should have enough sense to know I wouldn't let him go hungry, she thought a trifle self-righteously; yet, she was rather pleased to realize that she had some real power over the wench and Ada. The baby seemed to recognize her touch for he stopped crying and turned his face to nozzle at her bosom. He was such a tiny thing to have so big a voice, so fierce a will, she thought. A careless hug could kill him, yet he demanded care and trusted that someone would provide it. Shaken by a sudden wave of protectiveness and remorse, she climbed back in bed and bared her breast to his searching. She had used the baby's hunger to spite the wench and was shamed by the knowledge.

Rufel knew she ought to ask Ada about Mammy and the wench, too, but she could not bring herself to do so, Ada could act so funny, even when asked the most harmless question—as though anybody but Rufel would already know the answer. And in this case, Rufel would almost agree with her. She, Rufel, had been Mammy's friend and she was chagrined by her own ignorance. She would send for Ada after dinner, Rufel temporized, or go out to the kitchen herself after supper. She whiled away the day, angry at her own past thoughtlessness, unwilling to expose her present uncertainty to Ada's view.

Harker came to visit the girl after supper. On impulse, Rufel followed him outside when he left, calling to him as he crossed the yard. Harker had known Mammy and had brought the girl here. She hurried down the back steps, determined to have her questions answered. He waited for her at the edge of the yard, hat lifted slightly above his bushy head, pleasant-faced as always, yet conveying a certain guardedness that in turn made her feel rather awkward in his presence. Thus the question she asked now was not about Mammy as she had meant, but about the wench and more challenging than she intended. "That wench from Charleston?"

He hesitated, then admitted rather sheepishly, "No'm. You know some of them places so little, only people know of em is the ones that live there—and it's not many of them." A grin moved slowly and easily across his face. "We just said Charleston cause we thought you being from that area you might know something of the hardship she had to bear."

So it was to play on my sympathy, she thought triumphantly; then blurted, "Did Mam— Dorcas have any children?"

"Why— She never spoke of none that I know of." And then, with dawning comprehension, "You don't think Dessa related to Dorcas, do you?"

She didn't think so, but that question had been there in her mind nonetheless. Now she asked with more coolness than she felt, "Well, is she?" Almost she expected him to laugh; the question was so ridiculous.

He looked at her quizzically. "I wouldn't think so," he said slowly. "But I don't know so, either. Nathan might; and he'd be the one to ask."

"Nathan?"

"Tall, dark-skinned fellow—"

She remembered the darky at the creek. Dark-skinned; so that was what they called it, picturing the dusky skin that had seemed like jet to her.

"You want I tell him come see you?"

The darky's question startled her. "No. No." She felt slightly panicky at the thought of questioning the darky with Ada in the parlor or the wench across the hall. "No; it's not important," she said quickly. "Thank you, Harker," she said turning away. The darky was probably at the creek, fishing again when he ought to be working, she thought. She could look for him there herself.

After dinner the next day, Rufel made sure that both babies were asleep then went to look for the darky. The best fishing on the whole property was at the pool some distance downstream from the spot where she had seen the darky the day before. Bertie had given her that spot as her own; he allowed the darkies the use of some streams west of the fields but he had forbidden them the watering places close to the House. The darkies had generally abided by the rule as far as the spot on the upper creek was concerned but the fishing at the pool had drawn them like flies to honey. It had been one of the most frequent causes of punishment. There was no one at the pool that afternoon, nor at the spot upstream, and she had turned to go when the darky seemed to emerge from the trees.

"You sent at me, Mis'ess?"

"No," she said startled. Face to face with him, she was not at all sure of what she wanted to know.

"Well, not exactly sent." He paused as though waiting for her to speak, but Rufel could think of nothing to say. He continued, "Harker said you was asking about Dessa." He paused. She scrambled about in her mind for something to say, but found nothing. "He thought maybe there was something you might want to ask me about her."

He did not say he would answer, she noticed, just as he had made no excuse or move to go when she surprised him loafing yesterday. It was as if they didn't know how they should act in front of a white person, she thought, amazed and uneasy. She had never met darkies who seemed so unversed in what was due her place as these. Harker, Ada, Annabelle, none of them offered her anything that she had not specifically requested; they volunteered no act that she had not specifically directed; they never sought to oblige her. Mammy had attributed this to Annabelle's slowness and refused to see it in Ada, whose manner now, Rufel thought, often bordered on the presumptuous. Harker had never displayed any suggestion of Ada's cheekiness but she knew he volunteered his knowledge of the land and how to work it out of something other than loyalty or duty to her. She felt, too, in him a certain reserve; he would give this much and no more. He could just as easily have told me about that wench, she thought crossly now. Certainly he must know more about Mammy. Instead he had put her off on this stranger who was no more obliging than he. She eyed the darky with disfavor.

"He said"—the darky spoke as though in response to her look— "he said you was asking about Dessa and Dorcas."

She nodded, hoping her continued silence would force him into further speech.

"Dessa wasn't no ways related to Dorcas," he continued after a moment. "Not that I knows of, anyway. Dessa come from a plantation up around Monks Corner, mammy, pappy, sisters, brothers—all of em from up around that way."

"You-all said she was from Charleston." She still felt a sense of satisfaction in having at least exposed that fabrication.

He shrugged. "Charleston, Augusta; don't matter all that much. Ain't likely she'd know anyone you know. She—"

"You-all lied."

"Yes, Mis'ess," he admitted without a trace of guilt, "and we didn't mean you no harm. Dessa been through a hard time and if stretching the truth a little get her a spot of rest—" He shrugged his shoulders and spread his hands palm up.

As though that explained it all, she thought indignantly. She turned away fuming. "Wait," he said touching her arm suddenly, lightly; and withdrew his hand as quickly. He rubbed it slowly along his pant leg, looking at a point just over her shoulder. "I seen her when she come out that sweatbox they put her in. Know what that is, Mis'ess? It's a closed box they put willful darkies in, built so's you can't lie down in it or sit or stand in it. It do got a few holes in it so you can breathe, but plenty people done suffocated in em. They whipped her, put her in that, let her sweat out in the sun."

"That wench don't have a scar on her back," she said quickly.

He looked briefly in her face, and she turned away, uneasy at the boldness of that glance. "They lashed her about the hips and legs, branded her along the insides of her thighs."

Rufel shivered; that couldn't be true, it was too, too awful, she thought; and how did this darky know anyway? "How do you know?" she challenged; yet, she was interested despite herself. "How you come to see all this?"

He did not look at her this time, rather he looked toward her. "I was slave to the trader what bought her. He was buying up around Minifree when he heard about an experienced field hand, already breeding, for sale at Simeon. Master Wilson ride a pretty mile out his way to look at a proposition like that and he taken me with him. So I was there. I seen her when she come out the box.

"They'd just about whipped that dress off her and what hadn't been cut off her—dress, drawers, shift—was hanging round her in tatters or else stuck in them wounds. Just from the waist down, you see, cause they didn't wanna 'impair her value.' That's what her mistress told Wilson. She drove a hard bargain; I was there and I heard that, too." His face had a stubborn cast to it, as though he expected her to challenge this. "Mistress told Wilson out front that the girl was scarred and she still got four hundred dollars for her." He shook his head and chuckled ruefully. "Not too many could get the best of old Master like that.

"I don't know how long they had her in that box. Her face was swolled; she was bloody and dirty, cramped from laying up in there. I didn't think she could stand up; but she did." He spoke with quiet intensity. "She stood up."

Rufel could see the scene as he described it. The darky himself tying the wench's hands, looping the lead rope over the pommel of his saddle, walking the horse across the yard and around to the front of the house as she stumbled along behind, seeing the darkies lining the drive, some, as he said, hiding their faces, others staring straight ahead. Had her own people been there, Rufel wondered, her own Rose? She could almost feel the fire that must have lived in the wench's thighs.

"The mistress was standing on the front porch, talking to Wilson. He was already mounted up and when he saw me, he started off at a trot, calling to me to hurry up. I knowed that girl couldn't bit more run than I could fly and I didn't want to drag her. Well, Master Wilson, he rode back and hit my horse, *piya!* like that cross the rump. By the time I got the horse under control, Dessa'd been drug about the yard a good bit. And Wilson was right there beside me, his hand on my hand when I moved to help her up. 'No,' he told me. 'That her first lesson on this coffle. She got to keep up.'

"She was crying, you know, tears making mud on her face, dirt from head to toe so she looked like something bandoned longside the road. She picked her own self up and I know her skin must've been screaming. But she didn't ask that white man for no mercy; not then, not ever that I knows of."

"What a horrid story," Rufel breathed after a moment, imagining the agony of those thighs, to walk with that burning— "That vicious trader."

The darky shrugged again. "Master Wilson wasn't like some, cruel just cause he could be; he didn't believe in damaging goods, though if he could get em cheap enough, he bought em. That what he done then was mostly for show, impress the mistress with how slaves ought to be handled. Soon as we was out of sight, he let me take her up on the horse with me; she rode in the supply wagon till she healed enough to walk. He wasn't trying to kill her."

"I know," Rufel said softly. Which made it all the more horrible. To violate a body so. That's if it happened, she told herself. She had sat, at some point during the darky's recital, on a low stump; the darky sat on his haunches a few feet from her. Rufel rose now, conscious that they had talked a long time, brushing carefully at her dress, yet reluctant to go. "How did you-all get way out here?" she asked curiously.

He hesitated, then said tersely, "Escaped off the coffle."

Rufel looked at him in some disbelief. She had seen coffles; they were a common enough sight on the riverboats, the men loaded with chains, the women with scarcely enough rags to cover them decently, all of them dirty and desolate. She found it hard to reconcile that memory with the presence of this darky. They seemed to personify wretchedness; he glowed with life. For that matter, the wench looked remarkably healthy to have been through all the darky said. She looked at him sternly. "She must have done something pretty bad," she said, unable herself to imagine such a crime.

"I don't know about that." The darky rose also. "Some owners, it don't take much. Maybe Dessa's was one like that. Whatever she done, it wasn't enough to 'impair her value.' "

The gently gibing tone seemed to mock her and she retorted, "I bet she was making up to the master; that's why the mistress was so cruel. I bet that's what it was."

"Dessa was breeding when Wilson bought her, Mis'ess," he said. "What she was carrying laying right up there in your house now. No white man ain't had no hand in that."

"Well," thinking of the nut-brown face, but—"His hair," remembering its silken texture. "You not going to tell me darkies have hair like that," she said stubbornly.

"Mis'ess"—he was shaking his head and laughing softly—"every negro baby I ever seen come in the world got curls shine like satin . . . and nap up"—he snapped his fingers—"inside six months. You see that boy in a year, he won't even be able to get a curry comb through that crop."

"Truly?" smiling at the idea. He nodded mock-solemn; startled by his drollery, she laughed. Catching herself a little guiltily, she asked more sharply than she had intended, "Are you the baby's father?

"No, Mis'ess," he said steadily.

"*I* think you-all are sweethearts." She smiled at him encouragingly, thinking that would explain his evident protectiveness of the girl.

He shook his head. "Dessa ain't been in too much of a position to think about no sweetheart," he said without looking at her.

confusion, her hysterical insistence on her mamm...
because her mammy had loved her don't mean...
love me, Rufel thought, wanting desperately...
had loved her not only fully, but freely...
personally responsible for Mammy's pa...
it, not as the soother of hurt as Man...
but as the source of that pain. Sh...
knowingly hurt a hair on Mamm...
Rufel's footsteps slowed as sh...
had been the center of Man...
my's children—girls or b...
How did they bare su...
branding iron searin...
there was nothin...
under the lash...
merely move...
Mammy—...
prised a...
of her...
bea...

tears.

"Mis'ess?" She look...
to heart. She been through a ha...
through a hard time, too—your man gone, Do...

It was what her own common sense told her but she wa...
raged to hear herself compared to the wench. "I knew that little
hellion couldn't be no kin to Mammy," she said tartly.

"The mistress have to see the welts in the darky's hide, eh?"

"Ye—" His tone implied that her desire for proof was mean
and petty and she flushed hotly, as the image of herself inspect-
ing the wench's naked loins flashed vividly to life in her mind.
"Well—" How else was she to know the truth of what they said?
"I know it's more to this than you telling," she flung at him as
she turned to go. "And I'm going to get to the bottom of it."

Rufel hurried toward the house in some agitation, yet she was
relieved that the wench wasn't related to Mammy—though after
hearing that horror story she could well understand the wench's

ny's love. But just
that Mammy didn't
to believe that Mammy
as well. Almost she felt
in, personally connected to
my had always been for her,
, Rufel, who would never have
ny's head. It was not so, of course.
e neared the House. If anything, she
mmy's world—And the children, Mam-
ys? Had Mammy been taken from them?
ch pain? she wondered, thinking then of a
g tender flesh. Surely whipping was enough;
she had ever heard like the scream of a darky
Had Bertie stopped the beatings as he'd said or
them, as Ada had once implied, to the woods? And
Had anyone ever whipped her? Rufel wondered, sur-
how angry the thought made her. Why, the very quality
relationship with Mammy might have been grounds for a
ing with some masters, she realized with alarm, remembering
ammy's tart answers, her way of forgetting to do what she didn't
want to do when she felt such forgetfulness was in Rufel's best
interests.

It didn't take much: remembering the darky's words. Often it
had taken no more with Bertie than a broken plowshare (which
cost money) or a darky who didn't move fast enough. That was
only at first, Rufel protested to herself; Bertie had become a good
master. Why, she couldn't remember the last time a darky had been
whipped at the Glen; certainly she would have heard the screams
(unless Bertie had taken to whipping them in the woods) or
Mammy would have told her— Wouldn't she? Rufel recalled
Mammy's tight-lipped face the first time they had heard that peculiar, high-pitched screaming. The ashen skin and pained expression had seemed to demand that she, Miz 'Fel, do something. And
she had, hadn't she? Coaxed and pleaded with Bertie, though it
had seemed to do little good at first. But the screams had stopped,

she repeated to herself. This, with this wench, was unusual. And they had branded her, too. That's if she took the darky's word for it, branded her and sold her away. She must have done something pretty terrible. Rufel clung to this belief, although it gave her little comfort.

The wench was dozing on the pallet when Rufel returned to the House, the baby snuggled carefully in the crook of her arm, and Rufel stood a moment in the doorway watching them. They were as peaceful as a painting, the girl a vivid chocolate and jet against the whiteness of the sheets, the baby as bright as toast against the bedding and the darky's arm. The darky's tale of beatings and brandings seemed, in that moment, a lie to cozen the gullible and trade on the goodwill of the openhearted. Rufel stalked across the floor and knelt by the pallet. The wench awakened almost immediately, her eyes gleaming forth from the darkness of her face, quickly hidden as she ducked her head under Rufel's gaze. "What's your name, gal?" Rufel asked sharply.

"Dessa. Dessa Rose, ma'am," she said in a raspy voice.

Rufel was slightly taken aback; she had not expected the wench to answer so readily. "Why'd you run away?"

The darky kept her eyes downcast and plucked nervously at the coverlet. "Cause, cause I didn't want my baby to be slaved," she said finally in a rush and still without looking at Rufel.

Rufel looked at the baby, seeing in him the pickaninnies at Mobile. And that's what he'll look like, too, if I put you all out of here, she thought pettishly. "I mean, why your mistress use you so?"

"Cause she can," the wench said on a long shuddering breath as she turned her face away.

Rufel was stunned for a moment by the ring of utter truth in the statement, yet, almost of its own volition, her hand reached to draw back the covers from the darky's body. She drew back at Rufel's touch, her eyes popping open in alarm. Rufel blushed, thinking for the first time of how humiliating she would find such an inspection. "Are you—are you healing properly?"

"Yes. Yes'm."

Why, Rufel thought, this wench is actually afraid of me. Con-

scious for the first time that she herself could be in physical danger from these strange darkies, she realized that she had fallen into
the habit of thinking of the runaways as a slightly malicious means
of evening the score in their continuing estrangement in the neighborhood. Somebody somewhere was using the Sutton slaves; why
shouldn't she use these—especially since she had neither enticed
them away from wherever they came, nor encouraged them to stay
here? She associated even Ada with the stock cuts used to illus-
trate newspaper advertisements of slave sales and runaways: pants
rolled up to the knees, bareheaded, a bundle attached to a stick
slung over one shoulder, the round white eyes in the inky face giving a slightly comic air to the whole. She still thought Ada and
the others no more than casual truants, avoiding work or even
punishments. But this wench and that big darky—especially him,
she thought, remembering his size and self-possession—even that
yellow boy who came to see the wench, were all, no doubt, hard-
ened rogues. Had to be, to get clean away from a coffle as they
apparently had done. Yet this wench was afraid of her. Rufel sat
back on her heels, fighting a panicky urge to laugh. Like I was the
criminal; her mouth quirked involuntarily. Calmed by the wench's
fear, she rose and left the room.

ॐ

The wench began to sit up, to take notice of her surroundings,
though she said little to Rufel and that in a voice barely above
a whisper, eyes downcast. The darky's diffidence irked Rufel and
she was offended by the way the girl flinched from her when she
reached for the baby, by the girl's surreptitious examination of
the child when Rufel returned him after nursing. For all the world
like she was going to find some fingers or toes missing, Rufel
thought indignantly. Exasperated, she told the wench, "Just because one mistress misused you don't mean all of us will." She did
stop flinching at Rufel's approach, but it was plain to Rufel that
the wench did not like having to let her nurse the baby; and she
seemed incapable of even casual conversation with Rufel. Some-

times Rufel wanted to laugh—she had thought that "devil woman" business no more than a joke. At other times, remembering the silly, passionate argument over Mammy, she knew the wench's reticence and timidity were feigned, and was angry and bewildered by the deception.

The wench talked freely enough with Ada and the other darkies who came to see her. Rufel often heard the murmur of their conversation as she sat in the parlor; now and then she heard a soft chuckle or muffled giggle and was surprised at how envious the laughter made her feel. She watched the wench covertly when she was in the bedroom, wondering what she could have done to make the other darkies, even laughingly, call her "devil woman." There had been only admiration in the big darky's tone when he spoke of her, no hint of fear or amusement in his voice. Though it would probably take more than this little pesky gal to frighten that darky, Rufel thought, recalling the breadth of his shoulders and the hard muscled arms. Rufel sensed somewhere in the general outline of the wench's tale a deeper story and one not entirely unrelated to her concern for Mammy, though she could not say just how. She blamed the curious restlessness she felt on her unanswered questions about the wench and one afternoon she gave in to impulse and wandered out to the stream.

Rufel and the darky were each aware of the other's presence this time. He stood and touched his hat. "Evening." He bowed his head slightly.

She stood awkwardly, shifting her weight from one foot to another. "Fishing?" she asked.

He nodded, then as though remembering himself, "Yes'm," and touched his hat again.

"Nice spot for it."

He shrugged. "Not as good as the spot down by the pool, but quieter. Everyone trying to fish down there this evening," he explained.

It seemed somehow rude to tell him that darkies were not allowed to use either, so Rufel merely nodded. She saw the stump she had sat on the other day and sat again, tucking her skirts carefully about her. After a moment he picked up the pole he had laid aside, cast, and sat on the ground a short distance from her. They were silent.

She cleared her throat. "Why you-all call that wench—"

"Dessa?" he asked quietly.

"Yes, that darky. Why you-all call her 'devil woman'?"

"Where you hear that?" he asked sharply.

She shrugged, pleased to have finally gotten a rise out of him. "Oh, I hear things," she said airily. "It have something to do with you-all escaping from that coffle, huh?"

He grinned slightly. "That ain't nothing but something white folks made up," he said with an air of unconcern.

"Well, why they call her that?" she prodded.

"That's some mess— That's some of Harker's talk," he said annoyed. "Dessa done her part just like everybody else, just she was more easy to pick out cause of that big belly." He chuckled suddenly. "She did like to scare Master Wilson half to death when she jumped on his back—he screeched like a stuck pig and she was already yelling like a banshee. I guess white folks might of thought they was in hell."

"You-all did kill some white people, then?" she breathed, admitting to herself, finally, that this question had been in the back of her mind ever since he told her of the escape from the coffle.

"Mis'ess," he said looking at her steadily, "we ain't harmed no one didn't offer us harm first."

"You-all going to kill me?"

"No, Mis'ess." He sounded genuinely shocked.

"Don't suppose you'd tell me if you was," she said, still on a note of disbelief.

"Mis'ess," he said earnestly, "ain't no one here plan you no hurt or would do you or yours any harm." He cleared his throat. "We all know it's not too many white folks would let us stay round like this."

It was not exactly the expression of gratitude she felt the runaways owed her, but, somewhat mollified and reassured, too, she asked curiously, "Was it a big battle?"

"On that coffle? Not really," he said briefly.

"Well." Rufel was disappointed. "Did that wench—Odessa really jump on that trader like you said?"

"Rode him like you would a mule," he said, laughing outright. "Master Wilson a big burly man but she stuck to him like a burr to a saddle. Knocking him all upside the head with her bare hand, yelling to the rest of us, 'Get him, get him.' Oh, she was something," he said shaking his head.

"All you darkies from off that coffle?" she asked.

"No'm; I believe Ned from down round Lowdnes County; Red from round about Dallas County someplace."

Rufel had only a hazy idea of whom he spoke and an even hazier idea of where the counties he named were located. To cover her ignorance, she said sarcastically, "All you-all escaping from a cruel master, huh? Beat every one of you worse than what that wench's mistress beat her, huh?"

"No, Mis'ess," he said quietly. "Castor's old master died and the 'state was being broke up; stead of being sold away from everything he knowed, he runned off." He paused and looked at her in a measuring way. "Master Wilson cuff me sometime, throw a boot at me now then, but, sometime—sometime I get to wondering why Master can take his ease while I be the one that sweat, why the harder *I* work the more *he* gets. But I guess you wouldn't know nothing about that?" he added, cutting his eyes at her.

His lightly mocking tone recalled her earlier anguish over Mammy— Had she felt this way? Rufel rose hastily to her feet. How could you love someone who used you so?

"Ada say you come from pretty big people back there in Charleston."

Rufel paused. He was watching her, she saw, not in that disconcertingly bold way he had, but from beneath properly lowered lashes. She was instantly suspicious; he was trying to cozen her, of course. "They wasn't *that* big," she said cautiously, remembering that other occasion, yet, wanting to impress him, she added quickly, "Oh, we was accepted by society, but we wasn't real prominent."

The darky nodded wisely. "Ada say Dorcas was always talking about the parties and dances you was invited to."

"Well," she said slowly, "I did go to a lot of balls and parties," and remembered with familiar yearning the ballroom glittering with the flames of a hundred candles; the jewellike colors of the women's dresses swirled in a kaleidoscope before her eyes.

"Reckon he'll be home right soon."

The darky's voice recalled Rufel to his presence and she stared blankly at him. "What?"

"Your husband," he prompted. "Reckon he'll be home soon?"

"Yes," she said nervously. "Yes, I expects him home any day now."

"Must be some powerful big business keep him away so long."

What could Bertie do on the river, any river, that would earn him money, that would make him stay away from home like this? "—gambling."

It was not the first time Rufel had asked herself this question and for a moment she thought she had spoken aloud, that the one word she'd heard from the darky was his answer. She stared at him in disbelief.

He grinned at her. "Oh, yes, ma'am, Harker's old master was a gambler; won Harker in a card game. Master's cardplaying was how Harker got free." Rufel relaxed as soon as she realized the darky wasn't talking about Bertie; the darky continued unperturbed. "Harker ain't had to escape like the rest of us, least ways to hear him tell it. Seem like his master got caught with too many aces—you know it's only four in a deck, Mis'ess, and there was three on the table and two in his hand. Not that I think the master here would do anything like that," he said, looking slyly, or so it seemed to her, out of the corner of his eye, then continuing casually, "Seem like Harker's master was a regular cutup, a confidence man you know. Sold snake-bite oil and a magic elixir was straight puredee alcohol. Sold well, too—especially to spinster ladies and widders."

He paused for breath and Rufel grinned broadly at his fast-talking commentary. "You," she said clapping her hands, "you are the funniest darky—"

"Nathan," he said smiling. "My name Nathan, Mis'ess."

Rufel hardly noticed. "What," she asked laughingly, "what 'puredee alcohol' and 'widders' got to do with Harker escaping?"

Not much, as it turned out. Harker had not thought it prudent to stay around and find out what the other cardplayers thought of a five-ace deck, as he himself had several stashed about his person. These he had slipped to his master as occasion and circumstance permitted while he served the gentleman drinks. When his master failed to meet him as they had previously arranged, Harker, believing all to be lost, had fled the vicinity. He had been a wanderer ever since. "Until he happened onto the Glen and a kind white lady named Miz—" He paused expectantly.

Amused by his mock gallantry, she replied, "Rufel," automatically, and wanted to bite her tongue.

He tipped his hat slightly and continued, "—named Mistress 'Fel took him in."

Gratified that he showed no reaction to her use of a pet name and oddly moved by his use of the diminutive, she smiled.

"That's better," he said. "Nice Miz Lady like you not supposed to go round all sad," he said gruffly.

"Why, why," startled she stammered. "Thank you, Nathan," she said touched.

Now that she knew who Nathan was, Rufel seemed to see him frequently. He came every couple of days to see the girl and now and then she walked out with him afterward, pausing at the edge of the yard for a moment as he finished some amusing pleasantry or anecdote, before turning back to the House. Often they met at the stream. It had been her habit to sit by the stream in summer with her sketch pad. She had some skill, she thought, with caricature, but Bertie had not encouraged this. The form, she knew, was rather vulgar but she could not help preferring the whimsical figures drawn as much from her imagination as life to the crude still-lifes and landscapes that Bertie praised as ladylike. So she had seldom sketched; she had watched the play of sunlight on the surface of the stream, counted the various shades of green among the branches of the overhanging trees, dozed a little, dreamed, though she could not remember of what.

Sometimes now she took Clara, as she had once taken Timmy, and spread a quilt for her under the trees. Now and then Timmy and Dante, pausing between the vague but exciting adventures that drew them to the fields and woods, or taking a rest from picking the fruit that Ada had started to can and dry for winter use, would sit with her. Most frequently it was Nathan who bore her company. He took his turn at the plow, he assured her when Rufel laughingly taxed him ("Harker going see to *that*," he added with a laugh), but his luck with snare and fishing pole were valued more than any furrow he could plow. He had shown Timmy and Dante how to make snares to trap the small game that abounded in the woods. The two youngsters had yet to make a contribution to the pot, but Nathan's skill kept a variety of fresh meat on the table. And he told fascinating stories—animals that talked, trees that had spirits, people who refused to die, and tales that he swore were "true to life." Often Harker figured in these; between them, the two of them seemed to have done everything possible for a darky to do and much that Rufel knew to be impossible.

Nathan had a gap between his two front teeth that gave his grin an open, carefree quality, and little red-rimmed eyes that he could make dance or sparkle almost, it seemed, at will. His company came, in large measure, to replace the companionship Rufel had shared with Mammy. She could not see him as she had seen Mammy, almost as an extension of herself—his observations were, by and large, too racy for that. His opinions and positions were sometimes mildly outrageous—he would rather come back to life as an animal or bird with a chance to work his way back to human form than sit around heaven drinking honey; women were as smart as men; there were some people who could see into the future—but he could make even the driest crop report sound scandalously funny. He treated her with a semblance of the deference and indulgence that had characterized Mammy's attitude toward her. Now and then, she might speak of some incident she had seen or heard of in Charleston or Mobile, but she felt little need to talk about herself. Mostly she was content to listen.

Through talking with Nathan, Rufel came to know something of the people who lived in her Quarters: Ned, a young rascal given to playing pranks; Red, who longed after a "wife" down around his homeplace; Castor and Janet and the others—and once again became aware of the daily routine of the farm. She used him much as she had Mammy, as the means through which she participated in the life beyond the yard. These were not Sutton darkies, of course, so she was mindful of what she said. Nathan could shut his face just as tight and quick as Ada or that wench, but he was far friendlier.

Rufel still felt some resentment that the wench had destroyed her comfortable, and comforting, image of Mammy, but she no longer held that silly argument against the wench. However hateful and spiteful the wench had been, she couldn't change the way Mammy had cared for Rufel. Even if Mammy herself had been spiteful, bitter, secretly rebellious, Mammy, through caring and concern, had made Rufel hers, had laid claim to her affections. Rufel knew this as love. She would have said as much, but the wench's stiff civility made her hesitant to reopen the subject.

She had heard the story of the escape from the coffle and the wench's rescue from the cellar again and again from Nathan. She knew there must be some element of exaggeration as in his other "true-to-life" tales. She would not admire the action—one couldn't, of course, approve any slave's running away or an attack upon a master—still, something in her wanted to applaud the girl's will, the spunk that had made action possible. The wench was nothing but a little old colored gal, yet she had helped to make herself free.

Nothing Rufel said or did made either the wench or Ada more at ease with her. Once Rufel had entered the bedroom to find Ada combing the wench's hair. The older darky sat in a ladder-back chair; the girl sat on the pallet, her back leaning against the rungs of the chair. Her head rested on Ada's knee as Ada's fingers wove rhythmically through the stubby strands of the girl's hair. They looked so companionable and content that Rufel almost felt an intruder. The moment the darkies became aware of her they started nervously, the wench vailing her eyes and bowing her head, Ada rising clumsily. Almost, Rufel begged pardon for entering her own room.

When Nathan told her that the wench was trying to settle on a name for the baby, Rufel did not immediately suggest one. She called him Button, a name that Timmy and Ada had picked up from her, which seemed like a perfectly serviceable one to her. Almost, she offered it in jest, but it was obvious that Nathan took the matter seriously. He was all for naming the baby Kaine, after the baby's daddy, and Harker agreed with him. The wench wanted to name the baby in honor of her rescuers. The baby's daddy, like that part of her life, was dead; she would not rake it up each time she called her son's name. Rufel saw both sides and suggested, half humorously, that the baby be named for all of them, or at least a name that represented them all, and, on impulse, offered "Desmond" as a pretty compromise. "Des" for Odessa, "mond" to represent the men, Nathan, Cully, and Harker, who were responsible for his free birth.

Button became Desmond Kaine (called Mony because Odessa, so Nathan told her, felt him to be as good as gold) with little ceremony that Rufel could see. She said nothing, but felt that, as mistress of the place, she ought at least to have been advised. She added it to her secret count against the wench, which already included her coldness toward herself and the wench's growing chumminess with Ada. Now she took a private pleasure in having had some hand in naming Button, feeling repaid in some measure for the wench's continuing aloofness. Maybe this was what Mammy had felt when she had changed Ruth Elizabeth's name, that somehow she had snuck a little piece of the child for herself, had marked at least some part of him with something of her own making.

She sought Nathan's company more often—he at least treated her like a person—and took out her pique at the wench by teasing Nathan, insisting that he must be sweet on her. "You talk about her all the time," she would say innocently, as if she herself took no delight in hearing of the girl's exploits.

At first Nathan had ignored her teasing remarks, then laughingly denied them. One day, he burst out in genuine annoyance. "Course I'm sweet on Dessa. Cully have a crush on her and I'm 'sweet on him,' too." He laughed harshly. "You been through with someone what we been through together and you be 'sweet' on em, too," he said turning away from her.

Rufel realized with dismay that he was really upset. "Nathan," she said contritely, "you know I'm only teasing."

After a moment, he turned back to her. "You see so many people beat up by slavery, Mis'ess," he said wearily, "turned into snakes and animals, poor excuses even for they own selfs. And the coffle bring out the worst sometime, either that or kill you. And it didn't in Dessa." He sighed. "I feels bad for all them that didn't make it, worse for all them that didn't die, that even now living in slavery after we been free. But us three—we did it and we made it. It's gots to be some special feeling after that."

৵

"What going to happen when the master come back here?"

It was high summer, the weather hot, sultry. Rufel and Nathan had sat in companionable silence, sweating, speaking lazily, now and then, of one thing or another. This question made Rufel's stomach lurch. "Why—why nothing." She had not thought about Bertie in weeks and even now his name did not awaken the familiar terror over his whereabouts. Rather, she was uneasy that Nathan should ask about him.

"He going to give us a share of the crop like you did?" Nathan asked almost idly.

Share the crop. The words echoed in Rufel's mind. That might mean something this year. Harker said they were likely to make thirty bales of cotton and close to a hundred bushels of corn in addition to the oats and potatoes. Cotton was the only cash crop but it was ridiculous to suppose that Bertie was likely to share any part of the harvest.

"Or he going to try to claim us as his?" Nathan continued quietly.

Rufel looked at Nathan, unable to answer truthfully. He might, she knew; Bertie might do anything. Her stomach tightened at the thought. He would want to enslave them. He didn't believe in sassy negroes or smart negroes or free negroes; that was why he couldn't keep a field hand on the place. He drove them hard and stinted on their food and clothing. Rufel knew this without ever having really seen it. Mammy had made sure that any darky who worked in or near the House was clean; Bertie had not encouraged Rufel to roam much beyond the House and yard. She had seen the hands from a distance when she rode out to the fields with Bertie now and then. They did look wretched, he had admitted, but then slavery was a wretched lot. And she had accepted this as long as she didn't hear the screams. Rufel bit her lip. Could she be that blind again? And these people would not be beaten or sold. She licked her lips. "I—I wouldn't let him sell you-all."

He looked at her with a humorous lift to his mouth and Rufel flushed. She would have no more rights than they when Bertie came back.

"We don't have to be here when he come back," he said, leaning toward her. "Harker got a plan let us be far way—if you help us." Uneasy but intrigued despite herself, Rufel listened as Nathan continued earnestly, "Member I told you his old master was a flimflam man, a confidence man? Well, they had one scheme they used when they was down on they luck. They would go into a strange town and his master'd sell Harker, auction him off. After a couple of days Harker would run off and join him at a place they'd already picked out. They do that in a couple of towns till they got a stake together again. Harker figure we could go down in the black belt and run that scheme three or four times using me and him, maybe two or three others, we could make maybe nine or ten thousand dollars. And we'd split it, split the money. That'd be five thousand cash dollars for you; five thousand dollars for us to get away from here on."

Rufel was a little repelled by the scheme, yet amused, too. It was like Nathan, she thought, to propose that *she* do the very thing she wanted to keep Bertie from doing. "What would I do with so much money?" she asked skeptically.

"What couldn't you do?" he asked with a hoot of laughter. "You say your husband went off looking for a new stake; well, you'd have one waiting for him right here when he come back."

When he came back. Bertie would take the money. They would resume their trips to Mobile and perhaps beyond; they might finish the second story. He would buy more slaves, clear more land, plant more cotton and their life would begin again: the poorly timed extravagances, the arguments with the neighbors, the wild schemes and dashed expectations, the single-minded dependence on cotton. Nobody around here planted more than a few acres of cotton; Harker said the soil was too thin and sandy to nourish the hungry cotton plants. Rufel shook herself. Bertie had made a good home for them, she told herself staunchly; only a greedy, ungrateful fool would think otherwise.

"What if he don't come back? What you going do then?"

The question opened the door on the bottomless terror that, in the settled heat of summer, she had thought gone forever and she teetered at the edge of panic.

"Dorcas always thought you'd go back to Charleston."

His quiet statement pulled her back from the brink and she turned to him. Charleston. To go back without begging her family's assistance, without risking their rebuff—

Profoundly disturbed and unwilling to continue the discussion, she changed the subject nervously. "What, what did you do when you was slaved?" Aside from his true-to-life adventures, he never talked in any detail about his life and she had long felt a curiosity about him. "What did you do?" she repeated.

He was quiet so long that she thought she had offended him and he would not answer.

"Worked for a slave trader grew negroes by planting they toes in the ground. Made em drink ink at night to give em color."

She smiled, glad to see him restored to good humor, but unwilling to let him turn aside her question with a joke as he often did. "What'd you really do?"

"Loved pretty white womens like you."

Her head snapped around; he was grinning, the gap between his front teeth sparkling, the sherry-colored eyes dancing. The lie was so outrageous that she laughed. "No, seriously," she said, sobering a little, but still gasping for breath.

"Serious business." He watched her steadily, only the twinkle and the grin lurking about his lips belying his outward gravity. "It's a special kind of white woman can't keep they hands off a negro. Special breed of nigga won't let em."

She hadn't laughed like this, she thought, hearing his soft chuckle under her own, since, since she didn't know when. "All right," she said suddenly, "what did you all do with the babies?" not even marveling at her own language.

"I makes love," he said grandly, "not babies." He shrugged. "Other peoples makes carriages and clothes. White mens makes labor and"—he cut his eyes at her—"lust. Why can't I make love to a"—he coughed—"a lady?"

It was the funniest, most audacious spiel she had ever heard, though she doubted she understood half of what was going on. "What," she asked, "what, what did Harker do?"

"Oh, he raised sand."

"A grain," she squealed, giddily, "a grain that grew up to be rock."

"No, this was hell," he laughed, "and when he got through with that, he raised the devil."

"And Ada?" she asked. "I know Ada 'raised' something strange."

He sobered. "Well," he said. "You know womens don't never have such a good time as the mens."

She expected him to make some further joke, but he said nothing. They were both silent now, and awkward after the shared laughter. "Bertie was a gambler, wasn't he, Nathan?" she asked suddenly, remembering the avidness with which he had returned to the river, the previous absences from which he had come back flushed, excitable, or, as often, ill-tempered and silent. She hadn't known herself that she knew enough to ask this and she was frightened at her perception. But having asked she could not quit the subject. "Wasn't he?" she asked again as Nathan hesitated.

"Yes'm," he said. Sighing heavily, he looked at her steadily. "Yes'm, he is."

"Why didn't Mammy tell me?" Rufel wailed, feeling more betrayed by Mammy's silence than by Bertie's deception. Had they conspired against her, plotted together to keep her in the dark?

"It wasn't her place."

"She should have told me anyway," Rufel insisted.

"I spect she tried," Nathan said drily. "And what was you going to do way out here by yourself, if you had knowed?"

What mamma had written must be true, she thought, a wastrel, a petty scoundrel; how much had he borrowed over the years?

"Maybe Dorcas was wrong," Nathan said, "maybe she should have told you flat out front what she knowed. And maybe if she had knowed up front, before you was married, she might've tried to say something. But she didn't know and once yo'all got out here— You was happy; all that time, least she thought you was happy and that was what yo'all both wanted."

Rufel looked mutely at Nathan. He was saying that she hadn't wanted to know; that she had kept herself from knowing the truth about Bertie. She looked away. There would be no Mammy when Bertie came back to abet her in the pretense. "Well," she said rising, wanting desperately to be alone, to think, "I guess it's time for me to go."

He rose and touched his hat. "Mis'ess."

Rufel walked back to the house in a daze. She hadn't known Bertie either, had purposefully kept herself from knowing him. Even now she could not recall his features; oh, she remembered that he had blue eyes and dark hair, that he was handsome. But for the life of her, she couldn't see these features in any familiar configuration. What else had she refused to see? she wondered bitterly.

Bertie was dead. Rufel walked on, considering this possibility more calmly than she would ever have thought possible. He had gone off a week or two without word before. She had received not so much as a note during the whole time he had gone that first summer. But even he would not go off and stay so long without a word. Truely he must be dead. And if Bertie were dead— Five thousand dollars was more money than she could imagine.

Rufel entered the House quietly, deep in thought. Hearing a slight noise as she started past the bedroom door, she stopped, pushing the door open silently. The wench stood by the window, her back to the door. Rufel paused, uncertain; the wench wasn't supposed to be on her feet yet. "Just a minute, Ada," the wench said without turning and bent to step into her drawers; briefly her breasts and hips were reflected in the dresser mirror. Only then did Rufel realize that the wench was naked; her bottom was so scarred that Rufel had thought she must be wearing some kind of garment. "I know you said tomorrow," the girl said without looking up, as she secured the drawers about her waist.

Barely managing to suppress the quick gasp of sympathy surprised from her by that glimpse of the dark body, and acutely embarrassed, Rufel closed the door. The wench's loins looked like a mutilated cat face. Scar tissue plowed through her pubic region so no hair would ever grow there again. Rufel leaned weakly against the door, regretting what she had seen. The wench had a right to hide her scars, her pain, Rufel thought, almost in tears herself. Impulsively, she opened the bedroom door.

"Odessa—" and stopped, unsure of what to say. The wench had snatched up a dress and stood stiffly with it clutched in front of her bare chest. Rufel sensed the smoldering hostility beneath the girl's obvious embarrassment and flushed painfully, recalling how she'd tried to argue the girl down about Mammy. "That other day"—she stopped and cleared her throat—"that other day, we wasn't talking about same person. Your mammy birthed you, and mines, mines just helped to raise me. But she loved me," she couldn't help adding, "she loved me, just like yours loved you."

The wench watched her narrowly for a moment; slowly her

tensely held shoulders relaxed. "I know that, Mis'ess," she sighed. "I know that," she said without anger or regret.

Rufel, suddenly conscious again of the wench's half-nakedness, started. "I'll pull this door to so you can have some privacy while you dress."

଼ଡ଼

Rufel and Nathan made love for the first time later that week. Nathan came to the House in afternoon. Rufel was in the bedroom and heard him ordering Annabelle out. He walked into the bedroom without knocking, closed the door behind him, told her to take off her clothes. He spoke with such authority that almost without thought her hand moved to the drawstring at her bosom. She caught herself and laughed nervously as she dropped her hand. He took her in his arms. It was no laughing matter after that and she clung to him as he undid her bodice with practiced ease. He picked her up, his mouth already nuzzling at her breast. His tongue left trails of liquid fire along her flesh. He eased between her thighs, entering that nameless deep, filling that lonely cavern. Will-less, she gathered around him; the day exploded into a thousand nights and endless stars.

Nathan had told Rufel the truth, though he later assured her that his first mistress had been no where near as pretty as she and, by the time he knew her, she had not been so young either. Headstrong and smart, Miz Lorraine—he never identified her beyond this—had inherited a large fortune at an early age. There had been none to curb her wild nature and not until she was almost forty— near as he could figure it; she held her age well—had she allowed herself to be "stifled," as she called it, by "the chains of matrimony." Prior to that she had taken slave lovers, bought from friends or sent up from her own plantation off the Georgia seacoast. She took them young—Nathan was barely fifteen when he was sent up to town, but already the size of his shoulders, his hands, and feet gave promise of the man he would grow into. He was apprehensive at being summoned to the House, and totally unnerved when the back stairway Miz Lorraine's maid led him up opened into the mistress's bedroom. He looked around wildly for the maid when Miz Lorraine told him to strip, sure that he couldn't have heard right. The maid had already disappeared. Frightened half out of his mind—Miz Lorraine had on something he knew he could see through if he looked—he did what she told him; and was totally unable to achieve an erection.

Miz Lorraine laughed, gently, mockingly, and made him sit on the edge of the bed. She knelt before him and took his penis in her mouth. Terrified, he at first tried fumblingly to pry her head away, but already her mouth and tongue were sending such intense waves of pleasure through him that all he could do was hold her head and moan—and try to control the muscle that threatened to leap from his control. "Mistress," he whispered frantically, "Mistress," trying to pull her head away now, "Mistress, I'm, I'm—" not knowing how to say it so she would understand him but terrified of coming in her mouth. "Mist—" He could hold it no longer. The power of his climax rocked him back on the bed and he lay there, waiting for her to denounce him, to call the laws, but uncaring. She squirmed onto his still erect penis. Her lips still wet with his come, she sought his mouth. Faintly repelled but already excited by the pull of her vaginal muscles on his penis, he turned his lips toward hers. "If you ever breathe a word of this to anybody, I'll chop it off," she breathed then. He believed her, but the threat didn't deflate him; rather the knowledge that he lay in danger, not only of his member but of his life, sent him plunging up a peak of unspeakable desire.

Miz Lorraine took her bedmates young, saw that they learned some more conventional trade, and, about the time their fear of discovery and their awe of her abated, about the time they found their tongues with her and might have boasted to others, about that time she got rid of them, sold them off. Nathan was young enough when he came to her that it took a long time for him to reach that stage, at least in front of her. He believed Miz Lorraine implicitly when she told him, with a finger over his lips, that talking to niggers was like trying to get monkeys to talk (it was even longer before he thought to ask himself what fucking niggers was like), and she, for one, did not want to do it. By the time Nathan found his voice, he also understood (or thought he did) something of why his mistress chose her belly-warmers from among the lowest of the low. Nature was strong in her; she did not call on him that often, no more than once or twice every month or so, but when she did, she kept him awake most of the night and sometimes kept him for a day or even two. If she had tried to satisfy her sexual needs with white men, even ones outside her own class, she would have had no way of ensuring their silence. If a black man boasted, she could have his life. He never learned who else, if anyone, besides her maid knew of the mistress's habits. He talked to no one about what he did and no one talked to him. This was what Miz Lorraine wanted: to be in control.

She was not as freakish as some of the white men people whispered about; she would copulate orally with him, but only once did she allow Nathan to serve her so. He did so, not because he wanted to—he never did get used to coming in her mouth—but because he thought it was expected. He had been with enough women to know that, usually, they did to you what they wanted you to do to them. While this was a wholly new thing to him and still slightly distasteful, it gave him such joy that he was not averse to returning the pleasure. He nerved himself up and took her, and himself, by surprise, his tongue flicking across that little slippery piece he knew got delight from his fingers almost before he was aware of what he was doing. She had writhed and kicked but he held on till he felt the thick come against his tongue. She threatened to yell rape that night; to sell him, to have him flayed within an inch of his life. He never took the lead in sex with her again.

At what point Miz Lorraine began to take his silence for sense, Nathan never knew, but she kept him longer, she said, than she had any other slave lover and promised to put him out to stud rather than sell him. He hadn't looked forward to that. He was thoroughly enraptured by her and he liked Savannah. He loved his work as coachman, the driving, his smart livery, the horses. He felt also, but so dimly he could not have articulated it, that there was something demeaning in what she proposed. Then, she had decided, as far as Nathan could see on a whim, to marry and, contrary to her word, had sold him to Wilson. He understood the reasons for her betrayal—he had never dared boast of his relationship with her, but on that plantation, away from the twin goads of fear and desire, he wasn't sure he could have held his tongue, as he had not been able to once settled at the Glen. He had tried to be philosophical about the change in his fortune. Driver was a brutal job, but Wilson had not been an especially brutal master. He had rather favored Nathan; the latter did his job and knew how to return an amusing quip without seeming uppity. Had Nathan been more inclined toward harshness, he might have stood higher in Wilson's esteem. As it was, knowing something of the hardships to which most slaves were subjected, he would not complain. Miz Lorraine had given him what few niggers even dreamed about.

There was, he told the men in the Quarters late at night, nothing in the world sweet as that white woman's pussy and he knew because he had had his share of black women both before and after Miz Lorraine. It was not, as he liked to claim, that they had snapping pussy that held on to your dick until the last little seed was drained, then opened to let you fill again. It was the terror, he knew, that made it so sweet. If climax, as some men said, was like death, then a nigger died a double death in a white woman's arms. And he had survived it. He walked a little taller, aware of the power hanging secret and heavy between his legs.

Nathan was the color of eggplant, a rich, velvety blue-black; beside him, Rufel's skin took on a pearly glow. They sweated and rested, his face buried in her bosom, one leg caught between hers. She stroked his back; his fingers played purposefully in matted pubic hair, teasing the slick lips of her vagina. Supine, she waited for him to enter her again.

They never heard the door open, only the startled gasp: "Mis—Nathan!"

Surprised, Rufel saw the wench's face, wide-eyed with shock, over Nathan's shoulder and glimpsed Ada's bandanna.

"Nathan," the wench breathed again, striding into the room, "and Miz *Ruint*— Well, I knew you was a fool—"

"Dessa!" Nathan shouted, rising.

"What you call me?" Rufel cried.

"Miz Ruint!" Odessa repeated harshly, deliberately, struggling now in Ada's grasp.

Nathan was out of the bed then; together he and Ada got Odessa, breathing hard but no longer struggling, out of the room. Nathan closed the door and turned to Rufel. "What's that she called me, Nathan?" Rufel asked.

"Rufel," Nathan said, grinning slowly, widely. "Miz Rufel; that's what she meant." He held out his hand to her. "That's all she meant."

Rufel shrank from him. Ruined, that was what the wench had said. Ruined. That was what she meant.

The Negress

*"Ma négresse,
voulez-vous danser,
voulez-vous danser avec moi, ici?"*
—Taj Mahal,
"The Cajun Waltz"

Five

❦

I never *seed* such a thing! Nathan—laying cross that white woman— Black as night and so—so *sat*isfied. It was like seeing her nurse Mony for the first time all over again. I was *that* surprised to walk in on them. I seed the name upset her, so I said it again out of plain meanness; I wanted to call her something worse. All the while I was yelling at her, Nathan and Ada was hustling me out that room. And something inside me was screaming, Can't I have nothing? Can't I have nothing?

Well, I went, just about stumbling down them back steps with Ada fussing in behind me. I'd "gone too far," she say, calling that white woman out her name. Miz Rufel been "good to us." Oh, yes, the white woman was "Miz Rufel" to her then—when *she'd* been the main one started me calling the woman Miz Ruint in the first place. Anyway, far as I was concerned, that white woman was the one'd "gone too far," laying up with a black man. And Nathan. I was so mad at him, I could've *spit*.

Ada huffed at me all the way cross the yard: We was all going get put off the place; if I wanted that "fool negro," I could have him when Miz Lady was through with him. I turned round on that one. I could feel trouble all round me and in me, and pain;

she was talking like all I needed was a little belly-rub. "You put Annabelle name in this mess," she say. And forgot Mony; remembrance of him didn't come to me till then. I'd forgot him just that quick, when it was him we'd gone in that room to peek at in the first place.

You know, any other time, Miz Lady—which is what we mostly called her amongst ourselfs; to her face, it was always Mis'ess or Miz Rufel. But everyone, Nathan included, called her Miz Ruint, too—amongst ourselfs; this was the name Annabelle give her. Both names meant about the same to me, though Ruint did fit her. Way she was living up there in them two rooms like they was a mansion, making out like we was all her slaves. For all the world like we didn't know *who* we was or how *poor* she was. Them rooms was big all right, but it was only two of them, same as any poor buckra; and that stairway didn't lead to no other story. It ended right smack dab against the roof before it had gone ten good steps. We all knew *some*thing wasn't right up there. And any other time, she'd've been out to the woods someplace, way she did most afternoons when I put Mony down for nap. That's where me and Ada both thought she was when we seed she wasn't in the parlor. Setting out there in the kitchen the way we was, we never even seen the white woman, neither Nathan, go in the House. Wasn't no way in the world we'd've just walked in that room if we'd knowed she was in there— I'm saying "me and Ada," but I knowed Ada wasn't that much in it. I was the one had mocked the white woman in public.

For the first time I wanted to cry. I couldn't go back in that House, not to get Mony, not and see Nathan, see *him* and that white woman again. The remembrance of them in that bed kept stabbing at my eyes, my heart—black white red. I knowed that red was her hair, but it looked like blood to me.

I moved down to the Quarters that evening. Tell the truth, I didn't have that much to move, just Mony (and Ada'd had to go back to the House and get him) and the clothes I stood up in. Even these was gived to me by Miz Ruint, just like most everything else I had. It chafed me to be so beholden to her. For the life of me, I couldn't see no reason for a white woman to let us stay there—less it was for devilment. I'd only heard of "good masters"—I didn't know nothing about no good white folks—and none of them claimed Miz Ruint was a "good master." No "good master" would've let us stay anyway. So why she would do this was a puzzlement to me.

Letting us stay on the place wasn't zactly slave stealing, true enough, but I knowed she was posed to tell *some*body we was there. Wouldn't the white folks get her for keeping runaways? She couldn't be letting all these peoples stay just so she could lay with a black man, I told myself. Could she? And I was scared. Ada was right, Miz Ruint could make us all leave. I didn't really think she would do it—who was going pick that crop, feed that boy, mend them draws? But she could, you know; she was white and it was her place. I couldn't just go round popping off at the mouth any old kind of how—least ways not at her. I had plenty I wanted to say to Nathan but I hadn't seed him since he put us out that door.

The Quarters wasn't no better than what Ada had said—one room with a dirt floor; wasn't even no chinking in between the logs. Harker and them'd added a lean-to where the mens slept and I moved into the cabin with the womens. I had walked down to the Quarters a time or two when Ada took dinner down, helping her lug that big kettle once I got my strength back. I knew most of the peoples by sight, and all of them knew Mony. He never wanted for lap nor arm long as a person was in the Quarters.

There was three other womens: Flora, a big hefty seal-brown woman; Janet, a little string-bean woman (both of them worked the fields); and Milly, a old woman with a ulcerated foot who helped Ada with the laundry and tried to work that loom Dorcas had used. I kept the House, helped Ada in the kitchen, and did the sewing, mending really. I could do decent plain stitch and darn; this what our mammy taught all of us, so we knowed how to be neat. But I couldn't bit more cut a dress or do nothing fancy than a man in the moon. Even this was better than what Miz Ruint could do and I set some store by it.

There was eight mens, counting Nathan-nem. Uncle Joel and his grand-boy, Dante, belonged to the place. Uncle Joel had been sold more times than he could count; white folks just call him to the House and point to his new master. That last time, he figured his old master was using him to settle some small debt. He begged for Dante and the master throwed him in as a present to the new master's son. Being as his arm and leg was crippled on one side, no one valued Dante but Uncle Joel (though Dante could do just about anything peoples with two good arms and legs could do). Master Man, that's what Uncle Joel called Miz Ruint's husband; made it sound like something nasty, too. Master Man hadn't wanted either one of them and plained all the way home about getting the worst of the deal. Ned was a young fellow round about the same age as me; Castor and Red was both about the age of Harker. We didn't none of us know how old we was, but near as I could figure out, I think Harker must've been close to thirty. I wasn't no more than seventeen or eighteen myself. All the mens worked the fields except for Uncle Joel; he tended the garden which House and Quarters both ate from, and the few head of stock. Nathan mostly hunted and fished.

Evenings they sat in front the cabin; not everybody, every evening, but usually peoples sat out there a minute or so before turning in; sometimes Ada would sit a spell when she brought supper or walk down again after we'd cleaned up. Mostly I guess they was quiet—peoples don't talk too much in the heat, not after they been in the fields all day. Oh, sometimes they did talk, now and then trade stories, or Uncle Joel would play his mouth organ. I had heard it once or twice wailing faint through the night when I was laying up at the House. Sadder than a whippoorwill, more lonesome than a owl, it wrung my heart; it reminded me so much of home. But these wasn't like my home Quarters, and I sat there that first night holding Mony, feeling like a stranger amongst them.

The weather, the crop, this is what they talked about; Milly's foot, Mony—but Mony was sleep—the weather again. It was hot. Harker, Cully, and Red was off somewheres; I spected Nathan was up to that House. Even Ada and Annabelle was there, but Ada hadn't more than said good evening to me. The rest of them spoke and I could feel the ones had seed me bring my pallet down wanting to ask why I'd moved. No one did but they couldn't seem to keep a conversation going.

Long about the time Harker and Cully walked up, someone inquired after Nathan; after everybody say good evening, Janet inquired again. I didn't say nothing. Ada waited a minute, then she say, "Up to the House." No one said nothing to that; then she say, "Laying up with Miz Lady."

Don't nobody say nothing then; finally Harker slap his thigh and laugh. "Doggone it, Cully," he say, "I didn't believe old Nathan'd do it!"

Cully let out a big whoop. "Miz Lady bound to come in on the deal now!"

I couldn't believe my ears; had they planned this? "Nathan doing *that* with that white woman wasn't part of no deal I knowed about, Harker," I told him.

Everybody was talking at once, but he turned around when I said that. "What got you so mad, Dessa?" he ask.

"That's a white woman, Harker." They all quieted down when I said that.

"She willing," Harker say, dry as dust. That's the way he try to be, so calm don't nothing faze him.

Well, that give them all a big laugh, till Ada say, "That fool negro going to get us all killed."

"Ain't no such a thing," Harker say real sharp, "less one of us going tell it."

This made us all shut up. Wasn't none of us going tell and I reckon he knowed that well as I did, but I think his putting it so harsh made us see that we was all liable. Knowing about it, and telling, was about as bad as doing it—at least to the white folks. Then, just like he couldn't help hisself, Harker burst out, "West, here we come." And the men commence to dance around and laugh.

Harker come took Mony, gived him to Ada, and pulled me to

my feet. Trying to waltz me around, you know, but I didn't feel like no dancing and I shook his hands off. "This how we going work our way West," I ask him, "on our backs?" I got Mony and went on in the cabin and laid down.

I could hear them going on about Nathan and the white woman. Harker allowed as how he wouldn't mind being a fly on the wall do the white man ever come back and catch them. Not that he was wishing for them to be caught, understand; he couldn't wish that on no brother. But just so's he could see the white man's face. "Reckon his eyes would bug out?" he asked real serious. "You know that mouth would gape something scandalous, and he would get red. Got to get red. But he just might be carried off in apoplexy before he could do anything to him *or* her."

By this time, they was all laughing fit to be tied; I wanted to laugh myself cause it was true. A slave loving with the mistress, the *master's* wife, might be enough to give a white man the stroke. I could see my old master's face turning red—might even go purple—as the sight of that fly in his milk and death hit him all at once. Course his eyes would pop. Mine had. But I wasn't in no mood to laugh; Master might get red, but if Master lived, the slave was dead. Nathan could die tomorrow cause of this mess. I was mad at him for letting that white woman put him in such risk and I was mad at her for doing it.

Nathan and Cully, and Harker, too, sat with me the whole time I was out my head; Ada said that was the only thing kept me quiet—they hands, they eyes, they voice. These had stood between me and death or me and craziness. We'd opened to each others. Oh, I had a admiration for them—same as they did for me. We had *scaped*, honey! And they'd come back for me and we'd scaped again. You didn't do this in slavery. We laughed about it—they teased me about the white man what "kept company" with me while I was in that cellar; I said they'd been sparking the girls in the Quarters, that's what took them so long to see about me—but it was this that brought us close.

We talked about some of everything while I was laid up in that bed, and they was some talkers. Cully could have you dying about his old master trying to raise him as a slave *and* like a son—teaching him to read but not to write, to speak but daring him to think. Nathan would fascinate you with stories about outlandish goings-ons. And Harker got us all fired up about West. He could put some words together, make you see broad, grassy valleys, clear, sparkling streams, a river that divided slave land from free. And wasn't no pretense between us.

Mammy wasn't no more to Cully than breast in the night and he never knew enough to wonder about her till after he was sold. Somebody had carried him like I carried Mony; he'd kicked in a stomach same way Mony did in mine. But he might as well been carried in a bottle for all he knowed. Mammy wasn't even a face to him. Cully cried when he told us this and I was the one held him, right there on that feather bed. But we all heard; and Nathan, neither Harker was shamed of they tears. I never thought one of them could be so ignorant to something that hurt me so bad. White woman was everything I feared and hated, and it hurt me that one of them would want to love with her.

I thought "the deal" was a joke when Nathan and Harker first started talking about selling theyself back into slavery so as to get a stake big enough to where we could all leave from round there. This was a story they was telling to help while away the hours Ada made me stay in bed. Harker had the idea of someone posing as the master and of the peoples running away after they'd been sold and the "master" selling them again in another town. This was what his old master used to do with him when they was down on the luck. Harker's master was a regular scamp, gambling, mostly—he'd won Harker in a card game in Kentucky when Harker was about leven or twelve—and high living, but he wasn't above a swindle or a cheat now and then.

At first, Cully was "master"—except for that nappy hair, he could've been white, and he could read some and write a little. But anyone with half a eye could see he was too young to be out trying to sell a gang of negroes, and we joked about having Harker paint a mustache on him to make him look older. Harker had learned this from his master, too.

It was Nathan put that white woman in it. Oh, not by name; but once they got the idea wasn't but a step to seeing if it would work. And for that, like Nathan said, we needed a real white person, someone in want, to play the master. I didn't think about the idea of us selling ourselfs or each others back into slavery long as I took it for fun, you know. But I was uneasy, once they put the white folk in it. Wasn't no white folk I'd ever heard of would bit more go along with this cutup than a man in the moon—and if they did, it would just be to cheat us out the money in the end. These was the stories we'd all heard, that we'd told right there by that bed—bad jobs made good and the darkies not even getting thanks, promises of freedom or favor the white folks never kept. So it was hard for me to see this as anything but a joke. Even when Harker said he thought Miz Lady could use some money and Cully said he'd oversee the place—since he was so white—while they was gone, I didn't believe they would trust her. So I—just to keep the story going—I said I better go along to keep a eye on her. I didn't think they had the nerve to ask such a thing, but I begun to back off.

Who going nurse the babies? I asked them. It hurt me to my deepest heart not to nurse my baby. Made me shamed, like I was less than a woman. And to have him nursing on her . . . Oh, I accepted it. Wasn't no choice; but I never did like to see it. And she act like this wasn't no more to her than nursing her own child. Miz Ruint was so forgetful, I told them, till she just might forget herself if Mony cried and plump out that titty in public—trying to make a joke of it, but yet and still, trying to get them to see the point of how dangerous it was trusting in somebody could be that careless. Well, they laughed; thought I'd hit Miz Lady off real good. She did know the difference between black and white; I give her that. She wasn't that foolish. But where white peoples look at black and see something ugly, something hateful, she saw color. I knowed this, but I couldn't understand it and it scared me. But this was why Harker and them thought she might would go along with the plan.

Harker, neither Red encouraged too much conversation about Nathan and the white woman—Red say it was too much like talking in the man's bed. So, by and by, they started talking about West. They didn't none of them know that much about it, but Harker talked about it like he'd seen the forests and the streams, the river where slavery couldn't cross over cause everybody on that side was free.

I don't know if I really believe all that, land and rivers, and crossing over. It sound pretty spooky to me; yet and still, it appealed to me. Slavery not being allowed; everybody free. I'd traveled so far from my old home and still hadn't come to the end of slavery; Harker say we could travel that far and farther and still not come to a place where our peoples could live free. It scared me to think how much of the world was slaved.

I'd taken a dream out of slavery—the one Kaine gived me about freedom. Many the day I cursed freedom; it took everyone I loved in girlhood from me. It taken Kaine. I'd come out of slavery with nothing but that dream and I guess you could say, even laying there in them strange Quarters, that the dream had come true. I wasn't slaved no more; I'd slept in the white folks' bed and used the white folks' things, been used by them. Yes, freedom had come true, but in ways I'd never thought of and with hurts I didn't know I could bear. That dream had to be something worth living for, if not for me, then for Mony; West had to be better than here.

This what I thought when I listened to Harker talking about West while I was laying up there in the white woman's bed, joking with them about that plan. But out there in the Quarters that night, with Mony nested in the curve of my side, all I seed as I listened was Nathan sprawled in whiteness, white sheets, white pillows, white bosom. All he did was make them look whiter. He wasn't nothing but a mark on them. That's what we was in white folks' eyes, nothing but marks to be used, wiped out. Hadn't I seed it in Mistress, in that white man's eyes under the tree? We wasn't nothing to them. I couldn't trust all we had to something could swallow us like so many drops; I made up my mind not to put my freedom in no white woman's hand.

჎

Nathan stopped me that next morning as I was coming through the woodlot carrying Mony. It wasn't no more than just light, he was in the shadows leaning against a tree trunk. My heart did kind of leap up when I seed him; I was glad he'd come to me. Course, by the time I got to him, I membered I had some things to be mad with him about. I was finding out just how convenient it had been to live at the Big House. Oh, the mattress was the same—I'd taken that corn-husk pallet down with me—and I like to suffocate in that little hidey-hole Dorcas slept in. But I had to get up to the House early and I came back late on account of her nursing Mony. I started giving him a little grits in milk before I left the House in the evening and, after a while, he slept through the night. But he didn't the first night in the Quarters. I managed to get him back to sleep—Janet made him a sugar-tit from a corner of molasses she'd saved—but not before everybody in the Quarters was wake. They was too polite to say anything, but I could hear them tossing and turning well as they could hear me. So I wasn't in no mood to let Nathan know how glad I was to see him.

"Dessa," he say when I got up to him, "what is wrong with you?" Not "Morning," not "How do?" It was "What is *wrong* with *you?*" Like *I* was the one crazy.

I was so surprised and hurt—cause it was real evident to me *who* and *what* was wrong—that I walked on past him. "I'm a person," I said over my shoulder, "and you got to treat me like I got some sense."

"Why don't you act like you got some, then?" he said real snappy, but after a minute, he come to walk beside me and asked, like he want an answer, "Why is you mad, Dess?"

I thought he should already know that. I had told him what Master had done to Kaine and I knew he had seen how Young Mistress had used me. White folks had taken everything in the world from me except my baby and my life and they had tried to take them. And to see him, who had helped to save me, had friended with me through so much of it, laying up, wallowing in what had hurt me so— I didn't feel that nothing I could say would tell him what that pain was like. And I didn't feel like it was on me to splain why he shouldn't be messing with no white woman; I thought it was on him to say why he was doing it.

"Why not?" he ask when I ask him.

Well, that stop me right in my tracks. "Why not?" I ask. "What you going to do if her husband come back?"

"What *we* going to do if he come back?" he shot back real quick. "From what she say, he just as likely to lay claim to us and sell us all right back into slavery."

"And he sho will be disposed to do just that, he come back and find you sleeping in that bed."

He grinned. "So you think Master Sutton going give us a square deal, do I stop diddling his wife, eh?"

That lie-gap between his front teeth was gleaming and I couldn't help but laugh—which was what he wanted me to do. You know most mens feel if they can get you laughing and funning, talking a little saucy, you know, that they can do just anything they want with you. And I guess it is true that you catch more flies with sugar. But I was right; and I wasn't going be laughed out of it.

"You just liking her cause she white," I told him.

"Yeah," he say, "I likes her cause she white; I likes you cause you got that old pretty red color under your skin. Now what of that?"

I could've hit him, he was making me so mad. "You know what I mean!"

"If you mean that I'm getting something that the white man always kept for hisself, well, yes. I likes that, too."

"If the 'white man ain't no good,' how his 'likes' or his woman going be any different?" This was another thing he'd said there by that bed and I wanted him to member that.

"You know, Dess, Ruth ain't the one sold you; her husband ain't killed Kaine—"

"But he'd kill you or Harker, or anybody here, for less than what you doing. Maybe for less than what Kaine did," I added. I didn't like him putting Kaine in it; and I knowed he called that white woman name just to be cute. "Ruth," like she wasn't no more than his friend-girl. He could show off all he wanted to, try to make it seem like it was all in my mind. I knowed what had killed Kaine, the master's power; and poor or not, every white man had that when it come to a nigger. "Why you doing something you know can't mean you no good?"

"Felt plenty good to me."

"That ain't no answer."

"Why I got to have a better one?"

I just looked at him. To hear him tell it, he hadn't suffered as much as some people—he said he had belonged to a high-society white woman didn't mistreat her slaves, before he was sold—but he knew, had seen what others had been through. The reason he runned away in the first place was cause he couldn't stand having his own luck depend on having to hurt others. He didn't think I knowed this, wouldn't want me to know it, but I did.

Maybe there was some little black drivers in slavery. But every one I ever seen was big and black and they whole idea of theyselfs was in they strength; that was the white man's "arm" and that was the only way they knew to be. Well, Nathan was big and black but I don't think he knew nothing about no white man's arm until he was sold to that slave trader. Maybe he was too old to like it by then, maybe it just wasn't in him to like all that bullying and beating. But he had to act like he did or at least act like it didn't make him no difference. I think even after we got away from the coffle, he still didn't like to show too much of hisself that wasn't like what people generally thought a big, black nigger should be. But Nathan was different; and I knowed he was different.

I couldn't put into words all this that was going through my head. I didn't have the words, the experience to say these things. All I could do was feel and it was like my own flesh had betrayed me. Nathan and Cully, and Harker, too, had risked something for me and I felt bound to them—and them to me—as tight as blood-kin. Miz Ruint wasn't no part of that knot; the only way she could get in was to loosen it. Maybe I would have felt this way about anyone but this was a white woman—and a crazy white woman at that.

Well, with the answers Nathan was giving the questions I was asking, didn't neither one of us get no satisfaction. So I resented the white woman even more.

I took Mony and all my mending out to the kitchen yard. I wasn't going let my tongue run away like that again, but I didn't want to be round the white woman. I hadn't never had that much to say to her, no way. She was always strange to me, way she was always looking at me when she thought I didn't know it, other times acting like she was scared I would touch her. I didn't like her eyes—though they wasn't as bad as that writer man's had been. His was about as empty as a snow sky, just that pale and heavy; hers was gray as wet mortar. But, most times, it was like she didn't see you, no way—and be talking right at you. She left her dirty draws in the middle of the floor when that's the first thing you teach a child: Pick up behind yourself. She called Ada "Auntie" like they was some kin.

Ada said this was the way white peoples was. And what did I know—I hadn't been more than a mile or so from my home Quarters till I was sold. Most of what I knowed about white folk, I'd learned on that coffle. Ada had worked in Houses from the time she was old enough to know anything and I don't reckon it was much white folks could get past her. She had come out from a pretty strict-run House, the kind where the mistress weigh out the provision in the morning and lock them up at night; you know, order everything about the House just so. Her old mistress was one of these see-nothing, say-nothing white womens when it come to the master. And he slept with all the womens in his Quarters; said it kept them fertile. Ada was her master's daughter—though it didn't get her no special favor; she just happen to be one the childrens he kept. He didn't have nothing to do with Annabelle—only white on her had come from Ada—and Ada might would've been there still, hadn't've been the master started looking at Annabelle. That was his granddaughter, mind, and she not even thirteen. Ada tried to get the mistress to stop him, but mistress say, don't bring that kind of talk in her House. This was one of the first things Ada told me about herself: "He didn't have to be so low." Lips trembling, eyes like a bruise in her face, swimming in water, and I was back in my home Quarters hearing my friend-girl Martha's voice: "All he had to do was ask," after Master's brother forced her in the fields one day. Oh, I was spared much that others suffered.

And Ada tell you in a minute, white woman ain't got no excuse to be so trifling when all it take is they *word*. Aunt Lefonia and Emmalina had said about the same thing. They didn't have too much patience with white womens amongst theyselfs—though they never let on about this before any mistress; before mistress they was good slaves. Not that they talked that much about white womens in particular; they talked about everyone come near that House. But this was Ada's favorite conversation; Miz Ruint didn't know how to keep no House; wasn't for Dorcas, Miz Ruint'd be dead. Tell you the truth, I wasn't much interested in that white woman; used to be, quite a bit of the time, Ada would talk, and I wouldn't listen. But now, with Harker and them acting so closed to me, I began to pay attention.

Ada had been on the place even before the master took off. She'd come from up around Huntsville and she and Annabelle was pretty wore out by the time they got that far. They stole or grubbed what they could in the woods. This is what all the people came there did: run, beg, steal, starve, run. And all the time not really knowing where you going, just that you can't go back. See, they couldn't go to no House and ask for work, ask for food; sometimes, if there wasn't no dogs, they could get food in the Quarters. But it wasn't too many Quarters round there, wasn't too many farms. That's why Ada stayed around. White folks there didn't keep too close watch over black people; they thought it was so few up that way that they knew them all.

Well, Dorcas friended Ada; Ada taken a chance when no one else wasn't about and asked Dorcas for food, which Dorcas gived her. She and Annabelle had found a cave not far from the Quarters; they stayed round there in the day, slept there and only come out at night. When the master left, Ada moved into the cook-shack. So she had good reason to know about the white woman's business. And she did run on about her: Miz Ruint think that shiftless husband of hers a gentleman; she don't know nothing about slaves.

"Tell you, dearie, she can't come from too good of a peoples, she don't know how to talk to no darky." We was setting out there at that big slab-top table under the tree where Ada was canning. We had made up; she really was glad someone had said something to Miz Ruint. She just wished I hadn't called Annabelle's name—which, a course, I hadn't. But wasn't no use trying to tell Ada that; once she got an idea in her head, it was like trying pull hen teeth to get it out. I knew I wasn't entirely without fault myself—I really was trying to watch my tongue—so I just went on and begged her pardon. Anyway, it was that fool negro (meaning Nathan) that Ada was most put out with.

"You know this ain't the first white woman Nathan done loved with," she told me, like this ought to make some difference in how I felt. But I didn't believe her. Ada thought I was just jealous-hearted; she would say anything to get me out the way of making what she called a fool of myself over a negro didn't have no better sense than Nathan. He'd stayed with his first mistress because he was doing her "a . . . a service," she told me.

Well, I almost laughed at that. For a black man to even think under a white woman's clothes was death and here she was telling me Nathan had a *habit* of doing this with them? It was bad enough, his doing it with one; only way I could splain that was that they was both crazy. But, stead of arguing, I agreed with her about the sense part—though I knew for a fact Nathan had plenty. But, see, Nathan was one of these what you call red-eyed negroes. You know, the kind of negro get his shirt soiled in hell and go to heaven for a change of clothes—so he can go back and "study" hell some more. You knew this was wrong, but you couldn't help but admire it. And the mens thought Nathan's rutting up there with a white woman was a fine turnaround, so Ada said, after the way white mens was always taking our womens. Not all white mens acted animals towards us, understand, but enough of them did till this is what we always feared with them—and what our mens feared for us. I was spared this in bondage, but I had seen the way some white mens looked at me, big belly and all, when I was on that coffle.

The womens didn't get as much kick out of Nathan and Miz Ruint as the mens. Janet said Nathan should've raped her or at least knocked her round a little since this what he was going be cused of anyway. Even Milly didn't see how neither one of them could go round the place so unconcerned like what they was doing wasn't a danger to us all. By and large though, no one had too much to say. Harker said it was Nathan's business and if people wanted to talk about it, they ought to do it to Nathan's face. Ada told me this, you understand; didn't nobody say nothing to me. I was the "devil woman"; this was between me and "my mens." The rest of them was all trying to keep out of it.

I know the peoples didn't mean no harm by that name; in fact, they was proud of it—one of our womens helping to best the white folks, scaring a white man half to death. I didn't no ways look like I could do all that. I mean, I was sturdy—you had to be sturdy—but I ain't built big. All the peoples got a kick out of this, me so small, jumping white mens. But I hadn't never liked that name, not from the first time I heard Jemina say it. And now they begin to take this in another way and look at me like maybe that "devil woman" wasn't such a joke after all. This, where before they was saying Miz Ruint was the one touched in the head. Looking at me funny like I was the one ungrateful—or lame-brained, choosing corn husk when I could've had feather. Didn't no one just come right out and say this, you understand. They just act like it. Didn't no one say nothing to me; and Ada was about the only one I said something to. Still, they was uneasy about Nathan; man or woman they was uneasy. White mens would kill to keep something like this quiet.

We was all worried that another white person would find out about this—though really, the onliest white person I'd seen since

I'd been there was a peddler she bought some flower seeds off of. Didn't no one visit her. This is why we felt a little safe there; she lived so cut off. But this with her and Nathan—seem like it was something white folks would just know.

ॐ

White woman sent word by Cully that she wasn't going no place with me till I begged pardon for calling her out her name. Well, that was fine with me, I told him, cause I wasn't going no place with her, no ways. Ada hooted. We was setting around to the side of the cabin in the shade when Cully walked up, so I guess this must have been a Sunday. The others was about, mostly I spect down to the fishing hole cause it was hot.

Cully wasn't nothing but a boy, remind me of my brother Jeeter, way his wrists was always showing under his sleeves—big, heavy bones, look like they going pop the skin. Oh, they wasn't nothing alike in color; Jeeter look like midnight beside Cully's day. But something in the way Cully carried hisself put me in mind of Jeeter. I think this how I first come to note Cully. I wasn't nothing but a little girl last time I seed Jeeter and he was the age Cully look to be. Jeeter never got old in my memory and I call him up now, sharp as the day they sold him.

"Nathan put you up to this, huh, and Harker?" I asked Cully. He was like a little puppy dog when it come to them, wasn't nothing they could say or do was wrong to him. Used to be wasn't nothing I said wrong with him, neither, till all this come up. Oh, I had a lot to be hot with Miz Ruint about and I would've bit my tongue before I said sorry.

"This what Miz Rufel say," he told me, coloring up like a white girl, he was that light. It made him look about ten years old, which he knew, which made him madder—and redder—still. He hadn't even started hair on his chin, so wasn't nothing to hide that blush. For a minute I felt kind of bad about taking my spite out on him. But then I thought about him carrying word for her and I got hotter, adding just for spite, "Specially not on no cork-brained scheme like the one Harker talking about."

Well, this answer put them all out with me, cause they was all hot behind Harker's plan. Even Castor and Milly—they was the scariest ones—thought it was a good trick to pull on the white folks. Harker couldn't do no wrong, far as they was all concerned.

Castor and Flora and them had worked the fields all they life (me, too, come to that) and they could do that—hoe, plant, plow; but hadn't none of them ever decided when to plant or what or how much. They just knew how to work; they didn't know how to direct it, to set it up from plant to harvest of all the crops. And this is what Harker could do. He knew all these things about the land, about planting and keeping it healthy, but he wasn't so set up in his own opinion that he wouldn't listen to someone else experience. And he took what he knew and what they knew and put it together so the crop that year was looking to be double what they had harvested the year before. This was one thing made all the peoples respect him.

Even after Harker come to the Glen and decided to stay a spell, he wandered a lot. (This is one of the first things I noted about him, that he had been places. I had never known a negro who would just pick up and walk. I mean, I knowed ones to run; you know, trying to delay that lash, or go off to see someone—sweetheart, mother—but not just to go cause you feel like it. This was unheard of, far as I knowed. We all belonged to a place and seemed like you was born knowing not to move too far from it. But here was someone who walked around where he wanted to—more or less—wasn't scared to do this. It was one of the first things I come to admire about him, that he was not afraid of coming or going.) Harker had come upon Cully and Nathan about three or four days south of there. They had made it that far before Nathan's leg give out. Oh, yes, a bullet had pierced him in the leg when they scaped from the patterrollers that caught me. Neither one of them knowed what to do with it and it festered. Well, Harker stumbled up on them where they was hid in the woods and got them both back to the Glen, where Ada doctored his leg; quite naturally they thought highly of him. So, when Harker started talking about leaving everyone was all set to follow him. This was they leader, they saver, and they was some upset that I was scoffing at his plan.

I had a deep admiration for Harker myself but I really didn't like the idea of us selling ourselfs back into slavery. Though, to tell the truth, the plan wasn't so foolish as I made out. There was no doubt the peoples could be sold. White folks had asked the same question in every town the coffle went through, "Got any niggers for sale?" Oh, we would fetch some money. And white folks didn't really start thinking someone had run off till they had been gone a day or so and, on a big place, a new person might not be missed for two or three days. Only reason more didn't run away was there was nowheres for them to run to; and even no-wheres was a hard ways to go. There was terrible whippings if they caught you, which, having *nowheres* to run to, they mainly did.

But, by the time our peoples was looked for, they could be in another town, getting ready to be sold again. If they was caught, they would have a pass; and they so-called owners might not even recognize them. I had seen what Harker could do with a little of that greasepaint. He didn't make no amazing changes but he did enough so, if you didn't know the person, they looked enough different that you'd think you mistook them for someone else. All this was just in case; wasn't no reason for no one to be caught. Running away was how most everybody had got there in the first place. A gang of peoples could probably work this scheme several times without making no stir. No, there was no doubt it could work from our part, the ones who would be sold. It was the part of the one doing the selling that I had my doubts on.

I just knowed there had to be some way for us to get away without having a white person in it at all. And I knowed if Nathan and Harker thought about it, they could find whatever way that was. I put a lot of faith in mens' minds—I thought my brother Jeeter could turn the world around. And, generally speaking, I do believe that if you think about a thing long enough, man or woman, you will find some way to handle it. So that's what I was trying to say to them—to Harker especially, cause he was the one with the most ideas—find this way.

Ada argued that we had to trust someone, but I couldn't see placing all our dependence on a white woman, white anything for that matter. We all knowed they was wicked and treacherous— that's why we was in the position we was in. And even though I could understand Harker's point that *this* didn't necessarily have to turn on *that*, I didn't want no part of it.

"Miz Ruint ain't turned on us yet; this deal benefit her same as it do us," Harker said.

This was another evening, maybe a day or so later. We was setting out there front the cabin again; even Ada had walked down. Nathan was up there at the House and though no one mentioned it, we all knowed that, too. Still, the idea of her, a white person, working for negroes was so comical to me I had to smile. "She talk to herself," I told him, "Ada vouch for that."

"Maybe she ain't had nobody else to talk with," he say. "Dessa, she do got some stake in doing right by us."

"She crazy; we all know that. You put yourself, your freedom at the mercy of a crazy white woman?"

"It's not the white woman holding up the deal. She say she willing to do it," Ned spoke up. I could see Harker shushing him but I wasn't going to pay that old mallet-head boy no mind no way. He was always playing tricks on peoples—you know, tie your pants leg in knots, rig a bucket to dump water on you as you go in the barn. He was always getting up some devilment like that. Thank God he growed out of it, but he was a pest. And this the way they all act, like I was the only one could play the maid. Janet or Flora could do as well as me. But I was the one Miz Ruint was putting it on; I was the one had called her out her name.

"How you get here, wasn't for taking a chance?" Harker ask.

"You talk about chance," I told him, "but I know chance. Chance called master, chance called mistress." Wasn't for chance I be loving Kaine right now, I thought, be with my family today. He was right about chance putting me where I was that day. "How long you think we going last amongst white folks with Nathan in her bed?" I ask him.

They was all quiet for a minute; this was the first time someone had brung this up when we was all together like that since the night I moved down there. Then Janet spoke up. "Well, that is a dumb thing for a negro to do—" she start off. But before she can even finish, there was that old mallet-head Ned squawking about "Dumb? Dumb! Yo' all just jealous cause he not diddling you." Then he say under his breath, "Don't nobody want no old mule like you," but loud enough for everyone to hear. And somewheres in the darkness a voice went, "Humph," like it wanted to laugh but caught itself before the laugh could get out good. And then there was a silence. Silence and a fire-burst where Ned's head should've been when I looked at him. I had to close my eyes. Was this what they thought of us? Mules. I was so choked I couldn't speak. I used to warm my feet against Kaine's legs in winter; time they got me out that cellar, my heels was so rough they snagged a tear in them sheets up to the House. Janet had that kind of skin remind you of hickory—red-brown and tough; Flora's skin was smooth as peach peel, hands big and hard; Ada— But Ned wasn't talking about no color, no feel.

Mules. Milly who had birthed seventeen children in eighteen years and seen them all taken from her as she weaned them, been put outdoors herself when she went two years without starting another child. They had taken Flora's baby from her, put her out to nurse with someone else cause Flora could do much as any man in the fields. This is what broke Flora from slavery; this why she runned, so she could keep her babies for herself. Janet was mistreated cause she was barren; Ada's master had belly-rubbed with her, then wanted to use her daughter. I had been spared death till I could birth a baby white folks would keep slaved. Oh, we was mules all right. What else would peoples use like they used us? And still I wanted Kaine's lips to nibble at the kitchen on my neck, dirty and damp with sweat, would've cried to feel the hard chap on his hands catching in my hair. He had smelled like good earth after a short rain, kind make your mouth water for a taste of it and drive pregnant womens to eat dirt. I was glad he wasn't Master, wasn't boss—these wasn't peoples in my book. Had he really wanted me to be like Mistress, I wondered, like Miz Ruint, that doughy skin and slippery hair? Was *that* what they wanted?

I could see Ned when I opened my eyes, burr-headed and mallet-shaped as he was. I know Harker made him apologize; by him being young and so rude like that, somebody had to tell him something. But I don't know how long it took or how Harker done it. I'd come to a flash somewhere between "mule" and "humph"; and I was still shaking from remembrance, from feeling. This was the flash that'd nelly-bout killed Master and almost strangled Mistress, that rode me in the fight on the coffle. It scared me to see it almost loosed against one of us; and, pesky as he was, Ned was part of us. Yes, I trembled; that feeling, that anger was like a bloodhound in my throat, a monster that didn't seem to know enemy nor friend, wouldn't know the difference once it got loose.

Harker was speaking to me. He'd sent Red back down to Dallas county to bring out Red's wife, Debra, and they baby; she was still nursing and could nurse Mony while we was gone. All they needed now was for me and Miz Lady to come on in. I swallowed down; that bloodhound was still at my throat and my voice was rough. "Get another mule," I told him; "this one don't know how to be no maid."

❧

They finished stripping the corn and the work slacked off some; it didn't never just stop. Seem like it was always something to plow, plant, pick, or peel at that place. We rose at the same time but now they sat a little later and talked a little longer in front the cabin at night. One night they encouraged Uncle Joel to play that mouth organ. Music didn't flow there as I membered it doing in my old home. We got up with the chickens and nobody raised a call on the way to the fields and it was seldom and seldom anyone gave out with a holler as they worked.

Uncle Joel started out with a lively little tune and soon we was all clapping; Ned struck up a lyric and Annabelle got to cavorting. She was something to see there in the moonlight. She hadn't combed her hair since I knowed her—Ada said she was too tenderheaded and sometimes my fingers itched to pull a comb through her hair and fix it up regular, corn rows or seed plaits, least put a bandanna over them kinks. But that night all them naps looked like curls and ringlets hanging about her face. She was light as a feather on her feet, her body supple as a willow and it wasn't long before others joined in.

The nights could be like velvet there, like another skin, it would be so warm and close. This was like times at my old home, and somehow, that night, I was glad to have something familiar instead of sorrowing that the old times was gone. Something in me still listened for that banjo, but I was glad that I had lived to have such a time again and I sat there patting my foot.

Harker asked me to dance, bowing to me, smiling. I hadn't heard him the first time—he was standing off to one side of me and I was watching them dance off to the other. When I turned to him, he said, "Dansay?" Something like that. I didn't understand the word but I knew what he wanted and I looked up, smiling, my heart beating fast. I'd been acting like they acted, like it didn't make me no never mind that we didn't talk no more. But sometimes I'd see him or Nathan or Cully about the yard or round to one of the outbuildings and my heart would about bust, I'd want so bad to see them smile or have them say a word.

"That's French," Harker told me then, and dropped down beside me where I was sitting there on the ground. "How many times you been asked to dance in French?" This tickled me and he told me some more French. "Negro" meant black man; "negress" was black woman; "blank" was white. I laughed at that, thinking about Miz Lady. She could sure look like it wasn't nothing shaking behind that face. Harker had learnt these words down in N'Orleans, he told me. This was the way the black peoples spoke there; they said it was some islands way out to sea, somewheres out from there, where black peoples had made theyselfs free. This was what they had talked about on the coffle and I asked Harker why we couldn't go there, stead of West like he was always talking about, where it take so much of money to go.

"Maybe," he told me, "maybe there is some islands out there where black peoples is free, but we got to depend on strange whites to get us there. Once we get on a boat—which ain't no sure thing—but once we get on the boat, we totally under the dependence of the whites. Or, say we make for the north; probably Nathan, with the way he handle horses and all, and Cully, cause he young, could make a living, but me and the rest—including you—we farmers. Land expensive in the north and things I know to do in the city ain't zactly what the law allow. And I don't have no white man to front for me this time," he add, trying to make a joke. "There's a lot of slavery between here and there. And if they catch us up there, they'd just bring us back south."

I knew all this was true; I had heard it before; I had proved some of it myself. You could scape from a master, run away, but that didn't mean you'd scaped from slavery. I knew for myself how hard it was to find someplace to go.

"No, Dessa," he say, "I want to go West cause I knows for a fact it's no slavery there. A black man told me that. He been there, come back *from* there (and I never met no black man come back from these so-called islands). Slave catchers, neither patterrollers troubles no one there. But whichever way we goes, Dessa, going to take money."

It was like Harker was saying to me, here's the plan I found to handle this problem, and finally, that night, I heard him.

"Dessa," he say, "Ada tell me you and the mis'ess don't even much speak to each other."

I wasn't foolish enough not to say something to her, and anytime she spoke to me I answered. But if she sat down outside, I'd generally find something to do back at the House or down to the shed where Milly was struggling with that loom. So I said kind of careless like, "Slave don't generally have too much to say to the master that I knows of."

"She ain't your master."

"I knows that, but do she?"

Well he sucked his teeth at me, which, though I do it myself, have always irritated me with other peoples. "What have she done you?"

Well, put like that, I couldn't think of nothing right off and I got mad. "Why you taking her part?"

"It ain't taking no one's part to ask what causing trouble between two peoples."

"Why don't you ask her?"

"She say you called her out her name." Well, everybody knew that was true. "It fit her," I said. I was tired of them acting like I was the main one in the wrong. "Nice white lady living out here, alone, amongst all these 'darkies.' "

"Damn it, Dess," he start off and I stiffen up right away; I don't like no man to cuss at me. "Dess," he say and it was like he'd never called my name before, just "Dess," soft like that. "What going on here?" He sounded about as hurt as me. I didn't know myself what was going on; I just knew I didn't like it. "Walk out here with me a ways," he say; "I want to talk with you."

Wasn't no privacy to speak of round that cabin, so we walked out towards the fishing hole a ways. We stopped in a little clearing there in the woods and sat down on a log. We was quiet for a while.

"You liking Nathan for your man now?" he ask all of a sudden.

His asking about me and Nathan surprised me so much that I laughed. Well as he knew us, Harker ought to knowed it hadn't been no time for thinking about liking and belly-rub. Not that Nathan wasn't a fine-looking man—and I loved him. I had a powerful feeling for him, but as a brother; he was like a brother to me. Then I got angry; that was all they could think of when it come to a man and a woman: Somebody had to be lusting after somebody else. I had to be wanting Nathan for myself; I couldn't just be wanting him to have something better than I knew Miz Ruint was. "That's all it come down to, huh?" I ask Harker. "Somebody fumbling under somebody else's clothes?"

"I didn't mean you no offense, but— You must be liking him for something. So why you want to lose him as a friend?" I wasn't specting this and I sort of turned away from him, but he kept right on talking and his words stayed on my mind. "Maybe he think you ought to be proud of him for doing something like this," and "Maybe she wouldn't do it just for the money," and "All we know is she willing to do it."

"And what they going continue on to do?" This was a sore with me, that Nathan could be loving up with her all the while he posed to be my friend.

"I see this ain't no sense thing with you," Harker say then and I got mad.

"Sense? Why what he feel got to make more sense than what I'm feeling? You got all the sense in the world? Is Nathan?"

"Dessa, Dessa, I didn't mean it that way. What I meant is, you feel about 'sense' one way and he feel about it another; and that's that. And you-all going lose friendship over a white woman."

I didn't like it put that way, but still, "He seem like he willing," I told him.

"Who would you have gived Kaine up for if they had asked you?"

My heart about turned over when he ask that. "It's like that, he feel like that for her?"

"Maybe; I don't know. Nathan can speak for hisself. But you-all won't even talk to each others now. You know, I always did admire the way you-all was about each other. That's why I went back with them to get you. At first I thought you was his woman, some kind of relation to him or Cully, they talked about you so. And I admired it even more when I found out you wasn't."

I hadn't knowed he felt this way about us. I'd thought it was just the scaping, the idea of that that got his tention. Yet and still, "That mean I can't never say he wrong no more?"

"Dessa, you done said it."

"And he don't care."

"Care about as much as you do. Dessa, what you-all got between you don't give you the right to pick Nathan, neither Cully's woman."

I wasn't trying to pick Nathan's womens, I told him. "If I was,

I sho would find him a more likely one than her." Harker just
looked at me. "I be happy to talk to Nathan, anytime he want to
talk to me," I finally told him, "but Nathan, Cully, you—all you-
all seem like you don't have nothing to say to me don't have
something to do with some white woman or this plan." He didn't
say nothing to that either. After a while, I said, "You know she
wanted to see my scars?"

"I know," he said. "Nathan told me."

You know they would sometimes make the slaves strip when
they put them up for auction, stand them up naked, man or woman,
for all to see. They didn't like to buy them with too many whip-
scars; this was a sign of a bellious nature. This the first thing flashed
in my mind when Nathan told me she wanted to see them scars,
that Miz Lady had to *see* the goods before she would buy the story.
Nathan didn't urge me to do it, I give him that, but he, neither
Harker understood what a low 'ration this was for me. Maybe,
by her being a woman, they thought it shouldn't make me no difference; I know they thought I placed too much dependence on it.
And I held this against the white woman, too.

"I know she ain't the first person wanted to look under there,"
Harker said real rough. Then he was gentle, trying to get me to
see his point. "You ain't the only one been hurt by slavery, Dessa.
Everyone up in here have some pain they have to bear. Naw, Miz
Lady didn't have no right to ask, but what is that compared to
what she could've done—and didn't do?"

He stopped, but I didn't say nothing. "You know, girl, you didn't
have no business calling that woman out her name. We *been*
trusting her all along, just like *she* been trusting us. How you going
stop now?"

I muttered something about her trusting in her whiteness and
not our blackness. That's when he put his hand on my hands where
I had em folded there in my lap. "Dess," he say to me then, "I'm
glad you ain't liking on Nathan cause I think you great myself."

Well this about took my breath away; it was so long since anyone had been so forward with me. And he said it like he knew
just the way I wanted to be great and so was qualified to judge. I

got up off that log real quick. I was nervous and shy as a girl just come into her womanhood. "That what you call me out here to talk about?" I ask real sharp.

"You want me to say it in front of Janet-nem?" he ask real innocent like.

Well, this just seem to me plain foolish so I didn't even answer it. "What this got to do with Nathan and that white woman?"

"Well it ain't no sense in me trying to make up to you if you mooning round over Nathan and jealous of some other female on his account."

There didn't seem to be nothing else to say and we just stood there in the moonlight looking at each other. I was still flustered, wanting to stay and wanting to go, but when he started kissing me, I didn't stop him. It was the strangeness of him in my arms made me pull away finally. Kaine was slight built; hugging him was like hugging a part of myself. Harker wasn't big like Nathan—Nathan's muscles bulged like a stuffed cotton sack. He was tall as Nathan, but more rangy; even so, wasn't no way I could mistake his shoulders for my own. I pulled back from him; my head was swimming. I was wanting to laugh, wanting to cry, wanting to spite him somehow cause he wasn't Kaine, wanting to kiss him again. So I ran.

I never did like to admit I was wrong but the next day when I went up to the House, I apologized for being rude. I wouldn't say no sorry and I wouldn't beg no pardon, neither. I was raised in a one-room cabin, had worked the fields all my life. I didn't know nothing about knocking before you walk into a room. But *white* woman have a right to say who she want in her room; long as she didn't ask me, wasn't my business who she invited in there.

಄

Wasn't no "death do us part" in slavery; wasn't even no "dead or sold," less'n two peoples made it that. Far as two peoples loving with each other, it was any handy place if you was willing—and sometimes if you wasn't; or you jumped the broom if the masters let you marry. But you couldn't help dreaming. Dreams was one the reasons you got up the next day. Kaine had been my dream and I didn't spect to do no more dreaming about a man—least not no time soon. Yet, there I was, casting eyes at someone else. Seem like everyplace I look I seed the way Harker hair spring back like a sponge when he take his hat off; or how he move easy, easy when he walk. I tried membering how it was with Kaine. I was mad cause this wasn't him. I was scared and shamed of myself.

I had cried a long time in that box, from pain, from grief, from filth. That filth, my filth. You know, this do something to you, to have to lay up in filth. You not a baby—baby have clean skin, clean mind. He think shit is interesting; he want to show it to you. But you know this dirt. Laying up there in my own foulment made me know how low I was. And I cried. I was like an animal; whipped like one; in the dirt like one. I hadn't never known peoples could do peoples like this. And I had the marks of that on my privates. It wasn't uncommon to see a negro with scars and most of us carried far more than we ever showed, but I felt as crippled as Dante and I didn't want Harker nor no one else to see me.

He come and got me one night and we went down to the fishing hole. He spread a blanket under the trees. I wasn't no Christian then and he wasn't one neither. I sat up afterwards and kind of draped my dress across my hips and scooted so my back was against the tree.

Harker was laying up there, naked as a jaybird, calm as you please; his hands folded behind his head, his legs crossed at the ankle just like he was in his own self's bed, in his own self's cabin. "Dess?" Voice quiet as the night, "Dessa, you know I know how they whipped you." His head was right by my leg and he turned and lifted my dress, kissed my thigh. Where his lips touched was like fire on fire and I trembled. "It ain't impaired you none at all," he said and kissed my leg again. "It only increase your value." His face was wet; he buried his head in my lap.

Six

%

Kaine was like sunshine, like song; Harker was thunder and lightning— Oh, not in the way he act towards me; never in the way he act. But in the way he come into my heart, way he shook me. "I never wanted at nothing till I met you," he told me one time; we was down to that place in the woods. "I let the white man worry about how we going eat, where we going sleep. *I* always kept *me* a change of clothes and I knowed how to eat even if he didn't." He figured free negroes wasn't that much better off than he was and they had a whole lot more to make do and worry about. So Harker let the white man worry and never hankered after being free. And he never wanted at nothing, he told me, "till I wanted you."

He said, "I don't want to love you in the woods cause we don't have no place else to be." This was another time. Seem like I could be with him for hours and never know tiredness, never be weary the next day. "That's part the reason I pushed at you to go long with this deal. I want to see at that Mony child I helped you birth and give you more. I can't do that if I'm slave to someone."

And I knew he meant it. I had known him a long time by then; not in years, no. I had known him only weeks. But he had brought

me out that cellar, had birthed my baby and sat beside me while
I laid in that bed. We'd talked and I felt I knowed him deep. And
here he was promising hisself to me, talking about a future he
wanted for us, and this frightened me. Kaine hadn't done this. You
know, the future did not belong to us; it belonged to our masters.
We wasn't to think about no future; it was a sign of belliousness
if we did. So it scared me to hear Harker talk this way. I felt
sometimes that if I hadn't pushed Kaine to think about running,
he would never have hit Master. What was that banjo compared
to us? He could've made another one. Now here was Harker
showing them same signs. Oh, Harker knowed the laws and rules
was set against us, but he act like that was just so he could sharpen
his wits on them, make doing what he wanted to do more interesting, you know, a little exciting. And this was how he went at
that scheme, like all our fears about slips and what-if's was just
something to make everybody think a little deeper, a little faster.

He taken us over that plan time and time again while we waited
for Red to get back with his wife, Debra. Harker, Castor, Ned,
and Flora was the ones we sold. Most any one of our peoples would
bring eight or nine hundred dollars easy at public auction—so
Nathan said, and after three years with that slave dealer we figured he ought to know. I'd never had no experience of money before, you understand, so the number didn't mean that much to
me. What I went by was how he said it and he said it like it was
a right smart amount. Harker, neither Nathan wanted to sell any
of the womens, though we was likely to bring us much, if not more,
than the mens. Womens was subject to ravishment and they didn't
want to put none of us back under that threat. This the way it
was during slavery. The woman was valued more because her
childrens belong to the master; this why they didn't like the mens
being sweet with nobody from off the home place, because the
childrens would belong to someone else. Increase someone else's
riches. But the womens couldn't handle the harvest by theyselfs,
so Flora—big, roebuck woman with that brown, brown skin,
brown to the bone—she volunteered to go.

We figured to do well enough without selling me or Nathan,

and I wasn't sorry about not being sold. This was a scary thing to me, to flirt so close with bondage again. All the mens could see was the trick—those that stayed was put out. Even Nathan felt he would miss some of the "fun" on account of his driving the wagon. But I could see risk and slips, and wasn't for the West, I wouldn't've been in it.

We was to go by wagon to Wilkerson on the shores of Lake Lewis Smith and take a boat from there down the Warrior River to Haley's Landing, just over the line in Tuscaloosa County. Harker knew the country all the way down to Mobile and cross to the Georgia line—that's where all that gambling and scheming had caught up with his old master, in Opelika, not far off the Georgia line. And he had roamed all up and down by hisself. From Haley's Landing, we would go overland, working the towns between the Warrior and Sipsey rivers in Tuscaloosa, Pickens, and Greene counties.

Miz Lady would tell some story about her husband being laid up with the fever or a busted leg; a couple of times, I think he was dead. We was to meet at such-and-such a place, by such-and-such a day after the sale; we'd wait two days at a meeting place, then we'd all go on to so-and-so. We was not to come back for no one. We was not to talk. We had to be as careful with slaves as we was with the masters. Our life depended on no one speaking out of turn. We was slaves; wasn't posed to know nothing nor do nothing without first being told. She was Mistress; wasn't no Mis'ess, no Miz Rufel to it. If they was caught, they was to act dumb and scared and show the pass from Miz Lady, which they all had hid in the toe of they shoes. She was to act high-handed and helpless if she was in a tight spot. We would end up in Arcopolis near the junction of the Warrior and Tombigbee rivers. From there we would take a boat back to the Glen. We spected to be back before the second picking of the cotton in October.

Red, Debra, Janet, Uncle Ned, Dante, and Cully was to take care of what needed doing in the fields. Ada cut Cully's hair down so none of the kink showed and Miz Lady taken him into town and give out that this was her brother from Charleston, come to visit a spell. This was so there would seem to be a white person on the place while she was gone. Uncle Joel was known to belong to the place, so between them, we figured Cully and him would keep suspicion off. You know, a peddler or a traveler lost his way might stop by. But the House was off the Road and people in the neighborhood didn't visit her.

Harker had me fix up some belts for me and Miz Lady to carry money in under our clothes, and fix our petticoats so we could hide money in the seams. I grumbled about this cause, tell the truth, I didn't believe we could actually fill up all these things with money. Me and Miz Lady was to keep the money with us at all times; never pack it in our baggage, never leave it in a room less one of us was there, never accept no credit. Harker favored gold or "gotiable certifieds." He never did care too much for paper money.

He couldn't read nor write proper—though he could do this better than most slaves and he could cipher like nobody's business. He had made up some marks that wasn't writing but he used it like that and this is how he got us in the way of understanding where we had to be and what we had to do. He was something to watch; he made us feel wasn't nothing we couldn't handle long as we stayed on our toes. It scared me to want him so.

We drove out before dawn, silent as the dark we traveled through, fording the creek not far from the House and skirting the town. We wanted to be well out the neighborhood before too many peoples was up and stirring. Nathan drove the wagon and I rode up front holding the baby, Clara, setting between him and Miz Lady; Harker-nem rode in the wagon-bed.

I didn't want to leave Mony; he already knowed me and smiled when he seed me, and, oh, I didn't want to go nowhere without him. Specially since Miz Lady was taking Clara. But I was the one'd made the point about the nursing and I could see Harker's about white folks being more liable to take kindly to a white mother and baby, go out they way to help them.

I wanted to ride in back with Harker, but I was "Mammy" now, taking care of Little Missy, keeping proper distance between Mistress and nigger. I was with "Mistress" about the way I was with

Nathan. We spoke (Harker wouldn't allow no surliness)—good morning, how do, nice day—but I kept my feelings to myself. Setting up there between them that morning, seemed like I could feel them *want*ing at each other. Not with they hands, now; they didn't even hardly touch *me*. But it was something between them and it made me mad. I sat there hoping they'd feel *that*. This wasn't no time for fooling and I wished I had Harker beside me stead of one of them.

We didn't see too many peoples that day, nor houses; this was sparse-settled country and Harker was taking us a way not too many peoples came. We traveled along a ridge that sloped gentle in some places, sharp in others, and everywhere was forest. Now and then we saw smoke curling white against the sky. Once we saw a place where a big fire had burned; charred trunks fanned out from us far as we could see in one direction. About midday, Nathan pulled off into the woods and we shared out the food Ada had packed for us. I was glad for the chance to get down from between Nathan and the white woman. We ate, stretched our legs, then got back on the road. It was nothing more than a track really, and hadn't've been for Harker's saying so, I wouldn't've known it was there.

Round dusk we come up on a sizable plantation. The House didn't look near as grand as the Glen but it was built of regular clapboard, not chinked logs like the rest of what we'd seen, with what looked like two real stories. Miz Lady sent Nathan up to the door to ask shelter for the night. Far as I was concerned, we could've camped by the side of the road—we had bedding and provision enough to do that. You know, I wasn't particular about this in the first place and I wanted to put off the start long as I could. I think the others felt some of this, too, but we hadn't spoke much and the longer we traveled that day, the more quiet we got. When I mentioned about camping out, Harker said no. He didn't want us arriving in Wilkerson looking too wore out. Attract too much tention; white lady with all these negroes bound to attract enough.

We stayed that night at the plantation of Mr. Oscar; Nathan

was sent round to the Quarters with the rest of our people but I stayed with Miz Lady. This is where I began another part of my education. When I come to myself in that bed, I accepted that everyone I loved was gone. That life was dead to me; I'd held the wake for it in that cellar. Yet and still, I was alive. At first I couldn't put no dependence on what I was seeing—a *white* woman nursing a *negro;* negroes acting good as *free. I* wasn't even posed to be there. I didn't have no words to make sense of what my eyes was seeing, much less what I'd been doing. I was someone I knowed and didn't know, living in a world I hadn't even knowed was out there. So that bed was grave and birthing place to me. I had come into the world, had started on it the minute I said run to Kaine, said north, or maybe when he told me go see Aunt Lefonia. I had never been around white peoples much before I was sold away. Except to bow my head and be careful how I spoke, I didn't know much about how I was posed to do. That's how I could be so hankty with Miz Lady, cause I didn't know no better, and didn't know enough to listen to the ones what did. But when I walked into that parlor with Miz Lady, I began to learn what I had missed as a field hand.

Mr. Oscar's wife and two childrens was off visiting her peoples over by "Elyton," wherever that was, but he made Miz Lady welcome, inviting her into the parlor and ringing the bell for some tea. He was a big, what you call ruddy-faced white man, skin very red; he had a bushy, sand-colored mustache and he smiled a lot and seemed to bow before her almost as much as a negro. She smiled a lot at him and seemed to like the way he hovered around her. She told him she was Miz Sutton, taking some hands to help with the harvest down to her daddy's place on the Mobile River. This was the story she would tell until we got farther down country, then she would tell another one; she had several. Harker had drilled her on them same as he did me.

Mr. Oscar didn't have a lot of servants in the house; the cook had answered the door, then gone back to fixing on his supper—which he graciously invited Miz Lady to share and she graciously accepted. I'm standing there watching all this you understand, holding Clara, kind of shifting from one foot to the other cause Miz Lady ain't told me to go or stay. Well, long about this time, they had finished saying all this, a young girl come in and said Mistress' room was ready. "Mistress" got up out the chair and happen she drop the hanky she been using to pat her face with. Before she could bend down to pick it up, he grab her arm, say, "Allow me. Nigger," he say, turning round, "pick that up." I had my hands full with Clara, and he wasn't looking directly at me, understand. So I just stood there.

"Dessa!" Miz Lady hiss at me, yanking on the tail of my dress. "Nigger!" he say real sharp, and even I knowed he meant every nigger in hearing this time, but the other girl reached and got the hanky before I could move. He seemed satisfied with that. "Get them bags," he say over his shoulder. Miz Lady ain't have to yank my dress that time; I shifted Clara to one arm and picked up the small satchel. Other girl grabbed the two big bags and we struggled out the room behind them.

It was some more bowing and smiling up in the bedroom but finally he left. She closed the door, and I put Clara down on the bed to change her. "Somebody," Miz Lady say, looking all out the windows, "somebody better start paying tention, else they going ruin the whole thing." It made me hot that she could signify like that; yet and still, I knowed I'd been slow. This what Harker meant when he say don't speak out of turn, neither act out of it. I was slave; I was "nigger"; I couldn't forget that for the rest of the journey. And I was mad at myself that she'd had to remind me.

She taken a green dress out the bag and told me to go iron it. I looked at her. Black, brown, gray, dark blue, that's all Harker allowed, and hats that covered up that red hair. Harker didn't want her in nothing showy and didn't seem to me was nothing plain about that dress, way it was cut low cross the bosom. I picked up a blue one from off the top of the bag. "This seem more like what Harker said you should wear," I told her.

"That's a afternoon outfit," she told me; "you can't wear that to no dinner."

I didn't know nothing about all that, a course, but I knowed it wasn't part of the plan for her to be showing herself off before no white folk. "Harker said you posed to be quiet and respectable."

"Harker said I'm a high-class lady and to make everybody treat me that way," she say real sharp.

The girl knocked at the door just then with the tea and we both held our tongues while she set the tray down. Just as the girl turned to go, white woman shove that green dress in my hand. "Iron this, Odessa," she say. "You-all do have a flatiron, don't you?" smiling round at the girl. I felt like snatching her *and* that dress, but the girl was in the room and wasn't nothing I could do but take it. "Thank you," she say kind of careless like. Then, "Guess I wear the shawl, too." And she throwed *that* cross my arm, too.

Actually, I got that girl to touch up them clothes some; mad as I was I might would've burned them. It wasn't so much the dress itself that made me angry. I didn't think way out there what she wore could matter that much; I mean, Mr. Oscar had already noted her. It was just the idea of her acting like she didn't have to go according to plan; she could correct me but I wasn't posed to say nothing to her. I let her have that dress, but I was going speak to Harker about her ways.

There was a lot more to being a lady's maid than I had thought. It wasn't just the fetching and carrying, though Lord know it was enough of that. You be *toting* some hot water, let me tell you, specially in them two-story places. Which this was. Seeing at that baby wasn't no problem. She babble at you all the while you doing for her, then wrap them little pudgy arms around your neck when you pick her up. Never cried less she was hungry or sleepy or wet. No, Little Missy wasn't no problem. But seeing at Miz Lady liked to give me a fit.

White women wear some *clothes* under them dresses, child. Miz Lady hadn't had no call to rig out in full style since I'd knowed her, but she put it all on that night. There was slips and stays and shifts and hose and garters, petticoats and drawers (and I still feel that all this is unnecessary. You need all that to protect "modesty," person have to wonder just what kind of "modesty" you got). I didn't bit more know how to do up all them hooks and ties and snaps than nothing; she had to talk me through it. She wanted me to put her hair up, but I drawed the line at that. I still remembered that night I waked up with that stringy stuff all in my face, and I didn't want to touch it. She finally ended by braiding it in a big braid and piling it on top of her head—where it commence to fall right down.

After she left, I fixed my pallet cross the hearth, on the cool brick there that was even with the floor, hoping maybe I could catch some breeze down there. She woke me up with her giggling when she come in. I think that they'd been standing at the door saying good night for a long time, but she closed the door when she heard me stirring. The candle had guttered out long since, but I could see her by the light of the one she held. She was laughing. "Mr. Oscar the most engaging rogue," she say. "Why, I had to leave the table, he had me laughing and blushing so much." She hiccuped and laughed. Seeing her like that put me in mind of how she acted when I first seed her, all giggly and fly, like she didn't have two thoughts to rub together in her head. She'd been drinking, too; smelt like peach brandy to me. I hurried her out that dress and into bed, uneasy at having her like this—what if she'd slipped in front that white man? But steady, too. She wasn't acting no better than what I'd said and I had a earful I was going give Harker that next morning.

I was wakened by some muttering and it took me a minute to realize it was him and her in that bed. At first I was embarrassed and surprised. If she'd wanted to do that, I could have slept in the kitchen. And glad, too, cause this would show Nathan just what kind of old thing he'd taken up with. She get in heat and pick up with whatever was handy. Oh, I had a lot I was going to tell him and Harker, honey. Then I realized she was trying to get him *out* the bed; she was whispering but she still sounded angry, and scared. "Mis'ess?" I said; I didn't call out all that loud, just in case I was wrong, but she heard me.

"Dessa," she called. "Odessa, help me get this man out the bed."

Well, I got up and started looking round for something to hit him with. Nearest thing come to hand was a pillow and I started pounding him all about the head with that. We was all shouting and carrying on by then. I could tell he was drunk—letting two womens beat him up with pillows! We managed to push him out the bed, tried to stomp him to death with our bare feet. He crawled cross that floor and got out the room somehow. I slammed the door and we pulled a chest cross in front of it. We leaned against it, panting a little now.

"That what you was using?" she ask, pointing at me. I still had one them pillows in my hand. She did, too, looking like a ghost in that white nightgown, her hair screaming every which where. I started laughing, trying to keep it quiet, you know; and she was laughing now, herself. The more we tried to be quiet, the more we laughed. Well, that peach brandy commence to act up about then and she barely made it to the slop jar.

I helped her over to the bed. She looked plumb miserable setting there. I wasn't feeling all that good myself. What if Mr. Oscar hadn't been drunk? I asked myself; and, What if he come back? Knees shaking now, and just wanting to get to that pallet.

"Dessa?" Miz Lady, calling me, patting the bed like she couldn't think of the word for it; but I understood. I didn't too much want to be by myself right then neither.

I laid awake a long time that night while she snored quiet on the other side the baby. The white woman was subject to the same ravishment as me; this the thought that kept me awake. I hadn't knowed white mens could use a white woman like that, just take her by force same as they could with us. Harker, neither Nathan could help us there in that House, any House. I knew they would kill a black man for loving with a white woman; would they kill a black man for keeping a white man off a white woman? I didn't know; and didn't want to find out.

I slept with her after that, both of us wrapped around Clara. And I wasn't so cold with her no more. I wasn't zactly warm with her, understand; I didn't know how to be warm with no white woman. But now it was like we had a secret between us, not just that bad Oscar—though we kept that quiet. I couldn't bring myself to tell Harker, neither Nathan about that night. Seemed like it would've been almost like telling on myself, if you know what I mean. I was posed to be keeping an eye on her and something had almost got by me. Sides, I told myself, that bad Oscar had paid Miz Lady back twice over for coming on so hankty with me. But really, what kept me quiet was knowing white mens wanted the same thing, would take the same thing from a white woman as they would from a black woman. Cause they could. I never will forget the fear that come on me when Miz Lady called me on Mr. Oscar, that *knowing* that she was as helpless in this as I was, that our only protection was ourselfs and each others.

We reached Lake Lewis Smith and sold Harker and Ned there at Wilkerson. We hadn't looked to sell anybody so early but the man paid "sixteen fifty for the pair," which Nathan said was a decent price, what with the country about Wilkerson not being planted so much to cotton. It hurt to see Harker, even Ned, led off again, back into that prison house. But I knowed, I be*lieved* that if anybody could get out again, it would be Harker; he had that kind of mind, you see. And if it was anybody could keep that pesky Ned in line it was him.

Miz Lady used some of this money to buy me some clothes. This was Nathan's idea; he said I didn't look like I belonged to no proper lady, proper lady wouldn't own me as no maid. What clothes I had was cut down and took in from some of her old things. These was clean and neat as I could make them, but they did look pretty cobbled up. Good enough for a hand, yes, but not for no respectable lady's maid.

She bought me two dresses, a plaid gingham and a sumac-colored cotton, two bandannas for my head and a kerchief to go across my shoulders, three full changes of underwear, shoes (not them old russet brogans they used to give slaves—if they gave anything at all—but sho enough shoes, good as a white person would wear), and some stockings. These was the most clothes I'd had in my life and I treasured them the more cause they was bought from selling Harker and Ned.

She also bought some pepper and two little snuff boxes for us to carry it in; got so we could open them with the flick of a thumb, with either hand. And hatpins. A long one she kept pinned in the crown of her hat and a shorter one I wore in the folds of my shoulder kerchief, the point buried in the knot at my bosom. We wasn't troubled by no more bad Oscars again.

We could have sold Castor and Flora, Nathan and me, too, for that matter, several times over before that boat let us off in Winston. But we decided to keep to the story about Miz Lady's daddy until we reached Haley's Landing. This was a larger town than Winston, not big as some I had seen on the coffle but pretty big for that region. We waited for Harker and Ned in Winston at the south end of Lake Lewis Smith. They arrived shortly after we did and we went on to Haley's Landing.

Me and Miz Lady put up at the hotel there and lodged Nathan at the livery stable and Harker and them in the slave pen behind the jail. Then Nathan went with her to have some handbills printed up announcing a "private sale," "through no fault," of "likely negroes." Back in them days, every negro was "likely." "No fault" meant wasn't nothing wrong with the slave and in the bill of sale they was always "warranted sound." Sometimes, so Nathan said, dealers would say "no fault" in their handbills and print this in the newspapers to make people think it was a planter on hard times selling and they could get a better deal. The "private sale" was to keep from having to sell to speculators and traders or anyone else didn't look right. We didn't want none of our peoples in the hand of a trader. Only way we was likely to get someone off a coffle was to buy them—we didn't fool ourselves about how lucky Nathan and us had been before—so it didn't hurt to be too careful. For this same reason, the handbills always said something about first choice going to planters and city residents "who want for their own family use." (Nathan had all these sayings by heart and sometimes on a lonely stretch of road, we would pass the time making up rhymes with them. I can't member a one now, but the sayings from the handbills stays in my mind.)

Seem like every town we went through had a group of one-suspender white mens would sit in front the hotel or the tavern, lounge round the public fountain or the courthouse square. You wouldn't think there would be enough *interest,* let alone *money,* among them to buy a slave. But time an auctioneer put up that deal packing case and commence his spiel over the "article," there would usually be a sizable crowd. They hadn't tried to sell me from the block when I was on the coffle and I'd never seen an auction before. I'd heard about them, a course, how they looked in your mouth and felt your body. Often you was made to jump around and dance to show how spry you was. These was things I'd heard about, you understand. I'd never experienced this, never seen this for myself, till that day.

I stood in the crowd between Nathan and Miz Lady holding Clara and watched them mock our manhood. "Prime field hand," the auctioneer say, "look at that arm," jabbing at Castor's shoulder with his pointing stick. "Prime," he say with his hand up to his mouth like he was whispering a secret. "The gen-u-ine article," pointing now at Castor's privates. All the white men laughed; this was a big joke. Castor looked like he want to crawl in that box. "Guaranteed increases. Nary a sign of bad on him," turning Castor round, raising his shirt to bare his back. "Enin-ine hundra dolla, nin-ine hundra— Sold for nine seventy-five."

"Nigger went cheap," white man in the crowd say. I pushed Clara at Miz Lady and left.

I heard Nathan calling me but I never slowed. I didn't want to hear no message from that white woman. He caught up with me and pulled me into an alley. I was crying and he held me against his chest. "It's just these last few times," he say, "last few times and that's the end," he rocked, "won't none of us be sold no more." He was shaking; his tears rained on my head and neck. We rocked and crooned to each others, till we cried ourselfs out, then leaned against the wall, laughing a little, kind of shamefaced. "We been through some times, ain't we?" he say wiping his eyes. I nodded, wiping at my own face. Where would I be without this brother? I thought, wanting to hold him, to hug him again. "Dessa," he say, taking my hand. "Dessa, I was bred in slavery."

I snatched my hand back; I hadn't tried to make him see my part no more since that morning in the wood lot, and it hurt me that he would bring it up now. It was like he'd used the closeness I was feeling for him to bring that white woman between us. And it made me mad, too. "So now a person a slave master if they don't like what you doing?"

"I know you ain't nowhere near being like the white man," he say and grabbed my hand again. "Dessa— Dess, why can't I like you and her, too?"

It seemed to me that one rubbed out the other. Sides that, "I speaks to her," I told him, "what more you want?"

"I want you to be my friend."

"I wasn't the one stopped."

He looked at me and finally he grinned. "You a grudgeful little old something, ain't you?" he say.

You see what I'm saying? Whatever I said, he would have something to say. Oh, I could make him angry, I could even make him sad. Someday I might act evil enough to drive him away; he might get tired of me being so hateful and leave. Till then, he would keep at me: Say "friend," say "brother." And whether I said yes or no to him, it wouldn't never be the way it used to be. I guess this was always my pain, that things would never be the same. I had lost so much, so much, and this brother was a part of what I'd gained. Nathan—he wasn't grinning then. No, he held my hand and looked at me steady on. You know—and I swear this what I thought then—it like a darky to risk what he *know* is good on "chance," on "change," on new or "another." And what one did I know didn't have a little bit of that in them, from Dante on up? "Damn fool negro," I told him, yet and still leaning against him.

His arm tightened round me. "Hankty negress like you need a damn fool negro like me." And I laughed.

I don't mean to say that I ever got so's I liked the idea, black man, white woman. I don't think none of us ever liked the idea; and we was uneasy situated as we was; had to be uneasy. But I don't think Nathan and Miz Lady did more than hold hands or walk apart for a minute throughout that whole journey. This was business and Harker didn't even allow *us* more than that. I know I never felt that same kind of feeling flowing between them after that first morning. And, after a while, we was too close to hold hands, if you know what I mean, too mindful about everybody to show much that was special to one person. So I don't think none of us thought too much about them; and as for her—.

Well. My thoughts on her had changed some since that night at Mr. Oscar's. You can't do something like this with someone and not develop some closeness, some trust. And we couldn't help but talk, much time as we spent together. At first it wasn't no more than what we would do the next day, the peoples we seen; as time went on we talked about the sales and the stories Harker-nem was bringing back. We even laughed about that bad Oscar one night. Often, we was so tired from traveling and scheming we went to sleep with barely a good night between us. We was moving quick, honey—we watched every word; and the scheme went smooth.

Back in them days about all you had to do was put a rope and a collar on a negro and seem like every white person in seeing distance want to make an offer for him. We seldom had to hold auctions. At first we kept the stories simple—Harker's old master taught that the best lie is always the one closest to the truth. So Miz Lady sold them as just plain field hands—prime ones, now; they was always prime—and trusted. Family hadn't never meant to sell them, Miz Lady'd say, looking sad. By her always wearing some kind of dark dress, this gave the impression death was the cause of sale. Clara even got so she cried after them when they was sold. But (Miz Lady would go on), prime field hand don't go cheap. That's all she ever said they was, field hand. But the white peoples would just insist—"You mean he can't carpenter?" "He can't lay no brick?" "She must can cook." Till finally she started saying, "Yes, he a mason"; "he a drayman."

We sold Flora as a laundress and expert ironer when she hadn't even so much as seen a flatiron in them days. People could do these things was sold for more money. Sometimes they masters hired them out and collected they wages. Oh, I tell you, honey, slavery was ugly and we felt right to soak the masters for all we could get. And Miz Lady was good; she could hold and pacify Clara and bargain over a slave at the same time, matter a fact, she liked to do that to throw peoples off guard; they'd be up there playing with Clara and she had closed the sale. She bat her eyes and the sheriff want to put up handbills for her. She smile and a planter raise his price fifty dollars, just to be what she called "gallant." All that bat the eye and giggle was just so much put-on now, and it give me a kick to see how she used these to get her way with the peoples we met.

We always tried to have our noon meal off the road someplace so we could talk together, let down our guard a little. Harker wouldn't have us let down our pretense but just so much. Miz Lady always sat on something, a log, a rock, one of the bags, and I sat beside her, between her and the rest. And we all called her Mistress; that "Miz Rufel" and "Miz Lady" was only amongst ourselfs. Trusted hands, yes, but it wouldn't do for none of us to seem to familiar with her. Nathan and Harker kept things light with their back-and-forth and everybody played with Clara. (You know, she turned out to be no trouble at all. I hadn't taken up too much time with her at the House—that was Annabelle's job; she was the nursemaid. But Clara was a cheerful baby, go to anybody for a smile; and laughing and playing with her whiled away many an hour as we was traveling or me and Miz Lady waited in some hotel.) This was where we rested, where we planned and told tales.

The more money we made, the more real "West" got. What would we have to buy? When should we leave? These was the things we talked about. Should we head for St. Joe or Council Bluffs? St. Joe was closer but it was in slave country; so we settled on Council Bluffs. I was all set to leave as soon as we got back to the Glen, but Harker said no. This was a long journey and we couldn't just go rushing off. It would take a while to buy and pack all we needed. It would be winter by the time we was ready and we couldn't spect nothing but bad weather going north. (You know, I'm shamed to say I didn't know this where cold weather come from, the north. That I'd never seed no real meaning in birds going south till Harker pointed it out to me. This is what I hold against slavery. May come a time when I for*give*—cause I don't think I'm set up to for*get*—the beatings, the selling, the killings, but I don't think I ever forgive the ignorance they kept us in.) We couldn't start out much before the end of winter, and seemed like we need to buy some of everything cause none of us had nothing.

And the stories. Harker told about one place he was sold had a bulldog weigh five hundred pounds patrolling the Quarters, could see negroes in the dark; Castor about another one where they growed negroes so big one could eat half a barrel of flour and a middle of meat at one meal—and back that up with a barrel of greens and a water bucket full of syrup. One master tried to force his way with Flora—that was the way he broke all his women. But he was drunk and she "helped him," she say, "pass *out*," didn't even wait for morning to skedaddle out that place—and had been waiting for two days in the next town when we got there; was fixing ready to leave *us*. One of Ned's buyers sent him with a note down to the sheriff's to be whipped—this is what a lot of owners did in the cities and towns cause they didn't want to do this they-self. Ned stopped a white man and asked him what the note say; when the man told him, Ned give the note to the next negro he seen. Gave him two coppers to take it to the sheriff and wait for an answer. This wasn't a nice trick but it was what slavery taught a lot of people: to take everybody so you didn't get took yourself. We laughed so we wouldn't cry; we was seeing ourselfs as we had been and seeing the thing that had made us. Only way we could defend ouselves was by making it into some hair-raising story or a joke.

Somebody even tried to hold us up. We had just sold Ned—or was it Castor? We sold peoples so many times it was hard to keep count of them. Harker was the only other person with us, riding in the wagon-bed; I was sitting up there between Nathan and Miz Lady wishing I was back there with Harker. Seem like I could feel him touching me—oh, not with his hands; he hardly laid a hand on me. And sometimes I'd about swoon, my senses be so over-come with knowing he was near. That day, we'd set out later than we should, but was specting to reach the next town by nightfall. They'd told us at the place where we'd sold Ned, town was only a little piece the way down the road, but dusk found us still on the road with no house in sight. We figured later that they'd told us this on purpose and that it was somebody from that place knew we had cash money and thought they saw a chance to steal it. Well, they laid in wait for us in a canebrake, two of them, masked, on horses. One pointed a gun at us while the other held the mules by the bridle. "Put your hands up!" the one with the gun say.

Miz Lady carried a big, floppy, drawstring bag, sort of like a reticule, but big; carried some of everything in it, mostly Clara's stuff, but she had started crocheting for winter so that was in there, too. Well, Miz Lady cried, "What?! Why the i-*dee!*" just like these was some rude boys tracked dirt across her clean floors or was chunking rocks at her laundry. That's how she say it, "the i-*dee,*" and flung that bag in the horse's face. This was the horse of the man had the gun on us. It reared up and he dropped the gun trying to control it.

Honey, they wasn't no match for us, smooth as we moved together. When she flung that bag, Nathan shoved them reins on me, went flying at the one held the mules; I ducked down with the baby between the seat and the front of the wagon and pulled Miz Lady down on top of us. By the time I looked up, Harker had the gun on one and Nathan had a choke hold on the other. Miz Lady was brushing herself off and fussing about scoundrels picking on defenseless peoples. That's the way it was: bam, bam, bam, just like that, just like we'd done this a hundred times before.

We tied them up—Miz Lady still fussing; we didn't even take off they masks: Who was interested in knowing some good-for-nothing white mens?—run off they horses, and left them just like that for someone else to find there by the side of the road. "Let them explain that," Miz Lady said. "The i-*dee!*" and we fell out laughing.

A course Nathan and Harker fussed Miz Lady a little about the chance she took. Had to say something—it actually not that many bad mens a woman can stop with her purse. If they hadn't been there to back her up, she'd been in deep trouble. This was more understood than said, and what was said was more like a joke. We was feeling too good about ourselfs to take anything too hard. So, when Miz Lady brought up about me and her beating that bad Oscar with pillows, it was more or less to keep the joke going. By this time, Oscar was more funny to us than scary, but somehow we'd never talked about him in front the others. Well, by the time that story all come out, he wasn't so funny to Harker, neither Nathan. They'd thought about ravishment in the Quarters, but not about ravishment in the House, not under the white woman's guard, not of the white woman herself. And they was some upset that we was just now telling them—like that would've done some good. Harker jawed at me, Nathan at Miz Lady; I was sore at her for bringing it up in the first place. She was mad at all of us for being mad at her. And Clara was squalling; all that arguing back and forth woke her up. Everybody's mouth was poked out by the time we finished that ride.

Nathan had Miz Lady buy a little pistol in the next town, to keep beside the bed, and him and Harker taught us to shoot it. And our travels went on. King's Store, Eutaw, Yancyville, these the names I remember. Never stayed in none of them more than a day or two, and most of that was in some hotel, waiting. Sometimes we spent the night at a plantation house. Other times, we camped out. They tell you now about the gloried south; south wasn't so gloried back then, honey. Some of them places we went through wasn't no more than three buildings: the cotton warehouse, the cash-store, and the house where the manager or owner of the warehouse and store lived. Sometime, if they looked prosperous enough, we would stop at these places. There was one we seen had a bear chained up outside; this was their pet—big, smelly, hide gone all to mange, wallowing round the yard; he was some pitiful. We didn't stop there; didn't none of us want to be round someone would do a living thing like that.

No, being round her own people didn't make Miz Lady waver none in what we was doing. The money helped, of course. She was getting a good portion of money from the sales—not the largest portion, but a good share, you understand. Now, being round white peoples myself, I could understand how she was posed to be living up there in that half-finished House. With the money we was making she could go back to her peoples in style. And we none of us could help being some familiar with her. Castor and Flora was still kind of shy with her, but even they come to speak to her, sometimes without her having to speak first. I served her, yes, but she didn't treat me the way I had seen some treated on that journey, had never treated none of us with all that yelling and cuffing which was the way many masters did.

It had made me kind of scared to see the way peoples was treated at some of the tavern-inns and Houses where we stayed. I could go from one season to another at my old home and not see no more white folks than the overseer who bossed us in the fields, or Master from a distance. I just had no idea of all the cuffing and cursing we had to bear. I knew a rough word or shove wasn't nothing beside a caning or the lash; yet and still, it bothered me. And you was always darky or nigger or gal to them, never your name.

Nathan said the white folks mostly didn't mean nothing by all they carrying on and the black folks mostly didn't take it too much to heart. Miz Lady said only the most low-class white folks acted so harsh; most masters treated they slaves like they would other servants.

I didn't too much care to talk about slavery in front of her. Shy or not shy, nobody much wanted to disagree with her—though the time she said that, about low-class masters, Ned did speak out to say poor white folks didn't own no slaves. See, Miz Lady didn't believe most white folks was mean. She thought that if white folks knew slaves as she knew us, wouldn't be no slavery. She thought that was what'd ruined her husband—seeing how much money you could make if you owned other peoples. This is why she felt slavery was wrong, because peoples was no more to you than a pair of hands, stock, sometimes not even a name. When she said this, Flora say real earnest, "Please, Miz Lady, don't say nothing like that round no white folk." We all kind of laughed at the way she said it—Flora was being funny, you know; but she was serious,

too. She had seen white mens who said such things run out of
town for just being in close talk with other peoples' slaves. We
didn't want Miz Lady giving no white folks no reason to dislike
her. And she didn't see herself as no different from most white
peoples. If they just knew, she kept saying. Well, I believed this of
her, but I couldn't understand how she could watch white folks
buying up our peoples right and left and say this. As far as white
folks not knowing how bad slavery was—they was the ones made
it, was the ones kept it. Master could've freed me anytime and I
wouldn't've never said him nay. Maybe Nathan and them saw these
things, too, but no one said them to her.

Nathan stopped a runaway horse and buggy in a little town not
far from Arcopolis. Wasn't no one in the buggy at the time, but
he saved it from being tore up, sure, and the horse from maybe
running down somebody or hurting itself. The owner of the buggy
was real taken with this, and offered nine hundred dollars for Nathan right there on the spot. This had all happened so fast, you
understand, I'm still setting up there on that wagon seat holding
Clara and them reins. Miz Lady got her mouth open; Nathan and
the man was standing there waiting for her to answer. "Why, why,
sir, this here is my personal servant, my personal driver," she say,
drawing herself up like she was setting in the finest carriage.

"A thousand dollars, madam," he say before she'd even finished good. "I'm a horse-trainer myself and I never seen such a
fine hand with the horses. Courage can't go unrewarded."

All our eyes blinked at this. We hadn't sold no one for less than
eight hundred dollars but it was rare for us to get a thousand
without some kind of auction.

"Why sir, sir," she was stuttering sho enough now. "Why, sir,
who would drive my wagon to Arcopolis?"

"Tell you what, madam," he say cool as you please, "you throw
in the wagon and I'll call it eleven hundred dollars even. You can
finish your journey by stage."

By this time, I'm hunching her, reminding her that we got to
meet "Master" Harker in Arcopolis and he be real disappointed
not to see his favorite driver when we get there. And Nathan

wheedling, "Oh, please, Mistress," like a regular numbskull, devils dancing in them little red eyes. "Oh, please, Mistress; this master say he got a lot of horses."

I guess this what did it, eleven hundred dollars and them little devilish eyes. I had my doubts about selling Nathan and I guess she did, too, but Nathan was so set on it that if she hadn't said yes, I believe he would have tried to sell hisself. See, Harker and them would always come back with some kind of tale and it was plain to see when Nathan was listening to them talk that he wanted to get in on the venture, on the fun, as they called it. Wasn't nothing to guarding money, guarding womens and childrens. He'd helped spike them robbers, and now he wanted to do something of his own.

We'd come a long way from the time we'd watched Harker and Ned walk back into slavery. What we used to do with fear and trembling, we now did for fun. I told myself this was good, that it showed slavery didn't have no hold on us no more. Even me and Miz Lady had got in on the act with that bad Oscar, and Nathan deserved his turn. Bumping along the road in that stage, it was easy to believe this. With what Nathan had brought, we had made close to thirty thousand dollars—some fantastic number like that. The number really didn't mean that much to me. I had money wrapped around my waist, sewed into the seams of my petticoat, stuffed down the legs of my drawers. We had made so much money, and my mind about bust when I would think this was only a small part of the money in the world. This, I told myself, this what we come to get; this would put us beyond the reach of any slave law and the more we had, the better.

ॐ

The stage got into Arcopolis at nightfall. She taken a room in the best hotel and had them send up some food. We ate and went to bed. We was tired, tired. This was the end of selling, of scheming, of traveling and trembling. The end of watch every word. I was tired all the way to the bone and I slept very hard.

Things looked some better next morning. I knowed Nathan could keep care of hisself—and other peoples, too, if it come to that. That's how I'd got free in the first place. Long as he didn't hold us up waiting on him, I didn't think Harker would have too much to say about it. Fact, they'd probably all have a good laugh about me worrying so. No, I wasn't real, what you call *chipper* that next morning when we went to inquire about boats going upriver, but I wasn't down in the mouth neither. The man at the ticket office told us two or three boats left every day from the landing, and they wouldn't have no trouble putting us all up whatever day she want to leave. Miz Lady bought the tickets; then wasn't nothing else we could do but wait.

Before, time was important; we kept on the move and trusted to luck that no would track us. But now, in this final move, caution was most important. Harker and Flora-nem was all to take they time making sure they wasn't followed before they met us there. Roundabout as they was coming, we didn't spect to see none of them for four or five days. They was all posed to meet up outside of town and come to the hotel together, trusted hands reporting where they'd been told to go. Miz Lady was Miz Carlisle, meeting some hands her daddy was sending from his place to help her husband finish up the harvest.

So we waited; and while we waited, we shopped. This was something I had never seen done before. Oh, I had been in the cash-stores now and then on the journey, and that store where we bought my first clothes. But all of it was too new for me to see anything then and them cash-stores had such a mess of things, it was hard to see any one thing less you knowed what you was looking for. Well, the stores in Arcopolis was some different. These was emporiums and mercantile houses, selling everything from silk to steel, chock-full of stuff I hadn't never even heard of, let alone seen. Eggbeaters, apple corers, potato peelers (I thought these was going to be little mechanical fingers like the figures come out a clock. Oh, yes, I seen one of these, too, my first time on this trip), farina kettles, a bosom board for ironing shirts, skirt boards for the dresses, all sizes of flatirons. My eyes was just dazzled. It was hard for me to keep my hands to myself; I had never seen so much in one place.

Miz Lady bought for use at the Glen as well as our trip West and I learned a lot from watching her buy. She never let them clerks see in her purse. All they knew at first was that she knew what she was talking about, and only when she was satisfied that *they* knew what they was talking, did she buy. And then she bought a lot. (I know most times, colored womens can't do this; clerk don't want the colored person to know much as he know, don't want you to know nothing, far as that go; liable to get mad, you show you know *anything* at *all*. Cheat you better, you don't know nothing. But we not excused from knowing, even if we can't let it show in no way but keeping money in our purse and buying at the next store.) We bought all sort of provision—sugar, salt, coffee, tea, flour, molasses, plates, mugs, utensils, blankets, mattress ticking. And then we bought for the peoples, shoes and boots, hose, calico and kersey for dresses, jean cloth for trousers, heavy wools for coats and cloaks. She had all these things sent down to the boat landing to be stored until we left.

After we finished shopping in the mornings, we walked about the town some. The Tombigbee cross the Warrior River there at Arcopolis, so it was a lot of river traffic come through there. This was a good-sized town, two big, wide streets full of stores and a lot of going in and out. I have seed Decatur since that time, and St. Louis, so I know Arcopolis wasn't no real busy place. Fact is, there was more going on down to the landing than there was up there on that bluff. But I could've stayed in the streets for hours, listening and looking. Even so simple a thing as the dressmaker's, the barber shop, and the printer's—I couldn't see that printing machine often enough to suit me. The horses, the different wagons and carriages, the way the white peoples dressed. I'd seed some of these things from the coffle, I guess, must've seed them. But I didn't pay no tention to them; too deep in misery, too scared. And now my eyes didn't get enough of looking and I made excuses to be out in them streets. Course, I was looking for our peo-

ples all the while I was out there. This how Nathan'd done when
he was with us, sort of stroll around the town so the peoples could
spot him and know we was there.

Afternoons I would go out on some errand, down to the bakeshop to buy a pastry or to the dressmaker's where Miz Lady was
having some clothes made for herself. Sometimes I bought a paper
for her. Once I even mailed a letter; she was just writing to Cully
up at the Glen to say we'd be on directly, but this was something
I'd never experienced. Sometimes in the evenings, Miz Lady'd take
Clara and sit on the gallery there in front the hotel, trying to keep
cool. It was almost October now, the dead tail end of summer,
but it was still warm. I would stand behind her chair fanning them
with a big palm-leaf fan. I did this, too, when she went down to
dinner or supper—I fetched breakfast and we ate that in the room.
At night we would blow out the candles, open all the windows,
and lay cross the bed watching the streets below. She taken a corner room. It was noisy sometimes—there was a tavern down
the street—but that cross breeze from the windows cut the heat
some. Often we talked back and forth over Clara while she
slept.

We called up the comical things had happened on the trail. She
could mock some of them white peoples to a tee and it tickled me
even more that she would do this in front of me—and laughed
some more about that bad Oscar. Sometimes, there in the darkness, I'd catch myself about to tell her, oh, some little thing, like
I would Carrie or Martha; and I wondered at her, her peoples,
how she come to be like she was. Her husband didn't sound like
much of nothing and she didn't want to go round her mamma
without no money. She did ask about that coffle and scaping out
that cellar. I told her some things, how they chained us, the way
the peoples sang in the morning at the farm. But I wouldn't talk
about Kaine, about the loss of my peoples; these was still a wound
to me and remembrance of that coffle hurt only a little bit less. So
we didn't talk too much that was personal. I mean, I know I mentioned mammy-nem, and she talked about Dorcas—or "Mammy,"

as she called her. But this was a white woman and I don't think I forgot it that whole, entire journey.

Still, I think me and Miz Lady was in a fair way to getting along with each other, if it hadn't've come up about Council Bluffs. This happen one afternoon I was changing Clara's diaper. We hadn't been talking much of nothing, hadn't been that long come in from lunch. "I'm thinking about going on to Council Bluffs with you-all," Miz Lady say all a sudden.

Now Harker always wanted her to go far as the jumping-off place with us; much slave territory as we had to get through, it just made sense for us to travel with a white person long as we could. But Charleston was one way and West was another; it was a lot to ask anyone—even for what we was willing to pay—to go so far out they way for us. "Harker be real glad to hear it," I said. This the first thing come into my mind cause I knowed it was on his mind. "I know he set aside a good amount for someone to help us get through to Council Bluffs." I finished with Clara and stood up. Miz Lady didn't say nothing. She was standing in front one of the windows twisting a hanky in her hands. I guessed that was something to be uneasy about, traveling through so much slave country with a gang of runaway negroes.

"These white peoples act so hateful," she say, turning to me, smiling now, "maybe, maybe I just go West with you-all myself. What you think about that?" talking fast, nodding her head like she was agreeing with me. "What I got to stay round here for? I can't work that farm. Nathan say it's other womens have gone West."

She said some more, but I stopped listening at mention of Nathan. I hadn't thought that much about him and her loving in a long time. Mostly, we had too much else on our minds to be thinking about loving—least so far as everybody *act*. So it was easy to forget there was something more between them two. But now, when she said Nathan name, I membered setting up there on that wagon seat between them at the start of the journey. I could feel myself getting warm. "I thought you was going back to your peoples." I knowed she didn't set no store by her peoples, but that feeling of danger, of fear was back. Couldn't she see what harm her being with Nathan would cause us? Hadn't her peoples taught her nothing?

"I don't want to live round slavery no more; I don't think I could without speaking up," she say then, looking down at her hands like she couldn't look at me. But it was funny, cause that was the thing I had come to fear most from her by the end of that journey, that she would speak out against the way we seen some of the peoples was treated and draw tention to us. And what she was talking now would sho enough make peoples note us. "What you think about that, Odessa?" She was watching me, smiling. "About you-all coming with me?"

"I think it scandalous, white woman chasing all round the country after some red-eyed negro," I told her; and could've bit my tongue. She looked like I'd slapped her, face white as a sheet, them freckles standing out like hand-prints cross her jaw. "Speak, neither act out of turn"; seem like I could hear them words in my head. And it seem like I was bound to do one or the other. Oh, I had learned some on that journey. "Mis'ess," I say. And couldn't bring myself to say sorry; she'd risk us all for some belly-rub. I mumbled something about it not being my place to speak, something about getting some pastry.

I was almost to the door when she spoke. "Place," she say, "place"; but not like she was talking to me. "That's how they answer everything," she say, " 'Ain't my place, Missy,' " mocking us, you know, " 'Morning, Mammy'; 'Ain't my place.' 'Afternoon, Dessa'; 'Ain't my place.' Well, I ain't talking no 'place,' " she was yelling now, "no 'mistress.' " Didn't seem to me she knew what she was talking, and I knew if I heard much more I was going do more than speak out of turn. So I went on out the room and tried not to slam the door. "I'm talking friends," she scream and I heard something thud against the door. I stood there in the hall, breathing fast, wanting things back like they was when we come in from lunch, her Miz Lady and me the one she was partnered with in the scheme, wishing she'd come to the door and say what she'd said again.

Not talking "place," talking "mistress"; talking "friend." This what was going through my mind as I walked out the hotel. And, Swole all up, told me I didn't know a "dinner dress" from a "morning gown"— Like I don't know friend from slave just cause I spoke up about Nathan. I had swole up when Martha spoke about that Robert boy, how he bragged on the girls before the mens. I membered that and it was like a pain in my heart. That was what the white woman was talking about, being Martha, being like Carrie to me; and I was shaken. I'd slowed down, now I started walking fast again. This was the damnedest white woman. White as a sheet and about that much sense—sleeping with negroes, hiding runaways, wanting to be my friend. I slowed down again. Wanting to be my friend. Who wanted to be her friend anyway? I speeded up. It was like her to take for granted I'd want to be her friend, that *we*-all would want her to come West with us, that she could have what she want for the asking. Would "friends" put us in danger the way she had? And she want to be my friend. I stopped. This was something I hadn't thought of in her. And I wanted to believe it. I don't think I wronged her at first, but the white woman I'd opened my eyes to at the start of the summer wasn't the one I partnered with on that journey; I admitted this to myself that afternoon. Harker might would joke me; Ada probably call me a fool, after all the sand I raised, but I wanted to believe I'd heard the white woman ask me to friend with her. I wouldn't put no dependence on her holding to it, I told myself, not tarrying now, wanting to see how this would end. "Friend" to her might be like "promise" to white folks. Something to break if it would do them some good. But I wouldn't draw back from her neither.

I was almost to the bakeshop, when I thought I heard someone call, "Odessa." Miz Lady was about the only one call me that and this was a man's voice, so I kept going. And it come again, "Odessa." I kept walking, knowing they must be calling someone else, but walking faster and looking round trying to see where it come from just the same. All a sudden, a hand clap me on my arm and jerked me around. First thing I thought about was someone trying to steal that money. We didn't generally wear them money belts less neither one of us was going to be in the room. We didn't wear all them petticoats, neither; these was packed away in the bags. But—what with all that friend and place talk—I had come out that day and forgot to take the belt off. When I felt that hand on my arm, the money was the first thing I thought about, and I started fumbling for that pepper.

"I knew it was you," and I was looking in the face of a white man, wasn't too much bigger than me.

I knew he'd mistook me for someone else name Dessa so I tried to pull away from him, but without touching him, you know. I didn't want to be cused of disrespecting no white person. "Master, Master, I don't know you," I told him, but I was scared.

"Don't know me, eh?" he said grinning in my face. He had big teeth and no lips and his smile made him look like he was in pain. His nose look like a beak, it was that bony and sharp. His eyes was deep-set close beside it; they was empty as a unclouded sky. It was the white man, the last one, talked to me in that cellar. His eyes made me know him; when I looked into them I didn't see no reflection of myself. Oh, I knowed him. He knowed I knowed him; and he grinned.

I started jerking away from him in earnest then. White peoples had stopped, a course, was looking at us, and I tried to talk to them. "I don't know this master," I called out. "I belongs to Mistress Sutton staying down to the Hotel Gilmore." I was so upset I forgot all about Miz Carlisle and them hands. People was saying something, some of them was laughing but wasn't nobody helping me. The white man started pulling me along, back the way I'd come from. I jerked away and commence to run. "Stop her, someone," I could hear him yelling, "dangerous criminal, reward." Then something knocked me off my feet and something smashed into my temple.

When I come to myself, I was standing with my arms held tight behind me, heavy breathing rasping in my ear. I looked into the face of another white man and the floor about reach up and grab me; hadn't've been for my arms being held, I would've fell. I thought it was Boss Smith, had them same light eyes and sandy hair. But this white man was standing behind a desk. There was bars at the window behind him and I could hear other white mens behind me. At first I couldn't member what happened and when I did, everything inside me felt like it was coming unglued and I fought to hold myself together, just to draw breath. This was a jail; the white man was a jailer, a sheriff. I wanted to scream but all I could do was shake and lick my lips. A voice behind me was saying something and I could see the sheriff's mouth moving. Sheriff say, "Now just a minute, Nemi—"

Nemi. Never forget that name now, it's wrote in my mind. Oh, yes, I knowed the white man, now. "I belongs to Miz Carlisle," I said, "staying down to the hotel. I takes care of her baby, Clara—"

Sheriff say real rough to someone over my shoulder, "You can't keep kidnapping niggers off the street looking for that gal of yours—"

"That's all a lie, sheriff." This was said right in my ear; I jumped cause I didn't know it was Nemi holding me, and he yanked my arms backwards. "When I caught up with her she swore she belonged to some Suttons. This a dangerous criminal and I want her held."

Someone say, "He right, sheriff, I heard her say she belongs to the Suttons."

"Who are you, gal?" sheriff say to me. "And turn her loose, Nemi. Ain't likely she could get too far with all of us in here." He pulled out a chair, told me to sit down; he sat down on the edge of the desk facing us. The white man let go my arms and I sat down, thankful to have something under me, my legs felt that weak. I started to say again I belongs to Miz Carlisle, but the white man don't let me finish.

"Sheriff," he say, "she match the description in the poster." He took a paper out his coat and start unfolding it.

Sheriff say, "Speak up, gal."

"Master, I never seen this master before in my life," I said and it wasn't no act when I started to cry. "This master scare me so. I been stayed with Mistress Sutton— Oh please, Master, just go to the hotel and ask Miz Carlisle."

"The one I wants got scars all over her butt," Nemi say real nasty. "Let's have that dress off; let her prove she ain't the one."

It was several other white mens in the room and all them seemed to like that notion. "Ware the goods," I cried, scared to death at the way they was looking at me. "Ware the goods!" I didn't even not know what this meant then, but this what they said on the coffle when they got a pretty high yellow on the rope, "Ware the goods, Master saving that for the fancy trade." Only the trader would touch her then. And this what stopped the white mens: that I might belong to someone be upset about damaged goods.

"Damn it, Nemi, you had your last peep show in here," sheriff say. "All right, you mens, clear the office. This a jail, not no carnival." He sent one the mens down to the hotel to see could they find Miz Carlisle and everybody left but him and the little white man. White man say I had to be locked up and started reading from that paper. "Hundred-dollar reward. Scaped. Dark complexed. Spare built. Shows the whites of her eyes—"

Sheriff say, "Nemi, that sound like about twenty negroes I knows of personally."

"Branded," white man say real quick, shaking that paper, "branded, eh, sheriff, *R* on the thigh, whipscarred about the hips. What about that, eh, sheriff?"

Sheriff just look at him. "You ought to go on home, man; let the law take care of this."

"Like they took care of it already?" the white man yelled. "The law the ones let her scape in the first place!"

Sheriff sucked his teeth at that. "Come on, girl," he say to me, and I followed him through a wide doorway into the next room where the cells was. There was three of them, all empty. He locked me in one, then went back and sat at the desk.

I stood at the cell door holding on to the bars and waited. I was in puredee misery. West, the Glen, all our ventures, the whole last few months wasn't nothing to me then. I felt almost like I hadn't never left that first jail or this last white man. To come so close to what I had suffered for, to see, to have freedom in me—. I had to be real careful with myself.

I doubted everything. Harker and them would never scape bondage. And we had sold Nathan; I had let her sell Nathan. I had to sit down on that. Last time Harker and Nathan and Cully had come as answer to a prayer I was too numb, too blind to pray. But I wasn't blind then and I could feel every one of them scars, the one roped partway to my navel that the waist of my draws itched, the corduroyed welts cross my hips. And *R* on my thighs. This was the place Harker had kissed, had made beautiful with his lips. I would never have thought anyone would want to love this, that my blood would be stirred when they did. This was what would betray me. Nemi wouldn't even have to say nothing. Sheriff would see that for hisself. And these white mens would kill me.

I grieved for Mony, for Harker, for myself. I tried to tell myself I had Miz Lady—standing now, walking; afraid to keep still. White lady good as two or three negroes any day, trying to make a joke to myself, you know, keep my spirits up. But I wished she'd said "friend" while I was still in that room. No, I couldn't make myself laugh. Laughing was too close to crying and crying to begging, to screaming. If I let myself, I would moan; I would foul myself. I was being real careful with myself.

The white man stood in front of me, and I jumped. He was fingering that watch chain; that's what caught my tention, that clicking where he knocked his fingernail against the watch. That's what I heard above me the whole time I sat under that tree, him clicking that watch and breathing.

"Smart gal like you don't have to end on the gallows," he say, and it was like "Nice day," or "Morning." That's the way he say it, "Morning; know you been laid with some buck," licking his lips, "—won't hold that against you. Woman like you need," he say. I couldn't believe what I was hearing. This white man—and I'm backing away, you know, and thinking, stuttering; I couldn't be subject to this, not now, not no more. And he commence to curse at me. "Sly bitch," he call me; he wasn't no more than two, three feet in front of me, and quiet. "Caught you," almost whispering, but I heard him right enough. "Got you now." He tapped his chest. "Right in here. Roots, you lying sow," and all such nonsense as that. He looked plumb wild, way he was throwing his head back like a horse and brushing at that hank of hair. Closer he got to me, the more I backed up till I bumped against the edge of the bunk. He was right at the bars by then and he reached for me. I couldn't help myself. I screamed.

Well, the sheriff called him up sharp then, and Nemi went on back in the other room. He kept on walking in and out my view, brushing at the hank of hair; it kept falling. I stayed on the bunk. I didn't put no dependence on that sheriff but the fact that Nemi did mind him calmed me some. White man come on me so sudden he hadn't peared subject to no rules; least not the same ones I was. But he didn't seem to back-talk that sheriff too much. This gived me some comfort; I didn't think the sheriff would let him do me nothing till Miz Lady come.

I couldn't think of nothing good that would happen when she did. Nemi knowed me without looking at scars. I couldn't hide them no way and they told plain as day who I was. I didn't see how Miz Lady could dimple her way round that. The sheriff looked to be a steely-eyed white man; you know, the kind we always joke about know what's in a darky's mind before the darky even think it hisself; maybe he wouldn't care for big eyes and quick smiles, neither. He was kicked back in one chair with his feet propped on another one, whittling. He didn't put me so much in mind of Boss Smith no more, but I couldn't tell much else about him from just looking—though it was something that he didn't seem to care that much for Nemi.

The white man had taken a seat where I could see him and he could see me. He sat with his legs crossed. Now and then he would brush at his hair or flick something on his lap, but he didn't seem too concerned. This the way he'd always been with me at that farm, like he had all the time in the world and might lend me a little if

I would talk. And I had talked. I'd had to say something to get
out that cellar; now, I didn't know what all I had said. Just about
Kaine, I told myself, just about Master busting in his head with
that shovel. But I was scared I'd talked more than that, had to be
more than that. Else why this white man track me down like he
owned me, like a bloodhound on my trail?

White man hitched his pants at the knee and switched up legs,
crossing the bottom over the top one. I looked at his ankles showing gray and bony above his low-top shoes. I membered how he
sat on them cellar steps with his hanky stuffed round his nose. I
really hadn't smelled myself till then. Lawd, it'd shamed me to have
to sit up there in them chains and know I was the one he was
smelling. Sometimes I just wanted to go over and wave my arms
all over him or break wind in his face; you know, breathe on him
so he would know that he could be made dirty just like me. Now,
I thought, now his shirt don't even have no collar; his ankles dirty.
My eyes filled with tears then. To be brought so low by such a
trifling little white man. This what chance will do, children, tram-
ple over all your dreams, swing a bony ankle in front of you.

And I got warm. I mean, crazy white man, tracking me all cross
the country like he owned me. Why, he didn't even not know how
to call my name—talking about Odessa. And here he'd just taken
it on hisself, personal, to see I didn't get free. And he was crazy;
had to be crazy, walking round with no hose, no collar, his cuffs
frayed. This the first thing that gived me hope. They couldn't take
the word of no white man like that, not against the word of a
respectable white lady. I stood up on that. See, this had been a
precise white man; even when he took his coat off, his sleeves was
rolled just so. He'd sweated; you couldn't help but sweat, not in
that heat. But, I mean: The sweat did not bead; it wouldn't roll
down his face. And here he was sitting up here with no hose on
his feet. Course it was something strange in that. And sheriff said
he'd dragged other girls in there. The white man was crazy; I'd
make them see that. My fingers touched them money belts hidden
about my waist, there where I hugged myself. Miz Lady couldn't
let them see under my clothes. We wasn't posed to let no one know

we had this money; she would member that. Cept for them scars, it was the word of a crazy white man against a respectable white lady. This was how I calmed myself till Miz Lady come.

I heard her before I seed her: "Sheriff, what is this nonsense about my girl?" Sheriff come to his feet; even Nemi stood up. "I couldn't make no sense out what this man said." She had Clara in her arms, petting her back like she was pacifying her but she looked some upset. "Is somebody trying to steal Dessa? Is that what he was trying to say? It's just scandalous how peoples will prey on defenseless womens." She stopped in front the desk, turned, and saw me standing there, holding on to them bars. "Odessa!" she say starting towards me, "You come out there right this minute!" like she was going to open the cell herself; Lawd know I was ready for her to do it. Sheriff hurried round his desk and blocked her way. "Ma'am," touched his hat, "beg pardon, ma'am."

And there was the white man, bowing at her. "Madam. Adam Nemi." And smiling, reaching for her hand. She drawed back but that was all the mind she give him, too busy looking questions at me like, What going on; who is this?

"I don't even know this master, Mistress." Talking loud cause they wouldn't let her come no closer.

"But I know you," Nemi say, "know you very well," and he tapped his chest.

"Nemi," sheriff say, trying to frown Nemi down. "This the law job. Ma'am, this darky cused of being a scaped criminal with a price on her head."

Well this give Miz Lady a little setback. "Why, why that's impossible," she say, looking round them at me.

I couldn't tell what she was thinking, but she had to be surprised. Harker hadn't thought up no story for this. In all his travels, he hadn't heard nothing about no reward, not for me, not for none of our peoples. The cellar, the coffle, all that had happened way over east of where we was working; none us spected to hear nothing about it here. Oh, Harker said he'd heard some talk about a devil woman at one of the places he was sold, but this was like a hoodoo story to the peoples, a conjure tale. Something that don't have to be real to be true. The white folks hadn't made no mention of no scapes. "They mistook me for another Dessa, Mistress," I called out. "Tell them who I am, Mistress. Can't be no reward on me."

"This girl mines," Miz Lady say. "Can't be no reward on her."

"This gal belong to the state, madam," Nemi say. He hooked his thumbs in the arm holes of his vest, poked his chest out a little. "I put up fifty dollars of the reward myself."

"Sheriff," Miz Lady say, just like she hadn't heard Nemi, turning to the sheriff, smiling, holding Clara so Clara could play with his badge, "we just come in from Aikens to meet some hands my daddy sending to help with the harvest. He"—she looked over her shoulder at Nemi—"just mistook my girl for someone else."

"You would lie for her, madam?" Nemi ask real sharp.

Well, she drawed up at that; white man ain't posed to call no white lady a lie. "Sheriff, who is this person?"

Nemi told her his name again, and put two or three more high-sounding words after it. "He done dragged other girls in here, Mistress. And undressed them," I said quick.

Her eyes flew open at that and the sheriff turned red when she looked at him. "Sheriff, this true? What is going on here?"

"Evil, madam," Nemi say. "Oh, she pull the wool over your eyes; she pulled it on mines, too—at first. Nice white lady like you can't know the blackness of the darky heart. Sing and laugh, and all the time plotting." This not exactly what he say, you understand; what none of them said. I can't put my words together like they did. But I understood right on, now; wasn't nothing wrong with my understanding. And this what Nemi meant; I was something so terrible I wasn't even human. I had lusted with the master, then knifed him; this why I was sold. My heart about leap out my mouth when he mention Master. His voice didn't even not change, and it was a minute before the sheriff and Miz Lady caught on to what he was saying.

The white man could talk, I don't deny him that, open his eyes all wide, use all kind of motions with his hands, spoke in a whispery voice so you had to listen real careful to make out what he said. Oh, he was something; Miz Lady couldn't seem to take her eyes off him. And I was sweating now; some of these was things I'd told him. "I got it all down here," tapping his chest again. I'd strangled Mistress, he said, and conjured the white mens and laid with all the "bucks" on the coffle; I'd called up the devil there in that cellar. A danger to womanhood, he called me.

Miz Lady sniff at Nemi. "One little pesky *colored* gal do all that?" And she smiled at the sheriff.

"The law handle this." Sheriff, cutting Nemi off. "Maybe the gal Nemi looking for didn't do all that, but she done something, else wouldn't be no poster out on her."

"Well, it can't be my Dessa," Miz Lady say, like that settled that.

"She fit the description," Nemi say, waving that paper, grinning in her face. "Madam—" looking now, "madam, what you say your name is?" like he was studying on it. "Seem like I know you . . ."

Miz Lady drawed away from him but not before Clara grabbed that paper out his hand. "I bet that description fit fifty negroes." Real busy now, taking the paper from Clara. She give it to the sheriff, but she wasn't smiling so fresh. This was something I hadn't looked for, that the white man might know Miz Lady, that she might have something to hide.

Sheriff cleared his throat and turned a little redder. "They branded the one we looking for, ma'am."

"Yes," Nemi bust out, "let's look under that dress!"

Well, she was startled sho enough, now, cause all this time she'd thought it was some mistake, especially after Nemi started his spiel. But even if she never seed them, she knowed about my scars. "Why—" she say, looking at me and petting Clara real quick, biting her lip, and looking away. "Why, I— Sheriff—." Petting Clara and batting her eye.

They thought she was stuttering about Nemi being so crude up in her face, talking under a darky's clothes. I knowed she was wondering about the rest of what Nemi said. Lusting with mens, killing white peoples, working roots, this was what she'd thought about me at first, what she thought about all us. I'd laughed about how scary she was of us with Ada; and I had done some things to make her think the worst of me. I guessed she was membering that, too. And she knowed about my scars, about the coffle, something about how the white folks done me; Nathan had told her. But these was things I'd never spoke about to her. If one thing was true, I knowed she must be wondering what else was, too.

Sheriff made Nemi beg pardon, but Nemi stuck to his point; he could prove who I was by the brand on my thigh. Sheriff looked at Miz Lady. She was petting Clara, looking at me—and what could I say in front the sheriff, in front that dirty Nemi? All the time we'd rode together, all those nights we'd laid in the dark almost side by side, silent. Now we just barely knowed how to read each other's eyes, each other's smile. "Odessa ain't got no scars." She heist Clara round to the other side and commence to fan herself with a hanky. She bat her eyes at the sheriff; sheriff looking at his feet, trying not to pay her no mind.

"The law need proof," Nemi say. He smiling now, tapping that watch case. "Now I come to see you, madam, I believe—" looking at her close in the face and she was looking at him like a chicken watching a snake.

I really wanted to make the white man smell himself, like I'd smelled in my own nose. That's what he was to me, a stank in my face, tracking me like a bloodhound, setting mens on to peek under my clothes, offering a *re*-ward on me. "Mistress." She turned her head. I patted that money belt under my dress. I looked at her and down at the hand patting my waist. Whatever she thought about me, whatever Nemi knowed on her, that money was real. And what was he beside what we'd done? "Mistress." I looked at her and I looked at Nemi—that crumpled suit and stained shirt front, the shadow long his jaw made his face look dirty. And she looked at him, the suit, the shirt, like she was seeing them for the first time.

"Sheriff"—she put that hanky up to her nose—"can I talk to you?" No smiles now, no bat the eye now. "In private," she say when Nemi start to follow, and walked over to my cell. Clara reached for me and started babbling soon as she got near me. I grabbed her hand and looked at Miz Lady. She licked her lips and kind of smile. Friend or not, best she could do for me then was to prove I wasn't nothing but her slave.

"Sheriff," Miz Lady say, "we carrying a lot of money for the hiring of these hands. Open your dress, Odessa—" I unfastened it partway there at the waist and turned so he could see without Nemi seeing, too. "We traveling alone. This why I can't have my girl undress in front no one I can't trust." She looked over her shoulder at Nemi. "And I certainly not going have her make no show of herself before no man—like them other girls had to."

"I had a old auntie look at them." Sheriff was moving toward the door. "I send someone at Chole."

And Nemi howled: "You can't set no darky to check a darky, catch a darky; that's the mistake they made at the last place. You can't take no darky's word on this."

"You take the word of the law and be done with it, man," the sheriff say and went on out the door.

Nemi stormed up and down the room and Miz Lady looked at me. I just shook my head. I was scared but I'd take my chance on any auntie before I'd let Nemi see under my clothes.

Well, Aunt Chole came, old woman smoked a nasty pipe and mumbled a lot. I guess they called her auntie cause she still worked, but way she hobbled round she might've been a granny and then some. Sheriff made her known to Miz Lady and Nemi. Miz Lady say it's a outrage to shame a good girl on the word of just someone, looking at Nemi and sniffing. Nemi say, don't look her in the eye, granny; she got the devil in her. Sheriff say, see if this gal whipscarred about her privates. "Yes, suh," Aunt Chole say, bowing her head, mumbling; "Miz Ma'am," mumbling some more.

She had some cloth folded over her arms, and she put this up round the cell mumbling the whole time. I could hear Nemi: "I bet she got callus on her legs from being on that chain." And I did, too. My heart was beating so fast I couldn't speak but in a whisper. "Granny," I said; I was unfastening my dress. "Oh, granny, I was scarred as a child; girl was watching me dropped me in the fire. I'm much ashamed of them scars." I was trying to catch her eyes.

Aunt Chole looked at me just once; her eyes was so milky, I think she might've been blind, anyway. I still had the quarter coin to buy the pastry; I give this to her, then I pulled down the top of my dress and my shift. She ran her hand over my back, heavy, calloused hands; never forget how gentle they felt. When I reached to pull up my skirt she stopped me. She put the coin in her mouth, bite it, then put it down her bosom. "Masa Joel, Masa Joel," she called out, "I ain't seed nothing on this gal's butt. She ain't got a scar on her back."

"You lying," Nemi yelled. "Sheriff, I told you about these darkies." I could hear the sheriff trying to quiet him down. I finished fastening my clothes and Aunt Chole pulled the cloth down from round the cell.

Clara reached for me soon as I come out that cell and I took her, her little arm going around my neck, her little baby hand patting in my face. Oh, it was good to feel that baby in my arms again.

From being red, Nemi went white when he seen me walk out that cell. "You can't mean this, sheriff. You taking the word of some nearsighted mammy? Let me see for myself." And he reached for me. I dodged back and the sheriff pushed him into the next room. "Nemi, you out your mind? Leave that gal alone."

"I know it's her," Nemi say. "I got her down here in my book." And he reach and took out that little black-bound pad he wrote in the whole time I knowed him. I membered him reading to me from it; even in that heat, I'd turned cold when I learned he tried to write down what I said. The book made me fear him all over again. Miz Lady was pulling on my arm, but I couldn't move.

" 'I kill Mistress,' " Nemi say, reading, walking up on me, " 'cause I can!' That's what she say," pointing at me. "Here's some more"—he was flicking through the book. "Here," he say shaking it in my face. Clara reached for the book and knocked it out his hand. The pages wasn't bound in the cover and they fell out, scattering about the floor. Nemi started grabbing the papers, pushing them in the sheriff's hand, into Miz Lady's.

"Nemi, ain't nothing but some scribbling on here," sheriff say. "Can't no one read this."

Miz Lady was turning over the papers in her hand. "And these is blank, sheriff," she say.

"What?" Nemi say, still on his knees. "Naw, it's all here." He lurched to his feet and the sheriff grabbed him. "She walk on the insides of her feets from being on that chain. I know this darky, I tell you; I know her very well. Her hair fit like a cap on her head underneath that scarf. I know her. Miz Janet," he say, reaching at Miz Lady, "you understand. Science. Research. The mind of the darky." And he tap his temple.

We moved then. "You-all in this together"—grabbing at us— "womanhood." He was down on his knees, scrambling amongst them papers. "All alike. Sluts."

"Nemi, for God sake," sheriff say; Miz Lady sucked her breath and almost stopped, but I was behind her and kept on going. I could hardly see for the rush of blood in my head when we went out the door. Nemi was low; and I was the cause of him being low. He'd tried to play bloodhound on me and now some bloodhound was turning him every way *but* loose. He knowed me, so he said, knowed me very well. I was about bursting with what we'd done and I turned to Miz Lady. "Mis'ess," I said, "Miz—" I didn't know what I wanted to tell her first. And it was like I cussed her; she stopped and swung me round to face her.

"My name Ruth," she say, "Ruth. I ain't your mistress." Like *I'd* been the one putting that on her.

"Well, if it come to that," I told her, "my name Dessa, Dessa Rose. Ain't no O to it." I didn't even not think about my tongue. This was the way she was, you see, subject to make you mad just when you was feeling some good towards her. And she was good.

"That's fine with me." We was both testy. Clara started petting me in the face and I hugged her to me. I wanted to hug Ruth. I didn't hold nothing against her, not "mistress," not Nathan, not

skin. Maybe we couldn't speak but so honest without disagree-
ment, but that didn't change how I feel.

"Ruth," "Dessa," we said together; and "Who was that white
man—?" "That was the white man—" and stopped. We couldn't
hug each other, not on the streets, not in Arcopolis, not even after
dark; we both had sense enough to know that. The town could
even bar us from laughing; but that night we walked the board-
walk together and we didn't hide our grins.

Epilogue

&

I missed this when I was sold away from home. —"Turn your head, honey; I only got two more left to do."—The way the womens in the Quarters used to would braid hair. Mothers would braid children heads—girl and boy—until they went into the field or for as long as they had them. This was one way we told who they peoples was, by how they hair was combed. Mammy corn rowed our hair—mines and Carrie's—though she generally wore plaits herself, two big ones that stuck out like pigtails over her ears. My fingers so stiff now, I can't do much more than plait, but I learned all kinds—corn row, seed braid, chain, thread wrap. After we got up in age some, girls would sometimes gather and braid each other's heads . . . Child learn a lot of things setting between some grown person's legs, listening at grown peoples speak over they heads. This is where I learned to listen, right there between mammy's thighs, where I first learned to speak, from listening at grown peoples talk . . .

First time Ada braided my hair there at the Glen—her hands, her legs, the feel of the chair rung at my back, the woman scent rising faint behind my head—I membered so many other times between other knees, the feel of other hands in my hair; I cried.

Ada rocked my head on her knee, pet my shoulder; finished up that braid and went on to another . . .

She didn't too much like fooling with no one's head; kept her own hair short under that bandanna and never combed Annabelle's. Oh, she washed it now, and rinsed it in flower water, but you couldn't get neither one to put a comb to it; put her too much in mind of how she'd had to dress her mistress' head. She could fair turn your stomach talking about white folks' hair, way it flew every which-a-way; said it smelt like dog fur when it got wet. So Ada only combed my head a few times, just till I got strong enough to where I could do it myself. I don't say this to fault her. Slavery had sucked Ada about dry; what was left was tied up in Annabelle. That was her blossom, her flower. . . . No, I wouldn't press Ada about no hair; Debra was always glad to braid so we did each other's. Flora and Janet got so they'd come round and have they heads braided now and then. This seemed to make us more respectable, something more than just a ragtag bunch of runaways. The children have joked me about this, say anytime something go wrong, Ada take to cleaning house and I get to braiding hair. It do give me pleasure. Simple as it sound, just the doing of it, the weaving of one strand with the other, have seen me through some pretty terrible days . . .

Harker . . . touch me—even now; sometime, just get close to me . . . he still overcome my senses and never mock at me for my weakness, say I'm his weakness, too; say . . . He walked all round Council Bluffs looking for a wagon train would let us go West with them. No one want to take us, said West was closed to the black . . . Laws was against us everywhere on that trip. Even in the so-called free states; we couldn't settle, couldn't settle no place between slave territory and Council Bluffs, couldn't stop no longer than overnight, had to pay five hundred dollars to pass through a place. That madness, that hate roiling round in Harker, everytime a wagon master told us no; way he waited, trying to fall with that break, blaming hisself. And Nathan walked with him . . . They walk such a tightrope, such a tightrope. This country have set us a hard task . . . give us so much hurt. Only way Eck-

*land would take us on his wagon train was for Ruth to sign that
we was her slaves and she was freeing us to go West. That was
the last train left that spring . . .*

*We come West and Ruth went East, not back to Charleston;
she went on to . . . Philly-me-York—some city didn't allow no
slaves. I guess we all have regretted her leaving, one time or another. She couldn't've caused us no more trouble than what the
white folks gived us without her. . . . Miss her in and out of
trouble— (Do she call my name to Clara? . . . Negro can't live
in peace under protection of law, got to have some white person
to stand protection for us. And who can you friend with, love with
like that? Oh, Ruth would've tried it; no question in my mind about
that. Maybe married Nathan—if he'd asked her . . . but Ruth went
East and we all come West. . . .*

*I told that West part so often, these childrens about know it by
heart. Mony tell it to his babies like the memories was his, stead
of things he heard when he was coming up. —"There, darling;
finish."— That's the kind of story childrens like—Indians and
buffalo stampedes, even that devil woman stuff. After that last jail,
I couldn't mind Cully and them keeping up that name. Maybe,
like Ruth said, Aunt Chole was mumbling about the devil—but
she didn't put no woman on it.*

*. . . I have met some good white men—Eckland, he was al-
ways fair with us; Nathan rode for him on two wagon trains. Many
the time he have sat at my table. And Brim live down the road;
the Steeles down to the Junction. But none the equal of Ruth . . .
I hopes I live for my people like they do for me, so sharp sometime I can't believe it's all in my mind. And my mind wanders.
This why I have it wrote down, why I has the child say it back. I
never will forget Nemi trying to read me, knowing I had put myself in his hands. Well, this the childrens have heard from our own
lips. I hope they never have to pay what it cost us to own ourselfs. Mother, brother, sister, husband, friends . . . my own girlhood all I ever had was the membrance of a daddy's smile. Oh,
we have paid for our children's place in the world again, and
again . . .*

Reader's Guide

This acclaimed title is a Quill Book Group Selection. To read an interview with the author and suggested questions for book group discussion, please log on to our website:

www.harpercollins.com/readers

"I loved history as a child, until some clear-eyed young Negro pointed out, quite rightly, that there was no place in the American past I could go and be free."

—From the Author's Note in *Dessa Rose*

Dessa Rose was inspired by two historical incidents. One involved a black woman sentenced to death in 1829 for helping to lead a slave uprising. The other involved a white woman living on an isolated farm in 1830, reported to have given sanctuary to runaway slaves. What would happen, Williams wondered, if these two women had met?

To answer this question, Sherley Anne Williams begins a compelling fictional journey into the American past—a process of reclamation for the characters and for Ms. Williams herself. This story of a complex friendship between a slave woman and a white plantation owner dares to treat controversial subjects: a black woman who is proud, intelligent, and vocal; a white woman who chooses a black man as a lover; how these women unite, after guardedly circling each other, in a bold scheme to undermine the patriarchal systems that enslave them both.

Dessa Rose has been used frequently in African-American literature and in women's studies courses. It was with the publication of *Dessa Rose* (William Morrow, 1986) that Sherley Anne Williams, already a respected poet and critic, came to the attention of the literary establishment.

Williams was born and raised in the Central Valley of California. As a high school student in Fresno, she searched for books by and about black people. Upon her mother's death when she was sixteen, her sister Ruby became her guardian. It was Ruby who cultivated Williams's literary interests. Her first published story, "Tell Martha Not to Moan," appeared in *The Massachusetts Review* in 1967. Narrated by a welfare recipient whose gullibility in love relationships causes her problems, this early work showed Williams's ability to confront difficult issues that face a large portion of the working-class or welfare-bound black population. The story was also noteworthy for Williams's experimentation in creating a narrative voice free of the encumbrances of standard English. Later, she would give the characters in *Dessa Rose* "real" voices that stun us with their immediacy and power.

Following graduate work at Howard University, where she wrote her first book, *Give Birth to Brightness: A Thematic Study in Neo-Black Literature,* under the tutelage of esteemed professor, poet, and critic Sterling Brown, Williams received a master of arts degree from Brown University in 1972.

Now a professor of literature at the University of California, San Diego, Williams is a widely published author of stories, poems, and a play. She received a Caldecott Honor for *Working Cotton,* her first work for children, and her first book of poetry, *The Peacock Poems* (1975), was nominated for a National Book Award.

The Peacock Poems, grounded in the blues aesthetic and often expressing pain and anguish, established Williams as a writer who seriously employs indigenous forms of African-American culture. A major theme of the poems is the loneliness of black women, who, like female peacocks, are robbed of voice and, in the eyes of some, of beauty as well.

Dessa Rose can be seen as such a woman: When we meet her she's huddled in chains, heavy with child, sentenced to die, grieving her lover's death, desolate, angry, and alone. As the novel unfolds in three large sections—The Darky, The Wench, and The Negress— Dessa Rose literally finds her voice over the course of these three evolutions, redefining herself and claiming her full status in the world not only in the eyes of others but in her own eyes as well.

By the novel's end, we understand the liberating power of language and the imagination: Through her brilliant reenvisioning of history, Williams has given Dessa Rose a story to tell and a voice to tell it with: "Well, *this* the childrens have heard from our own lips. I hope they never have to pay what it cost us to own ourselfs." It is a history that is hard-won, but it is a history in which Dessa Rose, the author, and we—who live Dessa's story as it unfolds—are finally made free.*

For more information about this and other Quill Book Group Guides, go to the HarperCollins website at www.harpercollins.com.

*Selected portions of this text have been adapted from *Call and Response: The Riverside Anthology of the African American Literary Tradition*, by Patricia Liggins Hill, General Editor, published by Houghton Mifflin Company, 1998.